WINTER GRASS

WINTER GRASS

RICHARD S. WHEELER

SAGEBRUSH
Large Print Westerns

First published in Great Britain by ISIS Publishing Ltd.
First published in the United States by Walker

Published in Large Print 2013 by ISIS Publishing Ltd.,
7 Centremead, Osney Mead, Oxford OX2 0ES
by arrangement with
Golden West Literary Agency

British Library Cataloguing in Publication Data
Wheeler, Richard S.
   Winter grass.
   1. Western stories.
   2. Large type books.
   I. Title
   813.5'4–dc23

ISBN 978–0–7531–9125–5 (pb)

Printed and bound in Great Britain by
T. J. International Ltd., Padstow, Cornwall

To Otis and Teddy Carney

CHAPTER
ONE

As far as the man in the saddle could see, his fence had been cut, each strand of Glidden barbed wire, between every post. The wires drooped to the prairie, keeping nothing out and nothing in. Everything was changed. The neighbors he thought were his friends suddenly were not. The sequestered range he had counted on for winter pasture was being invaded. The good order of the Flatwillow Valley that he had taken for granted suddenly ceased to exist in that dry June of 1886.

John Quincy Putnam, or simply Quin to those close to him, glared bitterly at the sagging wires. There were eleven miles of fence along this eastern boundary of the Q Ranch, and another twenty along the northern side, still intact. Eleven miles of brutal labor, cutting posts, hauling them down the mountain, digging postholes, and stretching the treacherous wire taut. The enterprise had absorbed his entire crew for months, and a dozen Flathead Indians besides.

The armies had rolled. Clear to the Little Snowies to the south, peppering his tawny pasture, were ribby long-horns with a Circle B scorched upon their flanks. If Alex Birkenhead — Alexander Aristotle Birkenhead, if you please — hadn't done it personally, he had surely ordered his polyglot crew to do it. What had taken months to string up had fallen in hours.

"It's an ugly thing to see, isn't it?" Quin asked the girl on the rangy thoroughbred beside him. "Some people have souls like that, I suppose. Souls that can't stand fences. Nothing but downed wire inside them, holding nothing out and nothing in. The only thing is" — he was puzzled — "Alex Birkenhead isn't like that."

She said nothing.

He sighed, knowing he faced another ordeal, and that maybe this enterprise, like the others, would come to nothing. And time was running out for him, his doctors said.

He had not consulted his neighbors before building his fence in 1884. To those calculating men on the other side of his wire, who ran their beeves on the inexhaustible prairies, his fences were an affront to common sense. They had studied their ledgers at least as closely as Quin had, and had arrived at different conclusions.

Still, the murdered fence angered him. His whole way of ranching hinged on those three strands of wire which cleaved the Q Ranch from the open range stretching a thousand miles eastward, and from a thing he called rape.

"What are you going to do?" the girl asked solemnly.

"I don't know, Missy, I surely don't know."

There was fear upon her, the same desperation he had witnessed for five years, a fear that he had soothed and rebuffed in all the ways an old bachelor could imagine. He had enjoyed some success, but always, it seemed, the terror sneaked back into her and got hold of her again.

"If we rebuild it, they'll cut it," he said. "The wire's a dead loss. Too many splices . . . If we patrol it, there could be trouble. Well, I've faced trouble before, and I can again. And this time I'll face the whole grazing district, and not just the Birkenheads."

From where they stood beside the cold creek in the mellow morning sun, they could see the sagging wires stumble southward, up the tawny bench to the long coulees beyond, and finally vanish into the rising mass of the Little Snowies, dark-forested on the horizon.

It amused him suddenly. He had a way of discovering humor in the very things that would have enraged men who hadn't taken so many lickings.

"I think our good bunch grass was more temptation than all those pillars of rectitude could endure!" he joked.

Missy stared at him somberly, unable to cope with his peculiar humor, which seemed so desperately wrong.

On Quin's side of the fence the grass stabbed upward, tall and rank, drought-cured in the waxing June sun. On the Birkenhead side — open range — it had been gnawed down to the roots, and some clumps had been torn out entirely, roots and all. An ominous growth of silvery sagebrush lacerated the hills where the grama grasses had surrendered.

"Let me show you something, honey," Quin said as he eased stiffly off his blood bay, in the manner of a man approaching fifty. The fourteen-year-old girl slipped gracefully off her mare and joined him as he stalked across the line into the naked land beyond the wire.

The two were as unalike as could be. The man was slender and above average height, while the girl was short and wide-boned. The man had a fine oval face that revealed the refinement of generations of Beacon Hill breeding; the girl had strong Slavic cheekbones, wiry blonde hair, smoky eyes, a formless nose — which all melted into a winsome whole on the rare occasions when she smiled. The man had a high aquiline nose, cobalt eyes that peered intelligently from under the untrimmed gray shrubbery of his brows, and he was fast becoming bald, so that his gray-streaked hair covered only the back of his skull, and sunburned skin with liver spots marched up his high forehead.

He selected a forlorn tuft of clipped-off buffalo grass and gouged around it with his jackknife until he was able to lift it from the hardpan with its roots intact.

"When the bunch grass gets chewed over like this again and again," he explained quietly, "the root system shrinks up, too, and doesn't reach down to where the moisture is in a drought like this."

He beat the clump gently until the brittle clay crumbled away, revealing a thin root network only a few inches deep. The struggling clump was lifeless and sere. No water had vivified it since the snow had melted in early March.

He raced back to his side and selected a clump that the influx of longhorns hadn't touched. It was not as

4

brown as its neighbors; some silvery green remained around the bottoms of the high leaves.

Quin sliced carefully through the hot earth, digging deeper until he was able to pry out the whole clump. But in spite of his care he left root behind as he lifted, root that pierced on down a couple of feet. The healthy grass made its own case for the girl, and she examined it silently.

Quin was perfectly familiar with Missy's silences. He knew she was absorbing all that he was teaching her. She was always quiet when she was afraid, as she was now, with that haunted look in her gray eyes. He wished desperately that he could heal that ancient memory inside her.

"Learn all you can about the grasses, Missy," he advised, rising stiffly, "because all this will be yours someday, and you'll have to know."

"No, it won't. We won't have any ranch," she replied darkly.

That irritated Quin. She had always been a doomsayer, a little pessimist, and her gloominess about things never squared very well with reality.

"If you get to believing that only bad things will happen to you, then that's how your life will work out," he remonstrated gently. "Just a lot of unnecessary pain and grief. You've got to have hope, Missy, a hope that says you're not alone in the world."

She seemed to retreat even deeper into herself.

"Well, there's no escaping trouble when it comes," he sighed, sliding a hand across his sunburned baldness.

"Do you want to go? Eighteen miles of hard riding. You could turn back if you want."

"I'll go."

"We'll be late getting home . . ."

"I'll go."

He peered intensely at her from under the bushy gray massifs of his brow.

She smiled unexpectedly, transforming all her incongruous features, from her mashed-potato nose to her wide lips.

The Birkenheads' Flatwillow Station was far down the creek, to the east. Time enough, Quin thought, to sort out what he intended to say. Not that making a good case would have much effect. This wasn't civilization, where men weighed words; this was frontier Montana, where a man defended what he had with main strength.

"All our palaver isn't going to accomplish anything, I'm afraid," he said, mostly to himself. "But it's all got to be said."

"The Birkenheads are smarter than you are," she announced as she rode abreast of him.

He glanced dourly at her. She was no doubt right, but why was she rubbing it in?

"It's ritual," he explained, some faint amusement in his eyes. "If I don't go over there and jaw at him, he'll take me for a doormat and run another thousand beeves onto the Q."

A lot of people were smarter than he was, he thought huffily as they pushed through the brushy bottoms of the Flatwillow. But they weren't smart enough to have spare grass during a drought, the way he did. After he had built his fence in 1884, he had sold his longhorns and restocked with red shorthorn Durhams. They had more meat on them, but required more winter feed. The fence was a sore point among the open-range cattlemen of the Maginnis grazing district, and they were even less happy when Quin withdrew from the communal roundup altogether. He had never attempted to placate them, and that had been a mistake.

It was the same terrible mistake that had devastated his life before, he thought bitterly. Why did he always just bull ahead with his plans without consulting those around him? For a moment the faint, tintyped images of his little boys, Cabot and Jimmy, pierced him, and then the accusing eyes of their governess, Mrs Sturdevant, and worst of all, the solemn gaze of his own Abby, she of the porcelain complexion and chestnut hair. The burned house . . . the angry mob, all the more violent when they discovered that he wasn't in the house with his sons . . . The fire. Years of drift and shadow, the same flaw of character licking him again and again. Not even learning now. It had always been easier to build as he chose, without all the politicking that goes along with any enterprise.

And now it was happening again. He wished not to alarm Missy, but it was no use. She kenned his every mood, even if she didn't know the details. She had been slow to trust Quin after he had rescued her from the Piegan, but now every fiber in her discerned his emotions.

7

"He'll say that fencing public land was illegal," Quin muttered, "and that's why he did it." He laughed sardonically at the tattered clothes that were going to cover the naked act.

"It won't matter what he says."

He smiled at her childish cynicism. Sometimes she sounded like a jaded old man instead of a blossoming girl. Maybe she was right. Maybe the Q was his last chance. If a man had health there'd always be chances. But he didn't. Years before, Cambridge doctors had told him he had a heart murmur and would be lucky to make it to fifty. So little time . . .

Quin gazed fondly at Missy as she guided her mare expertly along the bottoms. All he had, and all that he did, was for her. He had struggled to keep her a proper girl, and not a tomboy. Miss Nicole had helped. Not that she was much of a mother, he thought dourly. But at least that bluestocking was better than nothing. And Missy loved her.

He had traded two beeves for Missy in 1881, a year after he had hacked the Q Ranch out of a wilderness. They had been riding down from the Snowies after a week of working cattle up there, and they surprised Little Calf's band of Piegans, who were roasting one of Quin's steers. Another carcass hung from a cottonwood limb. Raw rage had boiled through him, but he held it in check because he was appalled by the band's emaciation.

He knew their story as well as anyone. The Piegans, Blood, Cree, and Assiniboin had been herded into a vast reservation north of the Missouri, and there they

8

had starved. The buffalo had been slaughtered, and the crooked Indian Bureau agents fed the Indians half the beef they needed, and that full of maggots. The result was inevitable: an array of renegades, hunting parties, outlaws, and loners who raided the herds of central Montana, causing devastating losses.

Quin and Little Calf had stared blackly at each other for an endless minute while the hotheads on both sides furtively eased for cover. The squaws and children had somehow vanished.

"We have few weapons, and you would slaughter us," Little Calf mumbled wearily. "I will pay for meat."

He nodded toward his lodge, barked a command, and a moment later a gaunt Indian woman dragged a terrified white girl, in tatters, toward Quin. The child's eyes were as wide and untrusting as a doe's. She clung desperately to the squaw, and Quin was suddenly aware of how rough he and his crew looked after a week in the Snowies.

"The meat is yours, then," Quin said. He lifted the quaking child and felt her tremble like an aspen in a night breeze.

"She has been in my lodge one moon," Little Calf said. "I bought her from the River Crows, who stole her and some fat ponies from the Sioux. I bought her for this," he said, waving a hand. "For food and safety for my people. A white child is better than rifles now. The women have cared for her, and she is fatter than any of us. But she is full of ghosts."

Quin nodded. "John," he ordered, "give Little Calf a bill of sale for the beeves."

He rode back to his log home at the Q then, the child rigid in his arms.

He washed and fed the mute child as best as he could, while his Chinese cook patched her skirts. She was so terribly old — an old woman who had come to expect the worst from life. She said nothing at all, not even acknowledging with a nod or a shake of the head his many questions. But she understood, he was sure of it. He rambled on and on for three days about himself, the ranch, his crew, his family, and how much he cared for her. For want of a name he called her Missy. He fought the nightmares that whipped the dark with her screams and sent him rushing to her bed to give her a rough hug.

There was something in her cheekbones that made him think of eastern Europe. Perhaps, he thought, she didn't understand him after all. Each night, as he tucked her in, he recited the Lord's Prayer while she stared at him intently. On the fourth night, in the silence after the prayer when Quin was snuffing the lamp, she spoke at last: "You say it differently," she whispered. "We don't say the last part."

That was all. The little voice had shattered the silence and Quin's composure. He kissed her in the dark and fled. The next morning at breakfast the child gravely announced that she was nine and that her name was Antonia . . . Antonia Novak. She ventured outside that day.

She remembered few of the details of the previous months. But from the shards of memory, Quin was able to piece together her story. Antonia and her parents had debarked somewhere in the West after a long train ride. The parents had bought a horse, a wagon, and supplies and had set out across the vast prairies. One dawn Indians had come. From her blankets she saw her father rise up, pistol in hand, and then fall back with an arrow in his chest. Then she heard her mother scream, and the screaming stopped suddenly. She never saw her parents again. The Indian men — there were no women — plucked her up and galloped roughly away while she screamed and cried. She couldn't understand what they said, so she just cried. Later she was given to the squaws and fed. She couldn't remember all that happened after that . . . Other Indians took her away. She was terrified and begged for her papa and mama, but the Indians didn't understand. She recited her Our Father over and over, but it didn't help . . . And then still more Indians took her, and they were kind and grave but poor.

Through the following weeks with Quin, Missy — the name had stuck — was melancholy, terrified, and often in tears. Quin's gentle kindness, eventually healed the worst of it, along with time itself. The episode left its stamp on her forever. Even now, as Quin glanced at the blossoming girl on the big mare beside him, he could trace her dark moods, her pessimism and sudden gusts of need, to those roots.

In time, Quin launched inquiries. The frontier imposed its duties: if there were relatives, he had to find them. He did it halfheartedly but as sternly as duty required. There had been few leads through the following years. From a wolfer who knew the Sioux he learned it had been Moose Jaw's hunting party that had trapped the solitary Novaks in desolate country south of Miles City. From Missy's own recollections Quin deduced that the Novaks had taken the Union Pacific to Cheyenne. An outfitter there vaguely remembered a young couple with a girl. They'd bought a Red River wagon, a good gelding, and all the gear they could cram into the two-wheeled cart. The husband had an accent — Bohemian, he thought — but the wife didn't. The outfitter remembered the wife because she was tall, elegant, and obviously fond of her husband. The Bohemian had talked of going to the Montana gold camps, Maiden or Gilt Edge.

There the trail had died. Quin employed a canny Chicago investigator on the chance that the Bohemians there would know something of the Novaks. But that had also come to nothing, and Quin was overjoyed. He set out to raise Missy as his own daughter.

There was a terrible nakedness on the land as they jogged east toward the Birkenheads': tawny raw clay hills and skeletal rock, covered by nothing except an ominous carpet of sagebrush. Dust eddied up around the fast-moving horses, coating them and their riders. Occasionally they surprised a gaunt steer, making a living on box elder brush beside the restless creek. It was a desperate land, broiling under a bronze heaven. The spirit of apocalypse was upon that country: the prairie was dying before their eyes.

"It's over," Quin muttered. "It was over two years ago when I fenced, but they got a reprieve with the rains. A steer needs forty acres here, not ten."

"They don't care," she said. "They'll go back to England rich and leave us a desert."

"Why do you say that?" Quin asked sharply.

"I just know."

Quin knew it, too. He'd learned a great deal about the Birkenheads over the years. Their father, Josiah Birkenhead, ran the largest cooperage in the world. He had learned to mass-produce barrels using assembly lines, interchangeable staves, and cheap laborers to replace the costly artisans of an earlier time. The barrels, with a Circle B scorched into them, were famous around the world for their price, strength, and weight.

Josiah, scenting huge profits at low risk on the American frontier, had dispatched Alex, Augie, and Minnie to Montana Territory to conduct an enterprise that their liberal Manchester education had not prepared them for, but the enterprise had flourished nonetheless.

All three, Quin gleefully reminded himself, looked as if they'd been manufactured in Josiah's cooperage. Josiah had named them after his heroes. Thus Alexander Aristotle, the eldest; Julius Augustus, who loathed his first name and complained that it sounded like the name of a Dutch diamond broker, in the middle; and Minerva Venus, the youngest. That Venus name hadn't worked out so well, Quinn thought wryly. The Birkenheads had been islands of cultivation on the rude frontier, and Quin's dear friends — until now.

The travelers made swift work of the widening valley. Their thoroughbreds were unusual for ranch horses, but Quin had selected them with one purpose in mind: he loved a horse that would walk. Not just amble, but *walk*, in a mile-eating gait that propelled it faster than most horses would trot.

The sun was already north of west when they rode into Flatwillow Station. It was a bleak place save for the riotous flowers along the front of the rectangular clapboard barrack that was the sole building there. Half of it was the home of the Birkenheads; the rest was a bunkhouse and kitchen for the crew. There wasn't a shade tree in sight to relieve the vast sere prairie, but along the creek grew a strip of emerald brush — chokecherry, willow, plum, and box elder.

Quin eased down and stretched his aching limbs while a giant raven-haired Swede silently led the horses to the pens. Alex's crew was a polyglot array of immigrants who had gratefully hired on when they discovered that one Birkenhead or another could speak their tongue. And they usually worked, Quin knew, for half the prevailing wage.

"Ah! You're just in time for tea," Alex Birkenhead called from his threshold, "and Minnie has made some splendid tarts. She won the bet, you know. We each put up a pound. I wagered you'd be here the day after we cut your bloody fence. Augie wagered on the next day, and Minnie the day after. Minnie's won the pot. If you didn't come today, all bets were off."

Alex stepped aside for his guests.

"We were working the high country," Quin replied dourly.

14

"I'll save you time," Alex announced. "I'm going to make your entire case for you. I know it as well as you do, eh? That's what you're here for, eh? Then you can take the matter to your solicitors for action, eh? That's where it'll all end up anyway."

"And in the meantime you'll have used my grass — the only grass in the district," Quin replied in a voice menacingly quiet, a voice that contrasted with the high, plum-juicy articulation of the Briton.

"My dear Putnam," he retorted, "not your grass, but your government's."

CHAPTER
TWO

Quin knew that he had nothing fancy to say to the Birkenheads. He had always thought of himself as a doer, not a talker. Henry Adams, not Quin, had been elected Class Orator of the Harvard class of '58, he reminded himself. He settled tautly into a rocker, prepared to listen to Alex.

The memory of uproarious debates in this very parlor subdued him in any case. He was no match for the voluble Britons, and he could fashion a riposte or hone a point to some fineness only hours later, on the long trail home. Quin's nature was almost taciturn, which is exactly why his neighbors relished his company during their amiable uproars. But now these erstwhile friends had cut his barbed wire. The repair of it would demand sweat and expense, not theories and hypotheses.

"This is a difficult visit for you, eh?" Alex asked quietly. "Difficult for us, too. We've been at each other's throats for days. Unbearable. Hot days and hot tempers. Minnie was all for it, whilst Augie favored the Pax Britannica."

Quin nodded curtly. The parlor, which had been the site of so much bonhomie, mocked him now. It was plainly a temporary lodgment, with whitewashed plank walls. Only a lithograph of Victoria Regina and her consort, plus bouquets Minnie had arranged in five-pound Arbuckle's coffee cans, relieved the severity. And yet a scatter of periodicals, the London *Times*, Henry George's *Progress and Poverty*, steel-tipped pens, ink reservoirs, and assorted spectacles lent the room an aura of comfort. Life proceeded here in solid English amenity.

"And what did you favor?" Quin asked.

"Rectitude — fair play — on both your part and ours."

There was a grim cast to Alex's square, sallow face as he gazed evenly at Quin. His two hundred eighty pounds of beef were encased in his ritual garments, which he wore to roundups as well as to tea parties: boiled shirt, cravat, black suit and waistcoat, and a gold watch fob strung across his ample middle.

"And I presume Minnie won."

"She did. There's no moderation in the fair sex."

"The unfair sex," Minnie added, wheeling in a tea cart. "Good afternoon, Mr Putnam, and Missy, dear. Do have some tarts."

There were two Wedgwood teapots, one steaming, the other cold. For Quin and Missy she poured from the steaming pot. For herself and her brothers — Augie had not yet appeared — she poured from the other, and Quin was reminded that the Birkenheads embroidered the afternoon ritual: the amber fluid in their teacups was ninety proof and brewed in jolly Scotland.

"It's because we are persistent, realistic, and with fewer scruples," she explained. "You men should be called the fair sex, because that is what you are. Alex and Augie are such silly geese; all they could think of was being fair, you know. But I disabused them of all that."

"So it seems," Quin agreed.

"We intend to improve our fortunes, and you, dear Mr Putnam, are preventing it. Now that it's done — the cutting, I mean — you may pick up the pieces any way you choose, and by then we shall have rain. Missy, you look ill. Are you quite all right?"

Missy nodded sulkily.

There was a hauteur about Minnie that discomfited others. She knew it, and used it mercilessly. With the buttressing of whalebone stays she had contrived to turn herself into a perfect cylinder, now encased in a summery lavender tent. There was a bit of Venus about her after all, in her golden complexion and in her glossy dark hair parted in the center and hanging in ringlets.

"The first three years were simply perfect. Our fifty thousand quid doubled. But last year's prices cheated us of a profit, and now this awful drought. We'll have a devilish time of it getting the last fifty thousand. That was the goal. One hundred fifty thousand in five years."

Quin nodded.

"I intend to do it," she proclaimed. "We'll have our gain, to the last pence. I'm the only one here with any steel in my spine, and —"

"I thought it was whalebone," said Alex drily.

18

Minnie glared icily at her blasphemous brother. "Out! I'll cut you out of my frontier journal, Alexander. You'd bore London anyway. Too civilized and nasty. What they devour is cowboys, trappers, Geronimo, Molly Maguires, and Wild Bill Hickock. Have another tart, Mr Putnam."

Augie swept in then and deposited his shotgun on wall pegs. He was a softer version of Alex, with a middle that distressed his sweater and Harris tweed jacket, which he wore over knickers and laced hightops.

"Oh, Quincy! Teatime, eh? I'm sorry about . . . uh, have some Darjeeling. Excellent tea, eh?"

He filled his cup from the cold pot and smacked his lips judiciously. "Splendid, splendid," he announced.

There was one of those awkward pauses that occur when people confront a hard topic.

"You know, Mr Putnam," Alex said into the settling void, "when father put us on the White Star steamer at Liverpool, he bade us good-bye with these words: 'Don't come home till you've tripled our capital.' He was quite earnest, I assure you. We are all three homesick. Not that we don't enjoy your New World and the great continent — a grander experience by far than India, I'd say — but our home is the moist gray of Manchester.

"Josiah Birkenhead fully expected us to toe the mark. He had heard at his club, from such chaps as Lord Harrington, that fortunes could be made here on the continental steppes and that a man's capital could double in five years, but only an ignoramus'd be that slow about it. Free grass! Untaxed and unlimited land!

Longhorns so hardy they survive winters without hay
— and disease-resistant! Buy a herd, gather, brand, and
ship the increase east!

"Five years, he allotted us, and now four are gone,
and we're fifty thousand short. It seemed easy enough
to him, over mutton at Conway's, among gentlemen.
'Simple enough,' he told us. 'Put all that schooling to
some practical use. Make pounds as well as theories
and poetry.'"

Alex stared glumly into his teacup.

"Well . . . we'll be ignoramuses if this drought
doesn't lift. But we'll manage, Mr Putnam. Triple the
quid, one way or another. Two more Texas herds on the
way. Bargain prices, I say, and a chance to recoup.
One's near Cheyenne now, two months off; the other's
still in the Texas panhandle. We'll fatten them here, sell
out, and steam home."

"More Texas fever," Quin growled.

"Some Texas ranchers swear there's no such thing,"
Alex mused. "But of course they're wrong. The
longhorns carry it, even if they're somewhat immune to
it. It's a risk. Especially for your shorthorns."

"Two herds you'll fatten on my grass," Quin
snapped.

"Not your grass, Mr Putnam. Public grass."

"Quincy," Minnie broke in, "the thing's in motion
now — the new herds, the access to Q Ranch range —
can't be stopped. I hope that's clear."

"Perfectly."

"It'll rain soon, and all will be green again before the
herds arrive," Alex said.

"You're an optimist."

"No, a realist. Reality is all there is. It rained the past two summers, eh? But dry summers are not uncommon here, eh? So the odds are good. The range was in excellent condition when we first arrived; it could spring back with a little water, eh?"

"No. The grasses are weakened."

"Eh? Well. The only good grass in the district is under Q Ranch fence. Our solicitors tell us it is an illegal enclosure."

"They told you what you wanted to hear," Quin replied softly. "Two sides — east and north — are under wire, and they call it an enclosure?"

Alex eyes his guest thoughtfully. "In the opinion of our solicitors, the Little Snowies to your south and the Snowies to your west form a timbered barrier livestock can't penetrate. An enclosure. A rectangle of public land appropriated for private use."

Quin sighed. "You'd better explain why my uplands are full of sheep and sheepherders every summer."

"That's a matter for the court, eh? That's where it'll all end. It's our position that you've sequestered grass. Your Congress outlawed sequestration two years ago, and your Interior Department even invites people to cut illegal fence. Let me read from this circular, eh?"

He donned his gold-rimmed spectacles and withdrew a document from an orderly pile of material beside him.

"The department will interpose no objection to the destruction of these fences by persons who desire to make a bona fide settlement in the enclosed tracts but are prevented by fences, or by threats of violence from doing so.' "

"Are you making a bona fide settlement on Q Ranch range?"

Alex paused for a moment. "More bona fide, I'd imagine, than your drovers' homestead claims and Desert Land Act claims, with their packing-crate houses and their agreements to sell to you as fast as the land is patented."

Quin nodded. Missy stared darkly into her teacup.

"We'll cut your other fence, too —" Minnie exploded.

"Hush, hush," Alex rejoined. "We're not at war with Mr Putnam; we simply want access to public land."

"No," Quin said. "She's right. It's the survival of either the Flatwillow Station, or the Q Ranch. One or the other."

There was a somber silence.

"I hoped it wouldn't come to this, Mr Putnam."

"Well, it did."

"I'll continue our case, eh? We've researched the case law. There's one decision that favors us, and one that favors you. A certain Cabot T. Thomas left two openings — one on a lakeshore, the other across an impassable canyon. The court ruled it was an illegal enclosure. On the other hand, one Samuel Bean claimed he didn't violate enclosure laws because he left a mile-and-a-quarter opening in his fence, and a federal district judge upheld him."

Quin nodded. The tea was good.

"Now then, Mr Putnam," Alex continued with strained geniality, "I should like to make your case for you. I know the whole of it, save the trivial details, but I can spare us some unpleasantness by reciting it."

Quin nodded and shifted restlessly in his rocker. Words, words, words, he thought savagely. These geniuses had to *understand* everything, talk it to death. Well, he'd show them that words have other uses.

Alex sucked at his chill teacup and plunged in.

"You've an excellent case, eh? Blooded cattle, controlled breeding, winter feeding, hay meadows, irrigated land — all demand fences. A good point. You're surely the pioneer of what's coming. I daresay the open range is doomed."

"That's not what I came to say," Quin responded. "My point is simple. You have no grass. That's as much your fault as nature's. And now you're preempting mine, which I preserved at great cost against a calamity such as this dry spell. It's not yours to take."

Quin let the implication hang between them.

"Eh? Well, I see . . . Now then. To make your case for you once again . . . I shall argue that each of us has a home range. It's public land, but each ranch has certain proprietary rights based on first usage, eh? Q Ranch has a right to range it's used since eighteen eighty, eh? Perhaps I should be your solicitor!"

Alexander Aristotle Birkenhead would indeed make an excellent lawyer, Quin thought, picturing the man in the traditional periwig.

"What are you going to do about your stock on my range?" he asked tautly.

Alex sniffed impatiently. "Why, nothing until a court declares one way or the other —"

"Which'll take months," Quin replied, suddenly grinning. "Tell me, Alex, what would you do if I rebuilt the fence?"

"Cut it again!" Minnie snapped.

"And if we patrolled it with armed riders?"

Alex paused, measuring his words. "The stockmen's association would use whatever means are necessary to restore access to public land."

"And tear out the north fence, too!" Minnie bawled.

"Hush, Miss Minnie! You'll have another attack of the vapors. Pour Mr Putnam some of that tea, eh?"

"Augie, you're the silent one. How do you view all this?" Quin probed.

"I wish it'd rain, old chap."

Quin sighed. "Why didn't you come to me with a proposal to lease some of my pasture?"

"That was Augie's plan," Alex confessed.

"Leases cost money," Minnie replied. "And it's public land — not yours to lease. We're having a hard enough go with beef prices nearing three dollars a hundred."

"I sided with Miss Minnie," Alex said. "Cut all costs."

"And because leasing's a cowardly, lickspittle, toadying thing to do," Minnie bellowed. "The entire grazing district resents your fence. You're quite alone, and quite vulnerable."

Quin caught the threat. "There's not enough grass on the Q for your herd and mine, much less the two you're importing," he remonstrated.

"Oh, there'll be feed enough," Alex assured him. "Longhorns are famous scroungers. They'll scratch for it in rough country and go for browse rather than grass. We won't ship this fall. We'll ship in eighty-seven when prices are better, and then we'll go home. All we need is an open winter, eh?"

"And the entire Q Ranch," Quin added sourly.

"Better see a solicitor, eh? Nothing personal in all this, Mr Putnam. Just a question about the rules of the game. You're a good neighbor, the only cultivated chap we've been able to find."

Quin rose suddenly, feeling barely civil. "You have two days to move the Circle B stock off the Q," he said tautly.

"And if we don't?"

Quin simply stared.

"And if we don't?" Alex repeated.

Quin's silence was deadlier than a spoken threat.

Alex measured him carefully. "You'd better stick to the courts, Putnam. You stand alone, you know. There's no one in the association who'd support you. They hate that fence. You're likely to find yourself without any means to recover your strays."

Quin understood. The blacklist. The association updated it annually with the names of cattle thieves, horse rustlers, insolent sheep men, undesirable cowhands, ranchers caught mavericking, sooners who slipped out ahead of the communal roundup to brand strays, crooked dealers, and other odious persons. If a man was blacklisted his reputation was ruined; he was numbered among the scum of the earth. His strays were never returned; they were auctioned, and the proceeds helped support range detectives. Often he couldn't even ship beef.

"Two days," Quin repeated softly, revealing none of the explosions that Alex's threat had detonated in him. Missy looked stricken, and he judged that she understood his rage.

"As you wish," Alex said easily, ushering out his visitors. "You know, Mr Putnam, we're fond of you. Take that thought home with you ... Come visit us soon, young lady."

Missy's frank black glare caught him by surprise.

They rode home through the long June evening while the sun tarried in the north. Quin was oblivious to his surroundings as they ascended the slope of the Flatwillow Valley, and he did not notice Missy's troubled glances.

He turned to her at last, emerging from some far continent of the soul.

"They're smarter than we are," she announced.

Quin laughed shortly, but then he saw the tears smudging her cheeks, and sensed her humiliation.

"I wanted to help you, but I couldn't think of anything to say," she wept.

"I couldn't think of much, either," he admitted. "I suppose you're right. I wasn't the brightest lamp at Harvard ... But James Russell Lowell taught me more than French there; he taught us to observe character: 'In vain we call old notions fudge, And bend our conscience to our dealing; The Ten Commandments will not budge; And stealing will continue stealing.'" He grinned slowly at her after reciting the quatrain.

She gazed solemnly at him through the dusk, absorbing his mood.

"Not that character has helped me much," he confessed, sighing.

Again he slipped into his private reveries as night enfolded the wide valley.

"But not this time, Missy," he announced suddenly, without preamble. "I'm getting stubborn in my old age. I'm going to fight this somehow, because it's not just mine; it's yours. And I have something else to fall back on — and that's faith."

She rubbed away the wetness from her cheeks.

CHAPTER
THREE

"Quincy Putnam!" she exclaimed. "I've been expecting you."

"Miss Nicole," he responded fondly, pressing her hand.

"I heard about the Birkenhead stock," she said. "Zeke Pulford told me they cut your fence. He always knows everything." She studied him with her startling violet eyes. "You look tired. Are you well?"

"Things pile up," Quin sighed as he followed the elegant young woman into a book-filled, masculine office that would otherwise have been the parlor. Morning sun glinted somberly off a polished brass spittoon that stood beside a massive oak desk.

"I've already started the casework," she announced, waving a languid hand toward a stack of morocco-bound law books.

She settled lightly into an enormous leather-swivel chair and was engulfed by it.

Miss Nicole was more gorgeous than ever, Quin thought with awe. That thin olive face framed by glossy jet hair that hung in soft waves to her bosom; those amazing, intelligent eyes under their long lashes; the sensuous mouth with its quizzical upturn at the corners; the throaty voice; the lithe, petite body with no fullness at all except at the breast . . .

He sighed. She never failed to irritate him. That had been particularly true this last year, and he had found himself making all sorts of excuses to avoid the arduous trip to Lewis-town. Imagine employing a female lawyer! If she weren't the best in the territory he wouldn't dream of it.

What a pity, he thought. She was superbly cultivated, not with *Godey's Lady's Book* banalities, but with real ornaments of the mind: languages and literature and a lively mastery of the pianoforte. But she had thrown all decorum to the winds and become a bluestocking, he thought dourly. And a *lawyer*. She actually made a competent living at it. Next thing you knew, she'd be smoking a pipe and wearing pants.

Worse, it was a sheer waste of beauty. She was squandering her dazzling face and figure on books and briefs. Lawyers ought to look like lawyers, not like Eleonora Duse. Lawyers ought to have jowls and bulbous noses and bushy eyebrows, and vast bay windows adorned with gold watch fobs.

It was embarrassing, using her skills as if she were some hussy of the law books. He had received just compensation for his folly at the cattlemen's association meetings, where his choice of barristers evoked sly, wry, and ribald japes. Entering her law office, he supposed, was like sneaking into a bordello.

Things had come to such a pass that he could scarcely stand to be with her for more than ten minutes. Her beauty always savaged him, and worse, he was always filled with sulky admiration for her incisive mind. She was all too eager to discuss the whole world with him, too, but he had started to beg off, pleading the press of ranch business and turning his face to the windows to avoid seeing the open disappointment in her eyes. For one of the bewitching things about her, he knew, was that she could meet his mind on any frontier of intellect. There was no other person in rude Montana who so awakened his joy in ideas or who cherished literature as much.

Once, in a period of weakness, he had allowed himself to wonder whether marriage might be possible, how she might look adorning the head of Q Ranch's dining table, how she might mother Missy. But that, of course, had been folly. That bluestocking had no more mothering instinct than a longhorn bull, and probably lacked the skill to fry an egg. Still . . . he gazed at her miserably, discerning an unseemly joy in her face. She was too eager for his company, and that flustered him. He wished he were back at the Q, in his high-cantled saddle, with all the Big Sky country laid out beneath him.

Nicole was twenty-six, and Quin was scraping fifty. He was an isolated, ornery rancher, and she a child of gaslights and cobbled streets and fashion. He had inherited her from Jean Aumont, and if anything she was shrewder than her sire. That, Quin supposed, was the result of helping Jean research cases and write briefs ever since she'd been able to read, especially during the long years after his first stroke. Then there were the final years after the second stroke when she did everything for him except sign his name — and maybe she had done that. Now she was the only female lawyer he'd heard of, perhaps the only one in the Republic.

Quincy blinked and scourged those dour observations from his mind. There was business to be done, and he'd be quick about it.

If Nicole had any inkling of what she unleashed in him, she didn't show it. She simply waited behind her protective desk, which formed a critical barrier, emotional as well as physical, in her associations with all men. She never pumped him; she always waited him out, Quin knew, letting him inch toward the details in his own way.

"I brought Missy," he said. "She's at the rectory with Father Dolan."

"Ugh!" Nicole bridled. "Torture. If she ran away it'd serve you right. I'm glad my father neglected that part of my education."

Quin felt uncomfortable. His deepest instinct was to keep faith with Anton Novak by rearing Missy as a Catholic.

"You're frowning, Mr Putnam," Nicole laughed. "You know she'd rather be at the ice cream parlor . . . I hope you'll let me keep her a week or two."

"I thought you'd ask. I had her pack a valise and put it in the buggy. She loves to stay with you, Miss Nicole."

Nicole smiled.

It was good for Missy to have some female companionship, Quin thought. Not that Nicole was much of a mother, or silent Missy much of a friend. But the girl was too much surrounded by men at the Q.

"Now tell me about the great invasion," Nicole said.

Quin did.

"I threatened him. I told Alex he had two days to drive his stock off my grass."

"And?"

"He threatened me with the blacklist."

"That could hurt you badly, Mr Putnam."

"I know. It cooled me off. I was ready to start a war if I had to, but that simmered me down. And now a week's gone by and those beeves are still chawing my winter grass. I figured I'd better hustle over here for your counsel."

She leaned back into the leather swivel chair until she was swallowed by it, and gazed absently out the window toward the gloomy pine-clad mountains. What a tiny person, Quin thought, to be armoring so large a ranch.

"I've looked up most of the case law regarding enclosures," she said at last. "In my opinion you're legal. Only two sides fenced. The question is whether the mountains south and west of you are impassable so that, in effect, you have an enclosure. I don't think so. Sheepmen invade your summer pasture all the time."

Quin nodded.

"The Interior Department actively encourages fence cutting where enclosures exist," Nicole continued. "You'll get no sympathy from Grover Cleveland. No doubt the Birkenheads proceeded on that assumption. But, of course, by the time all this is settled, your grass'll be flesh on their stock, which is what they intend."

As usual, she had it precisely, he thought. She had inherited that cool, analytical mind from her father.

"I might get an injunction if I go to White Sulphur Springs," she mused, "but I doubt it, given the color of the court there. And there'd be no way to enforce it here, so far from Sheriff Earley. It might give you legal footing, though."

It was a long trip to the county seat, Quin knew, and given the politics, a futile one. Ever since he built his fence, he'd rubbed against the cattlemen's association — which elected judges.

"What are you going to do?" she asked. "Bring suit, of course, but what else?"

"I'm debating it," he said. "If I rebuild the fence, at great expense, I'd have to patrol it, also at great expense."

"And they'd cut it anyway."

He grinned suddenly, remembering a notion that had been mounding up in his head for several days. It was reckless, but the more he weighed it, the choicer it became, compared with the alternatives.

"You've got that wicked smile again, Quincy Putnam, and that always means a lot more work for me," she observed wryly. "What are you up to?"

"I'd better not say," he drawled. "The canons of your profession would require you to divulge my plans."

She arched an eyebrow. "If you're going to do anything illegal, Mr Putnam, I'll be well paid bailing you out."

"The fine is small," he mocked her. "But the stockgrowers offer a five-hundred-dollar reward. The fact is, Miss Nicole, I may build another kind of fence, temporarily — one that can't be cut or penetrated — and when I do, the howling will never cease."

"Quin," she pleaded, "don't do anything foolish. Not you. I care very much what happens to you."

"Of course you do. I'm your best client. I'm half your income."

"No, you're not my best. You're my worst. You're such a mule sometimes. But you're my favorite."

Her violet eyes were full of mirth as she and Quin enjoyed what had become their ritual joke. There was something coquettish in the flash of her eyes as they caught his.

Quin suddenly felt acutely uncomfortable. She was being more familiar than he preferred her to be.

"Let's get back to business' he rasped.

The words sliced the humor short. She gazed at him sadly for a moment.

"Quincy, Quincy . . ." she whispered, and then stiffened up in her chair.

"I've got a ranch to run," he added relentlessly. "Can't lallygag around here."

"You're all business these days," she rebuked him. "We used to be friends."

"I hire you for your advice," he snapped. "I don't hire you to entertain me."

She paled, and Quin saw whiteness in her small olive knuckles as she gripped the desk. He was sorry. He had rampaged through the china shop of her soul, smashing teacups and cracking plates. He straightened up in his chair like a man recovering from a stumble.

"I'd hope you'd find a fine young man your age," he said. "There are precious few who'd be worthy of you."

"You have it wrong, Mr Putnam. There are few I'd be worthy of, or fitting for. You don't really know me, do you? But thank you anyway. I'll treasure your compliment."

She sat rigid and guarded in her chair.

"I'll go brew us some coffee," she said at last, "while you decide what you want me to do about the Birkenheads."

She smiled suddenly at him, her violet eyes blooming with affection, and then vanished into the bowels of the house.

Quin watched her go, wondering how she lived back there in her inner sanctum. Neither he nor any other adult had ever been invited beyond the parlor of the rambling frame house. Only Missy had, and Quin had shamelessly pumped all the information from her that he could about Nicole's private life. He knew, from what Missy had told him, that much of the downstairs was a library, except for a salon with a grand piano, a music stand, and a harp. Missy said that Miss Nicole trudged to the post office in the dry-goods store twice a week and usually returned with armloads of newspapers, magazines, and books. Sometimes there were so many she made two trips.

He also knew that she did all her own domestic work; that no one, save Missy and a few neighboring children such as Zeke Pulford had ever been fed by her;

and that, at least in Missy's opinion, Nicole could cook well when she chose, but scarcely bothered with food most of the time. Often Missy did the cooking because Nicole simply forgot or was absorbed in the law. Quin reckoned he knew more about her than anyone else did.

She was a legend throughout central Montana, this maiden lawyer, in part because of her seclusion. Cowboys, miners, tradesmen, all flocked to her, sometimes not for genuine legal help but just to gaze upon her. She had frequently counseled them without charge, patenting land, nursing them through employment grievances, drawing wills.

She often untangled life for bewildered immigrants. She was fluent in Spanish, French, and German, and she could understand Italian. They came to her rambling white house, spoke her name reverently and protectively. She was rumored among the Mexicans to be holy. The Italians noted her warm complexion and called her a madonna. On some feast days they left garlands on her door. None of them dared court her, this unapproachable woman with a mind so wise and heavenly that it grasped law, philosophy, business, languages, politics, music, art — and almost everything else. They spoke of her in hushed tones: the miss, the signorina, the senorita. If a miner or cowpoke disparaged her purity, he took his life in his hands.

But in truth, Quin knew, this romantic fascination was suffocating Miss Nicole. She was a prisoner in her clapboard house, and she was none of the things they took her for. She was simply a great oddity on the frontier: a truly cultivated woman. A rarity even in Boston, but a phenomenon here. Occasionally they had discussed things other than Quin's legal problems, and in those sunlit moments he relished an intellect honed much finer than his own, furnished with all the tapestries of high civilization. She'd done more work for him than he could remember, land claims mostly. She knew the plats of his ranch as well as she knew her own house.

He heard clattering pots in the kitchen and knew well enough why she hadn't married. Who'd want some bluestocking lawyer for a wife? She'd be a terrible mother. Why didn't she just abandon the law? he wondered restlessly. It was wounding her. Was she sheer innocence, this bookish child of Jean Aumont? Was she so secluded that she had been unaware of the bloom of her body? Surely there must have been chances. Her beauty was beyond cavil, and those violet eyes had become a legend around a thousand Montana campfires.

Quin's curiosity about her was well-nigh insatiable, and now, as he sat in her chambers, it was a passion in him beyond endurance. What on earth did she do here every day all alone without friends? And the nights. Did she sleep well? Missy said she read late and sometimes the clock chimed one before she turned down the kerosene wicks. It was almost as if she were afraid to sleep. How barren her bookish life must be, he thought. Dry and dreary.

If Nicole had ever had a serious suitor, he didn't know of it. Frontiersmen found her intimidating. Her gentility was too much for them. There was that delicious story about Jake Purcell, who walked in and proposed to her right out of the blue. She had told him, so the gossip went, that such a marriage would be impossible. What would they share? What would they talk about? He had replied that palaver wasn't so all-fired important; he just wanted a good sturdy woman to fetch his meals, tidy up the shack, milk the cow, churn some butter, weed the garden, and give him a passel of young 'uns, so why should she take notions agin' a nice life like that? She had simply laughed, hands on hips. But kindly. Nicole was rarely unkind. Where the yarn came from, Quin couldn't imagine, unless old Jake told it on himself in his cups. Quin had heard several versions of it, and suspected it was true.

There was, Quin knew, a true tale about Nicole that had become a celebrated episode in the history of the territory. After her father died, Nicole wished to practice law in her own right, so she boarded the stage to Helena, seeking an audience with the three judges who served as bar examiners for the territory. And there she was turned down cold. "It's not fitting work for a woman," intoned pale old Justice Hiram Angus Semple, while the other two humphed their black-robed agreement. She retreated to Lewistown, discouraged. A whole legal education lay wasted, and the iron corset of tradition would confine her to some sort of miserable marriage. So she prepared to leave Montana.

But word was bruited around among the Judith Basin cowboys and argonauts, and one Sunday they gathered, three hundred strong, and resolved that

Nicole Aumont was going to have a fair crack at a bar exam. They petitioned the august judges and got nowhere. Women had other duties and virtues, the jurists retorted. But frontier democracy has a way of riding roughshod over such obstacles, and one balmy January day in 1884 over two hundred of those brawny gentlemen descended on Helena with Nicole virtually a captive among them.

At one o'clock in the morning they thundered on Justice Hiram Angus Semple's door and informed him that he would learn another kind of law, lynch law, unless he convened his colleagues and administered the bar exam — immediately. By three o'clock he had assembled his owly colleagues in court under the baleful eye of the rude assemblage. A flustered Nicole apologized at once: "I am as much a victim of these events as I am their beneficiary," she began. By noon she had waltzed past the most formidable questions the rattled judges could muster, and the examiners knew they were fairly whipped.

"You've responded well," said the stern Scot, nervously clearing his throat. "We find no deficiency to prevent you from practice, Miss Aumont. This duress" — he waved a bony hand at the mob — "hasn't extended to our conclusions. You've passed the examination and may be admitted to the bar —"

A wild whoop erupted from the galleries, lubricated by a night of passing the jugs, but the bald old judge rapped his gavel fiercely.

"You'll have great difficulty, Miss Aumont. Some facets of law are not fitting for a woman, and you will blush to consider them. Divorce cases, certain homicides . . . Some of the judges will find against you, and some juries, for all sorts of reasons . . .”

The ancient Calvinist peered down on a wan Nicole and shook his head sadly. “Worst of all, you’ll pay a dear price all your life for abandoning your natural and appointed role. What will you feel when you’re old and alone, without children, without grandchildren? But the die is cast. So be it.”

The galleries were suddenly subdued. No Texas cheers now, for what had they wrought?

Quin smiled, remembering the hubbub.

She caught him in his reverie as she returned with coffee in demitasse.

“What were you thinking about? That expression —”

“You,” he said quietly, “and your bar exam.”

She waited, quizzically.

“And Hiram Semple’s prophesy about your future. He was right, Miss Nicole.”

“There are too many people thinking about my life and my future,” she rebuked him. “Who knows? Maybe I’ll go back to Saint Louis. With Jean dead, there’s little for me here.”

“I hope not.”

“What is there but books and more books?” she demanded hotly. “I’m so bored with them! I threw Tennyson through the window last winter.”

She retreated to her swivel chair behind the great desk. Routinely she used that sea of oak to steer matters back to law. Quin had watched her do it over and over, and understood the need.

"Have you decided what you want to do about the Birkenheads?" she asked.

"Yes."

She sipped from her demitasse, waiting him out.

"I don't want to do anything at law, now that I think about it."

"But Quin —"

"Words won't work."

"Words! Why, if you sue them, you'll —"

"Sure, I'll win . . . in a year or so. If they're still around."

"Mr Putnam, have you lost your mind? Your whole ranch is threatened."

"Exactly. And what am I going to feed those shorthorns next winter — legal briefs? I've got to shove those beeves off in days — a month at the most — or I won't have a ranch. I'm going to sting them some other way."

She was plainly puzzled, but he offered no more clues.

"You're a mule." She smiled wryly. "You're the most impossible man I know, Quincy Putnam."

He laughed easily, knowing she had surrendered.

"They're expecting law from me," he announced mysteriously, "but they're going to get another kind of heat."

She shook her head at his odd conundrum.

"When shall I expect Missy?"

"She should have been here by now."

"Catechism on a sunny morning. You're heartless."

"I'll keep the faith," he replied simply.

He slurped the last of the thick black coffee.

"I'm keeping you from your torts and suits and briefs," he muttered.

There was disappointment in her face. "Please stay. It's a light day," she pleaded. "Stay until Missy's free, at least. I don't see you half enough."

He shook his head. "I have a ranch to run, Miss Nicole. Take care of my girl, and if she's not helpful, tell me."

"She's too helpful. I wish she'd just go skip rope sometimes. She just glooms around here, not even making friends."

"She picks up your habits," he replied dourly. "We'll fetch her in a week or two."

He plunged outside, irked at himself and wondering why he was in such an infernal rush to escape.

CHAPTER
FOUR

The wizened ranch foreman, John Durham, found Quin in his study staring at the blank slope that rose behind the house.

"I brought ye the mail," he said, easing his rheumatic frame into the Morris chair. "Bunions was t' Grassrange fetching some horseshoe nails, and brought it."

Quin nodded, lost in some reverie. The old carrot-topped Scot with the watery blue eyes waited patiently until he had the full attention of his old friend.

"Have ye been doon to the hay meadows of late?" he asked at last. "I'm afraid the grass has headed out at eight or ten inches and we'll be having no hay."

"No hay?"

"Too short t' cut, and with the seed forming it'll not grow even if it rains."

"Do we have much of last year's hay?"

"A little, for the horses. But not the fifteen hundred tons we'll be needing."

Quin sighed unhappily, running a hand over his baldness. "And the Birkenhead stock all over our winter range," he added.

"I thought t' run the horses into the hay fields and hope they can crop it doon before it rains."

"Yes, of course, John."

"And I thought ye might consider reducing the herd, with the shorthorns needing hay all winter if the snow piles up."

Quin nodded. The heavy red Durhams didn't forage as well as the longhorns, and Quin's whole operation was geared to winter-feeding them.

The foreman eyed him quizzically, waiting for something.

Quin laughed shortly. They'd worked together so long and so affectionately that words weren't always an important part of their communication.

"You're wondering what I'm going to do about the Birkenhead stock," he added.

Durham's watery stare, which mesmerized rowdy young drovers who made the inevitable puns or bawdy jokes linking Durham's name to the ranch's breed, now settled skeptically on Quin.

"Wait for a gentle west wind, I guess."

"Ye got me treed," Durham confessed.

"Build a big black fence." Quin was enjoying his advantage.

The wily foreman said nothing.

"Fire," Quin announced. "Fire a strip of grass maybe a quarter-mile wide along the east fence, after driving all the Birkenhead stock to their side of the line."

"Fire?" Durham was visibly rattled. "Prairie fire?"

They all lived in terror of raging grass fires, whipped by murderous hot winds, killing every living thing in their path and leveling every building besides. There was a fine for setting them.

"A stinking black strip like that should hold them off awhile . . . until it rains. They can't cut it or tear it down, and it doesn't cost anything."

"But it'll burn feed!"

"Less than we'd lose with several thousand Birkenhead beeves on our range."

"You're already in trouble with the association! You'll only buy more grief."

"I'll risk it."

"But the range —"

"Have you ever seen burned-over range in the spring, John? All velvet green, all the sagebrush and weeds burned off, all that potash from the fire turned into good fertilizer to help along a carpet of grass . . . It's beautiful! And necessary, too. That's what lightning does to the prairies naturally every few years."

Durham shook his head unhappily.

"I'll touch the match myself, John, so none of you violate the law. I'll drag a bundle of kerosene-soaked rags on a wire behind my horse. We'll wait for the right wind, and plow a firebreak."

He sighed. "They're bringing in two more Texas herds. So far, our fence has kept Texas fever out, but once they mix their trail herds with our Durhams, it could destroy us in weeks. Texas fever! What else is there to do, John? Rebuild the fence? They'd cut it. Shoot their stock? That's war. I'm a rancher, John. I don't lead armies. Negotiate? I've done that. Go to law? Too slow — they'd have our grass. This news about the hay meadows makes it even more urgent to keep 'em out."

Durham shook his head. "They'll just go around your burned strip and come in from the north across the nester fields, or from the south over the Little Snowies."

Quin disagreed. "Not from the north. Lars Hilleboe, Coffeecan Pentecost, McDougal, and the rest wouldn't stand for it. The south? Possible, but our crew can haze the beeves out again. No. All we need is a gentle west wind."

Durham shook his head. "I'll have to think on it and give ye the common sense of it," he grumbled. He rose stiffly. "Be a little cautious about a thing like that," he counseled. "They'll all be hating you the worse, burning feed in a drought.'

"I can live with it."

"I'm not so sure," the old Scot growled, limping out.

Quin settled back into his desk chair unhappily. No hay. He'd have to sell off stock. And with prices ruinously low . . .

He stared at the envelopes on his rolltop desk. Invoices mostly. That's how things went; there always seemed to be more expenses in a bad year. Salt, for instance. The cattle devoured it in a hot, dry year like this. The envelope from Chicago, addressed in a spidery hand, caught his eye. He recognized the handwriting at once, though he hadn't seen it for five years. The letter was from Andrew Bird, the retired Chicago police inspector he had hired so long ago to look for Missy's relatives. Thank God there were none. He slit the envelope open uneasily, a crabbing fear rising up in him:

My dear Mr Putnam,

I am writing in respect of the matter in which you engaged me in the fall of 18 and 81, and which yielded no fruit at that time. I now have information about a certain Anton Novak who may well be the sire of the damsel in your custody.

I discovered the facts of the case while pursuing a confidential matter for Henry L. Dearborn, the prominent capitalist whose Chicago Traction Company provides horse-drawn trolley service for this metropolis. It is not uncommon in my métier to stumble upon information quite by accident. It was divulged, in fact, by Mrs Dearborn, Adelaide, who informed me that her daughter, Miss Ruth, had eloped with a dashing Bohemian immigrant named Anton Novak in 18 and 71, causing a great scandal.

According to Adelaide Dearborn, the young man was in domestic service, employed at a debutante party which Miss Ruth attended. Somehow they were drawn to each other. Soon they succumbed to that inflammation of the senses that overrides the sober judgment of young ladies and gentlemen. So it was with Miss Ruth, who was described by her mother as frivolous and headstrong.

The liaison was concealed because of young Novak's origins, poverty, and religion, all of which were anathema to Mr Dearborn, a man of means, a 32nd Degree Mason, and an elder in the Presbyterian Church. Mrs Dearborn, whose nature is more bounteous, told me she would have enjoyed the dashing Bohemian as a son-in-law, but as for her husband — it was impossible.

Nature took its course. When Miss Ruth, with child, could no longer conceal the connexion, she eloped. Mr Dearborn was distraught, broke all ties to his daughter, and forbade his wife to see her. But Mrs Dearborn did keep in touch furtively for a year or two, and out of her sketchy memories the rest of the story emerges.

Anton Novak found employment in the stockyards, out in the pens caring for cattle. Miss Ruth was happy even in her straitened circumstances because Anton was a splendid, manly husband, high-humored and affectionate. The child, Miss Antonia, was born some five months later.

Anton befriended the drovers from the West who came on the trains with their cattle and spun fine tales about frontier life on the prairies and mountains. Anton never forgot those yarns, nor the drovers in their finery, even though he advanced to higher tasks indoors.

We can only surmise that one day, perhaps after saving from his slender means, he and his little family embarked for the West and a better life.

If the child is in fact the daughter of this Novak, then her sole known relatives are the Dearborns. In spite of Mr Dearborn's animosity toward Miss

Ruth, I am sure he would be delighted to recover a lost grandchild, and would rear her as his own, with every advantage.

I am pleased to bring your case to a successful conclusion and I submit a small invoice for the additional service.

Your Humble Servant,
A. Bird

P.S. Mrs Dearborn assured me that there is nothing confidential in her account. It was a scandal in its day.

Quin stared vacantly at the blank slope rising behind his house, a view as void as his future. He was feeling old again — much too old.

In the safe beside his desk was his will bequeathing the Q Ranch to Missy. And in Lewistown, he presumed, Miss Nicole was preparing adoption papers. He had never quite nerved himself to sound out Missy on that topic.

The obligation hung there, a stern duty to write the Dearborns about the death of Ruth and Anton — and to surrender Missy to them.

Loss. All his life, the things he loved most had been ripped away. Now it was Missy. And the Q Ranch, besieged by drought and cupidity. Oh, Lord, Missy. His own Missy. Weariness engulfed him, the first flutter of the wings of the angel of death.

Quin rose, desolate, and stared at his friends the books, thousands of books that offered no counsel now.

Then he stared sightlessly at the ledgers on his desk which had recorded the painful progress and setbacks of a large enterprise. He eyed the comfortable Morris chair where he had whiled away the winter evenings, his feet to the stove, reading and planning a future for the girl who illuminated each day of his life. Was it his fate that everything he had ever loved or set out to achieve would end in calamity?

He would have to show the letter to Missy, of course. Or would he? There was more to this than just duty. He'd have to prepare her carefully for her good fortune and splendid new life. He'd have to mask his own grief from her. That would require some delicacy. He didn't want just to ship her off to strangers. Hadn't she borne enough loss for a little girl? And how would she, used to the rough and easy ways of the West, respond to the rigid comportment that would be expected of her in the Dearborns' circles?

Quin glared around him irritably. At the very least, he had to break the news gently to Missy. He'd have to see Nicole about all this. Nicole had steered Missy through the crises of girlhood that an old bachelor couldn't cope with; she'd be able to untangle all the bewildering aspects of this new development.

Missy was probably down at the corrals, expertly cutting out steers for the crew to vet, anchored to Snowflake, her Appaloosa mare, as if she'd been born to the saddle. Quin had fought that at first, bought a sidesaddle, tried to instill ladylike behavior, forbidden her to wear dungarees. She had ignored the sidesaddle, and Nicole had finally resolved the clash by sewing a fine pair of riding culottes, so that Missy looked to be wearing proper skirts in the saddle. How could he take a girl like that and resettle her in a great city?

He bolted restlessly through the sunny parlor and out onto the long veranda that ran the whole width of the rectangular clapboard house; and sank into a wicker chair there. Before him was a view so grand that it never failed to balm his wounds or calm his spirit. He had chosen the site for the house, snugged up against the northern lip of the valley, as much for that noble prospect as for the burbling spring, good garden soil, and central locale.

Far across the tawny Flatwillow Valley, shimmering in the dry heat, lay the dark ridge of the Little Snowies. From the veranda the ridge looked to be an unbroken line, but Quin knew it was rugged country, broken by steep canyons, pummeling creeks, and dark slopes forested with somber ponderosa, or the brighter firs — spruce, lodgepole, and glades of aspen.

Off to the right were the Snowies themselves, where most of his Durhams were summering. Closer at hand, perhaps a half-mile south of the creek, a grassy bench marked the extremity of the bottoms. There were fenced hay meadows in the bottoms, pallid green now when they should have been emerald. From the brushy bottoms, the meadow rose gently to the ranch buildings, which were snugged into a grove of ponderosa for cool shade and protection from the howling north winds. It was a place where a man could drink in the glory of Montana on a golden day, or watch a storm boil over the mountains, or gaze at the snow racing across his meadows.

Here a certain peace stole through him, as it always did. Here he could see design and purpose in all that he had built; the whitewashed board-and-batt barn with the great hayloft; the stout corral made of poles sledged down the mountain; the long log bunkhouse where his eighteen drovers lived; the original log home, with gun ports and heavy shutters against the rampages of Sioux and Blackfoot — now occupied by John Durham. And the great house at his back, sited so that every window, save those on the north, opened on a majestic vista.

He had built it slowly and carefully because he intended for it to endure beyond him. He was over forty and alone when he began, and yet he had built for generations to come. It was an act of faith. He had little time left, the doctors had warned him. True, he felt well. He lived normally, except to avoid heavy or prolonged labor. But only two years ago, over in Butte, Marcus Daly's own doctor had confirmed the murmur — and with a new listening tube he called a stethoscope, too. The copper king's doctor was the best in the territory.

Still Quin dreamed. To stop dreaming now was to die. He wanted five more years. Time to raise Missy, get her set for life, finish the ranch. Time to marry if he could. He had built the house for a wife, built it with an abiding faith that he would find someone and bring her here. It was quixotic, and yet he clung stubbornly to that dream. He needed a woman to love, a woman who would love him.

52

The whole house at his back was an expression of that hope. The parlor would have gladdened the heart of any woman. He had furnished it with a graceful melange of Queen Anne, Sheraton, and Hepplewhite antiques that his peppery octogenarian mother had selected for him in Boston and shipped west after the NP arrived in Billings. On the floor was a cornflower blue and gold Aubusson carpet. On the other side, across a central foyer, were a dining room and kitchen, and behind the foyer, off the parlor, was Quin's study, the heart of the ranch, redolent with the smell of books and leather. It was an extraordinary home for frontier Montana in 1886, and even more remarkable for a single man approaching fifty and eternity. It was, above all, an expression of Quin's optimism, his hearty belief that life was good no matter what trials it might bring.

The view, which spoke to Quin of a majesty and purpose in the universe far beyond his own immediate desperation, quieted him. Always in the past he had been forced to let go of the things he had built and the things he loved. It had been a recurring pattern in his life. But now he would not let go. He would fight for this place to the end, even to death. He was getting on; he no longer had the strength to start over. Here was he rooted; here would he live and die. He would fight for the Q . . . and fight for Missy.

He walked quietly through the silent house to his dark study and closed the door firmly behind him. There at the desk was the oval miniature of his beloved Abby, the tints brighter than his faded memory of his Concord bride. There had been a second wife in

Madison, Amelia Bardenouve, whose passion for him had blossomed in lockstep with his success as a railroad financier and right-of-way buyer. It had cooled just as rapidly as his fortune dwindled after the Panic of 1873, and after she ran off with a stockbroker he had quietly divorced her and headed for that place of lost memories, the frontier. He had lived alone now for thirteen years, save for Missy.

In the somber room, lit only by the north light of the waning day, the agony crept back into him, twice over, piercing, deepening into despair. What tormented him was the thought that he had Missy's well-being to think of as well as his own. Was it right for him to keep her? To conceal her from her relatives? To separate Missy from every social advantage and opportunity that good society could provide?

He stood heavily, hearing Missy on the stairs beyond. At least, he thought, he could be cautious. He would seek Miss Nicole's counsel first. Not that a bluestocking could be trusted with such matters. It was urgent that they set out for Lewistown and the gingerbreaded house of the only woman in the territory, perhaps in the Republic, who practiced law.

CHAPTER
FIVE

"When are you going to drive off the Circle B stock?" Missy asked at breakfast. "It's been days, and you haven't done anything. I despise those people."

Whatever Quin loved, she loved all the more, and whatever troubled Quin, she hated ferociously.

"Now, Missy," Quin objected, "it's no good to hate. The Birkenheads are friends — delightful friends — in spite of our big trouble, which I hope will pass soon."

"They're using our grass, and you're not doing anything," she accused. "Dingdong, more coffee."

She had taken to ordering the Q Ranch's manic Chinese cook, whose name rude occidental tongues had reduced to Dingdong, around like a slave.

"Please," Quin instructed.

"Please, please, please, please, please!"

"It's being done now, Missy. The boys have pushed the Circle B stock over to our east line and are holding the critters there. When the right moment comes, the Birkenheads will get a painful lesson. A burning lesson. And a message from me as well." There was a sudden hardness in his voice.

Quin looks tired, she thought. She'd never seen him like this, his face seamed with worry, rage glinting in his eyes.

"We'll be riding to Lewistown tomorrow," he announced softly. "By saddle, not buggy, so pack some duds tonight. I need to see Miss Nicole about . . . about several matters, and I want you to spend some time with Father Dolan . . ."

Missy regarded him uncertainly. This weary tone was new, and it raised a prick of fear in her.

"I'm sorry. I shouldn't have said those things about the Birkenheads," she muttered.

Quin smiled wearily. "Tell me, Missy. Would you like to be my daughter legally? Would you like me to adopt you?"

She stared at him, her fear soaring.

"Quin, I" — she stumbled, "I already am. Aren't I?"

"You're my daughter in my heart, yes. According the the law, no."

"I want to be."

Quin gazed at her. "But suppose you could have a better life with other people, grandparents maybe. Lots of friends, all the advantages of a city and polite society, a chance to marry a fine man, travel to Europe, do everything . . ."

She stared at him blankly, fear clawing at her stomach.

"But I love you, Quin. I don't want anyone else. I just want to be here on this ranch! I don't need friends. I have Miss Nicole and Mr Durham and Bunions . . ."

56

She was clouding over now. "You're going to send me away. You don't want me anymore."

"I hope to adopt you, and Miss Nicole is preparing the papers. But sometimes plans don't work."

Quin looked miserable, and nothing in his face allayed her fear.

"Are we going to lose the ranch and be poor?" she asked.

"I don't think so, but it's possible."

"Is that what you're going to talk to Miss Nicole about while I'm at catechism?"

"Yes, among other things."

"You look tired."

"I am. We've no hay this year, and we'll soon have no wintergrass, and if I sell the herd at these prices we'll take a licking . . ." He sighed, ran a hand over his baldness, and stood up.

"I could sell Snowflake."

Quin smiled. "There's no need. But I consider your offer a fine one; it tells me you have strong character."

"I do?"

"Yes. Sacrificing what you have to help others — that takes courage."

She didn't know what to make of that. She had wanted only to help save the ranch.

"Missy," Quin continued, standing at the window, "sometimes the things you love most get torn away from you. It's hard to give up what we really care about — like this ranch, which I built from nothing. It's even worse when people are torn away."

She sat at the table long after Quin had gone outside, puzzling over his strange talk. He said he wanted to adopt her, but he talked about loss, separation, grandparents. A dark anxiety settled in her soul.

Missy wished she knew who she was. She wasn't anybody. She wished she could be Antonia Putnam, and join Quin's family. The memory of Anton Novak, her father, was dim and now she tried to conjure it up. There was not even a tintype to help. He was blond and laughed quietly. She could remember his voice better than his face, because of the accent, the way his Rs jiggled. He was so happy sometimes, kissing her mother, teasing her about his riches. That was a private joke they shared. Mama told her she was once very rich, but she never said anything more, and always said "hush" when Antonia asked.

Novak was such a strange name. So was Antonia. Maybe she liked Missy better; she wasn't sure. But Quin was an odd name, too. He had told her he was named for a friend of the Putnam family, John Quincy Adams, the president. She wondered if meeting a president would be like meeting Quin.

She wondered what it would be like to be a Putnam. Quin said his father practiced admiralty law, whatever that was, and now he was retired and working at being an old curmudgeon, writing terrible letters every day to the *Boston Globe*. She had to look up "curmudgeon" in the big Webster's, and then she wondered why anyone would want to be one. And Quin said his mother was the best gossip on Beacon Hill and knew all sorts of things that weren't even so. Missy decided she'd like that. She wanted to meet Quin's mother. Maybe she would stay with her and Quin's father after the Q Ranch failed.

Missy sniffed unhappily. Papa would never marry Miss Nicole because she was too smart and even earned a living like a man. Everyone gossiped about her and said she was peculiar. But Miss Nicole always knew everything. She'd tell Quin if he was going to lose the Q Ranch. Missy wondered if she would have to go to an orphanage then.

Tomorrow they'd go to Lewistown and see Miss Nicole. She had to pack for that, and remember to take clothing for church. Missy didn't like Father Dolan very much. He was soft and white and seemed to blame her for being so far away and not coming on Sundays. It would be more fun just to visit Miss Nicole. But then she remembered Quin's strange mood.

They set off before dawn, he on his blood bay, she on the black. The days had been uncommonly hot, so Quin chose the high trail rather than the shorter wagon road to the McDonald Valley. Not only was it cooler, he pointed out, but it never failed to lift his spirits.

He had broken out his Sunday meeting clothes: slim black gabardine suit, boiled shirt with celluloid collar, bow tie, and shiny leather boots. Missy wore a white blouse and her comfortable doeskin culottes for the long ride, and was secretly grateful she didn't have to make the whole trip sidesaddle.

There was a bulge in Quin's coat pocket, and Missy knew he was carrying his small .22 revolver. He rarely wore his old Peacemaker now that the Indian troubles were almost over. But he did have his long gun, a Winchester 50–95 Express, in a saddle sheath for protection against wolves, or grizzlies, or renegades. The wolves were the main menace, and she dreaded to think what they could do to her if he weren't armed. Quin had once told her that wolves killed fifty or sixty of his calves every year, but it was getting better now that the territory was paying a dollar a pelt for them. She gazed at his possibles bag behind the cantle, knowing she'd find in it everything a person might need to survive in trouble or bad weather.

He smiled at her, but she didn't feel much like smiling back, and she didn't want to talk at all. They climbed the north fork of the Flatwillow and turned off at Potters Creek, which bounced over rocky slopes flanked by ponderosa, lodgepole, and aspen. They stopped at three beaver ponds that turned the creek into a staircase, and let the horses blow and drink. Some of Quin's red Durhams were there, and their calves were gathered in a nursery behind a chokecherry thicket.

They crossed a wooded divide that smelled pungently of cedar and wet earth, and then rode down to the headwaters of Surenough Creek, which twisted north and west through brushy thickets and then hunkered down between long ridges that formed the tree roots of the Snowies. They descended into open country, and it got hotter.

Missy felt so desolate that she scarcely noticed the way Quin glanced at her now and then whenever the trail widened and they could ride abreast.

"What's the matter, honey?" he asked quietly while they rested their mounts.

A flood of tears instantly dimmed her eyes. "Something's wrong," she gulped. "You're going to send me away. You're going to lose the ranch and not want to keep me anymore."

"Missy!"

"You're going to be poor. I just know —"

"Missy, Missy," he groaned, helpless in the tempest of her fear. He lifted her out of the saddle and hugged her, an arm tight around her shoulders until her snuffling stopped and she felt the peace of the high country steal into her.

They nooned on sowbelly and beans there, although it was early, and then rode on down the Surenough between bald hills and aspen groves.

She felt calmer. His eyes told her how much he loved her. He began to talk, though she didn't really want to listen, so wrapped up was she in her premonition of loss.

"The way I see it," he was saying, "is that the grass is more important than the cattle. I'm really a grass grower, not a stock grower. The cattle, they're just mowing machines. We can keep improving the breed — putting more meat on, getting faster growth, better fertility — and where do we end up? Limited by feed. And only feed. That's a pretty radical view, and I suppose I'm the only one in these parts to embrace it. I imagine a century from now it won't be much different. They'll still be trying to breed up, and they'll still be ignoring grass."

Missy liked his quiet talk.

"Well, I don't want to take anything away from breeding up. Do it myself. It's just that . . . we ought to have a real look at these grasses. Some of them doubtless have more feed in them, more power to make beeves grow. Maybe chemists will figure out what it is someday. Missy, have you ever noticed how the stock will eat some grasses and scorn others? Eat the top of a bunch and leave the rest? I guess they have some kind of instinct for what's best for them, something more than just taste. I'd sure like to know what the grass has got — whether it's a type, like bluestem or buffalo or wheat grass, or whether it's something in the soil."

He droned on as they slipped into Forest Grove, where a few families scratched out a living in the pinewoods by foresting, sawing, and gardening. A tired-looking woman waved heavily as they passed. They hit a wagon road where Surenough joined the south fork of the McDonald, and headed westward, upstream, toward the high rim of the vast Judith Basin.

"Grass, Missy! Now that all the long buffalo grass is gone, these ranchers are saying that the stock prefers the short grass anyway. Well, it's true; they do. But those fellas are avoiding the truth when they make a case like that to excuse their overgrazing.

"If a man's a grass manager, he'll never have to fight sagebrush or jimsonweed or erosion. Out beyond our fences are new gullies that make me sick. Every time I look there's another one. Just sick. Once they strip the grass off, the whole country gets torn up by every good gullywasher."

Missy knew he was teaching her how to ranch, and that somehow reassured her. If only he'd keep on talking.

"I wish I could protect the whole Q, just to control the grass. We're working on it, patenting all we can. Every man in my crew's got claims I'll buy just as soon as they're proved up. It's costly and slow, and I don't mint money the way the Birkenheads do; most years I've barely broken even. And patented land is taxed, too. But I'll have — you'll have — a place someday that'll care for itself . . . if I can put that land in my pocket before the government makes me tear out fence."

Missy gazed at him quietly, even more reassured. They loped across a high plateau, and the vastness of the rolling land and endless skies quieted them. Far off to the south, across a rolling wild, were the majestic Snowies, the eastern sentinels of the main chain of the Rockies. But they vanished from sight as the road twisted down a long coulee and into the Judith Basin.

"We've had to prove up everything. Pay for surveyors. Build homestead shacks on each claim. Plant trees for the Timber Culture Act. Dig ditches for the Desert Irrigation Act. And then buy it all from the crew. It's a load, Missy, and I'm crazy to do it when all the rest of them ranch on free land that's there for the use. But it's for us — you and me — and once we have it, no one can take it away."

He grinned. "Maybe it's for Miss Nicole, too. All those land claims are half her living."

They reached Big Spring Creek, which rushed icily toward Lewistown, fed by a giant upwelling of water at the toes of the mountains.

The legislature had created a new county, Fergus, and at the end of 1886 Lewistown would become its seat. But as Quin and Missy drew close to it, in the slanting sun, it looked too modest for such a future. Its locale was exquisite, set in a broad plain cupped by forested mountains.

"When I first came to this country there was hardly anyone except Nelson Story," Quin reminisced. "But now look at it! Fifty or sixty buildings, and that's nothing compared to Maiden. Twelve hundred people mining quartz gold up there now. I saw in a stockman's journal that there's more than one hundred thousand cattle and one hundred thousand sheep within a sixty-mile radius of Maiden."

Missy stared at the somber peaks to the northeast, where Anton Novak might have taken her. He had talked of Maiden.

"It'll die when the gold peters out," Quin ventured, "but Lewistown'll live. Half a dozen stagecoach routes join here, and lots of ranches to supply."

East of town they struck Main Street, which angled southwest toward the old stage route from Carroll to White Sulphur Springs. False-front buildings lined the rutted avenue, and behind them nestled modest clapboard or log or board-and-bat homes and outbuildings.

Drovers sauntered along the boardwalks, and Missy watched, enthralled. Lewistown was the drovers' Paris, and they always dressed their flamboyant best: high-heeled boots, bold-colored flannel shirts, silver-mounted cartridge belts for their pearl-handled six-guns, wide-brimmed beavers creased to individual preference, and florid bandannas.

Quin stowed the horses at the livery and engaged rooms from Prosperity Pulford, who owned the Traveler's Rest. But Missy didn't fall asleep until very late, and then she dreamed of her mother, all in white.

CHAPTER
SIX

That tattletale boy, Zeke Pulford, had blabbed to Nicole last night that Quin and Missy were at his father's hotel. No doubt they would be here first thing this morning. She had risen early and washed her hair, and now she brushed it until the raven waves glowed. She selected the sternly pleated snowy cotton shirtwaist, a summery dress that framed her olive face and emphasized the rosy hue of her cheeks better than anything else in her cedar-lined closet. And the fitted bodice would reveal a girlish figure that she dared hope Quin would notice. Her father's gold pocket watch, which she wore suspended from a necklace of cunningly woven gold, was a hallmark of her profession. It had to do. She whitened her high-button shoes where they had been scuffed and decided she was ready to face the man she loved.

It would not be easy. She had finally decided to go back to Saint Louis, because Quincy Putnam just wasn't interested in her. Saint Louis was where she had prospered the first sixteen years of her life, in that old brick rectangle of a home that had served as her father's office as well as the Aumont residence. How vividly she still remembered the night her father had roughly awakened her. "Pack a bag," he hissed. "Hurry!" She did, fumbling in the shadowed lamplight, and then they raced through the dark spring chill down to the wharves, where they boarded a river packet that would head up the Missouri the next morning. Her father hustled her down into the cargo hold of the paddle-wheeler, and there they cowered through the night and well into the next day, until the ship had steamed well above Saint Louis. Only then did he escort her up to cabins he had reserved.

They debarked at last at Fort Benton, Montana Territory, the head of navigation on the mighty Missouri. From there they traveled by stage the short span to the new, raw metropolis of Lewistown, purveyor to the gold camps in the Judith and Moccasin mountains as well as to the most opulent cattle ranches in Montana. And there, after a few taut weeks, the Aumonts settled down and practiced law.

She knew, partly from guesswork and partly from the gleanings of old correspondence, why he had bolted from Saint Louis in the black of the night, abandoning a capacious home and a lucrative practice. Nicole smiled bitterly. Her sensual father had not been an entirely honorable man.

Now she'd go home again. But anguish burdened that decision. She had to, before Lewistown tore her to pieces. Still — and this was her anguish — she loved Quincy and would gladly stay here if only he wanted her. Quincy Putnam, that strange, tender, tough, gentle, bold, balding man with his overstuffed conscience always getting underfoot. And dear Missy, the child of calamity, clinging to life only because Quin loved her in fee simple. If only he would propose! Could he ever love a bluestocking like herself?

She had scarcely gulped down a bowl of oatmeal when he was there at the door, lean and agitated.

"Quincy Putnam," she smiled. "Where's Missy?"

"At the hotel. I couldn't bring her here. Not this time. And Father Dolan's at Maiden."

There was something metallic in his voice that disturbed her. He scarcely glanced at her as he settled himself in his customary chair. She touched a hand to the rosebud she had clipped into her hair, wondering.

"Well," she said tentatively, "what is it, Mr Putnam?"

The tautness in his weathered face surprised her. He ran a hand unconsciously over his baldness.

"I've got a grief that's weighing me down so much I can't bear it," he exploded.

She waited expectantly. It was always best to let him crab toward his revelations.

"It's Missy!" he blurted.

"Missy? Is she ill?"

"No, no."

Nicole was suddenly alarmed. There was a haunted look on Quin's face that she'd never seen before. Jerkily he plunged a hand into his breast pocket and thrust an envelope toward her. She lifted the little gold-rimmed spectacles that rested on her bosom, suspended by a ribbon, and perused the letter carefully, never wavering until she had grasped every sentence. At last she looked up.

68

"I know exactly what your overstuffed Harvard-Unitarian conscience is goading you to do, Quincy Fiddlehead."

"I haven't said much to Missy yet," said Quin, "but she knows something's happening. I'm upset, she's upset, and I don't know what to do."

"Of course she's upset!" Nicole exclaimed. "You're all she has, Quincy. Away from you there's nothing. No relatives. Think what it must have been like for that shivering little girl. You became her food, her shelter, her home, her confidant, her father and mother . . . and she knows you're no relative. Only love binds you to her."

"Well, she'll soon have everything: blood relatives, privilege, wealth, friends her age, cultivation, neighbors." Quin glared at her. "There's nothing at the Q for her. Nothing! No other girls. No one her age. No school. And Lewistown's thirty-five miles away. Nothing."

"Quincy Putnam!" She stood up suddenly. "You're working yourself into writing the Dearborns. Stop being so noble. I won't let you. Over my dead body. You think it's your duty. Duty! Doing what's right for her! Don't be so lofty and resigned to suffering. What makes you think it'd be right?"

A rosy tint suffused her face.

"Quin," she said tenderly, "you're making yourself miserable about it because you love her so much you can't bear to let her go. You'd lose . . ." She paused. "Sometimes I can read your mind."

Quin smiled wanly. Too many people were reading his mind these days.

"You wrestle too much with virtue," she rebuked him. "Quincy Putnam, what you need is to be an ordinary, garden-variety sinner. You're so impractical sometimes, throwing life and happiness away . . ."

She settled back into the swivel chair.

"Missy's coming along well enough without childhood friends," she assured him. "I didn't have any either, not one giggly girl. I got along well enough. In fact, I did better. I learned law."

She gazed pensively out the window. "But sometimes I'm not so sure . . ."

He followed her gaze, past the gingerbread latticework of the porch to the dark, mysterious mountains, and then his eyes settled on her again.

"If all this information is correct, which I doubt, we've got to move fast to protect you and Missy," she mused. "Adoption would ratify your years together and provide a legal bond that Henry Dearborn couldn't sever. I'll have to see what bearing known relatives, such as grandparents, would have on the process."

She wrote a note to herself in a fine feminine hand.

"You're not protected, Quincy. If the Dearborns find out about Missy, they might try to take her from you, and that would tear you to pieces."

"Miss Nicole, that's my point! Restoring Missy to her true relatives would be the right thing —"

"Mr Putnam!" she interrupted. "Stop that! The right thing for Missy is what you've given her. You can be such a dunce when your head is stuffed full of principles."

70

"That's what I employ you for — the best legal mind in the territory," he replied drily.

She smiled. "A woman reads the law her own way, I've discovered. No, I'm not talking about the law at all. In spite of all you've built out here, you don't really have much, do you? You rattle around in your house, alone except for the girl who brings you your only real happiness. All right, then, be noble, be miserable, be lofty. The one you'll hurt most isn't yourself. It's Missy."

Quin sat quietly, subdued by Nicole's fervor.

"I don't know," he grumbled. "I don't like sneaking off to court like that."

"Mr Putnam, there are times when I — Look, once you adopt her and she's safely yours, there's nothing to keep you from telling the Dearborns about their granddaughter. She could visit them, try out their life. They might come to love her . . . as a grandchild. But, Quincy, she'd still be yours. She'd still be able to come home if that life was wrong for her, or simply if you wished her to come. Don't you see? You don't have to lose her."

Nicole had never been so adamant. She had often disagreed with clients, but she had always acquiesced in the end.

"I think it's the other way around," Quin said slowly. "If I kept her from this chance to join her family, if I condemned her to a life as a drudge on a lonely ranch, just for my selfish pleasure — when she could be the belle of Chicago, with every privilege — then she'd never forgive me. She'd find out someday, and I'd live with her rage and hurt the rest of my days. I'm not being virtuous or lofty. I'm doing —"

"What's best for Missy," she replied sarcastically. "Mr Putnam . . . Quin, don't torture yourself. The simple, natural thing is to adopt her. The best thing for you both is exactly what you've shared for five years. Time alters things, Quin. You've built a bond through time. It's alive; it shouldn't be torn apart. Don't you see what separation would do to her? She'll think you abandoned her. She'll think she was always the stepchild, the orphan, alone. It could crush her, Quin."

He was silent and seemed to be remembering things.

"It's a hard decision, and I don't want to push you," she said, actually wishing she could shove him. Something slackened inside her. She'd never really fought a client. Not until now. She'd laid out alternatives, described the things that might happen, and left the final decisions to those who employed her.

"I'm going to do the right thing and write —"

"I won't let you," she snapped. "I won't let you fob her off. I won't let you peddle her like a sack of potatoes to Henry Dearborn. You'll have to get another lawyer, because I won't do it! I won't!"

She sat bolt upright behind her desk, trembling, while Quin gaped at her.

"You'd . . . quit me?" he gasped.

"Yes, I would, Quincy Putnam! Yes, damn you!"

He slumped in his chair, plainly shocked to the bone.

Nicole was astonished at herself. Never in her life had she cried out so passionately. She decided, suddenly, that women shouldn't be lawyers. She was too emotional. She shouldn't practice law! It was male business!

Then he did a strange thing. A great wild glitter rose up in his eyes, and he laughed.

"You always said I was a mule," he joked, "and now you've whacked me between the ears with a two-by-four."

The ice that had collected around her heart broke into floes.

"I'm sorry we haven't proceeded faster with the adoption," she said shakily. "It got pushed aside. It always seemed less urgent than the mounds of other work crying for attention."

He rubbed his head ruefully. "When a man goes against his principles, he's just killing himself," he muttered, "and he pays for it ten times over in the end. If I don't do the right thing —"

"Oh, hush!" Nicole laughed. He was grumbling and muttering like a storm that had already passed over.

"All right," he sighed. "I want to think about it for a while. Nothing'll happen anyway, and I can sort out the right and wrong of it. Oliver Holmes used to say —"

"It's not the rights and wrongs; it's the loves and hurts," she retorted, knowing she'd won, even if it took him a while to reconcile himself. But rage still brightened her violet eyes.

He subsided quietly.

"How are you going to answer the letter?" she inquired.

"Why, I'll thank him and pay him. No sense saying anymore."

She nodded, worried about Quin's vulnerability. She wished she could complete the adoption immediately, even before he replied to the detective. But there was no pushing Quincy. If you hit a mule too hard, he just backed up.

"I've got to fetch Missy before she buys out Seth Westring. You'll join us for lunch at the hotel? Pulford's chow isn't fit for a coyote, but there's not much else in town."

"Quincy? Goodness . . . yes, I'll join you!"

It was the first time he had ever asked her anywhere. All their companionship in the past had risen out of business conducted in these chambers.

"High time I squired a lady out on the town," he grinned, rubbing the prow of his forehead. "And high time you got sprung from this calaboose."

"Quin!" she laughed. "Is that what you call my nice house?"

"It's a cage, at any rate," he said somberly.

She saw Quin to the door. Then she retreated in her swivel chair, plucked up her skirts, and lifted her whitened shoes to the desk. It always tickled her to do that, to lean back like a man and stretch out her legs.

She was tired. The confrontation had drained her. And she was curiously pleased and in a melting mood. She never got invited anywhere, and now he'd asked her to lunch. It was like going to dinner at Delmonico's or some swank place like that. At last! she thought. At last he cared a little. A delicious warmth stole through her. That mule! She'd bean him between the ears again, if she had to.

74

She had intended to tell him about St. Louis — the Great Decision. But this changed things, this lunch. At least for now. She couldn't just leave now, could she? And anyway, she hadn't planned to go until fall, after she'd lined up a replacement who'd buy her practice.

Quin simply melted her. Why did she just turn to butter? "Melted" was the only word she could think of. He was such a grand man! Her father had respected Quin, even though the two were as unalike as Cain and Abel. "There aren't many with Putnam's character," he had once told her. "He'll do well if all that ethical baggage he shoulders doesn't collapse him."

Ethical baggage! That was Quin. Too burdened with ethical baggage! Maybe that was what melted her, she thought. She always had the feeling that he needed to be cared for a bit; someone stronger and maybe meaner had to help him out from time to time. Funny that it should be Miss Nicole Aumont, she mused. Someone so petite.

She hadn't had much chance to care for anybody, she thought. She would gladly do his worrying for him; that's what lawyers and wives were for. Now, for instance, she was going to worry about how long it would take Henry L. Dearborn to find out about his granddaughter. Private detectives traded in information, she knew. Information that had brought a price from Quin would fetch an even greater price from the financier. It would only be a matter of time, she guessed, and then Andrew Bird would peddle his facts once again.

She yanked her feet down suddenly. She was going to have to browbeat that mule to finish up the adoption before real calamity smacked him down. "Andrew Bird," she wrote on her memo pad. It would remind her to keep the heat on Quin — beginning at lunch in a few minutes.

She smoothed her skirts and washed. Did she look her best? She peered anxiously into the glass, not content. It irked her that Quin had paid so little heed. Was he simply immune to women? Had he never, ever, looked at her in that way? Usually she didn't like men to look at her like that. She always retreated behind her desk and spoke brusquely when they did. But Quin . . . how she hoped he'd examine her just like that, slowly and warmly. She smiled as she pinned on her ostrich-plume hat and plunged out the door.

CHAPTER
SEVEN

The west wind wafted incense to Minnie Birkenhead, but she didn't think that was unusual. There had been smoke on the breeze through much of July. The summer had been tinder dry, and fires had raged on the prairies and up in the timbered mountains. The scented south wind had brought acrid grass smoke and pungent sagebrush smoke and sweet pitch pine smoke. But this was the first west wind in weeks, flowing gently, persistently out of the Snowies. She imagined the air was a few degrees cooler today.

She had driven about two miles west of the station, seeking subject matter to paint. Flatwillow Creek vanished there into a dense mass of reddish brush. Curious, she had barged through the thickets until she struck the stream, which widened into a snug pond before it curled lazily under a cutbank. It was a cool bower, even on that ferocious day. The pond was overarched by plum, chokecherry, and box elder, so that only a patch of turquoise showed overhead.

An hour later, refreshed by her sojourn at the creek, she set out for home. The shadows stretched long, and the acrid aroma of burning grass was more persistent. Just before abandoning her glade, she'd been startled by a steer that had splashed squarely down the creek, rolling its eyes. An odd day, Minnie thought; something more for her burgeoning journal.

Each of the Birkenheads had a light wagon, fashioned from tough ash and hickory — a rectangular box for a chassis and above it a bench seat on leaf springs, designed for two, but ideal for just one Birkenhead. They had learned to drive their wagons almost anywhere a horse could go, save for steep coulees and cutbanks. With a deft celerity they wheeled along to roundup camps with the cowboys, who found the little wagons handy for spare gear.

Across the arch of the western sky, as Minnie squinted at the amber sun, lay a pall of brown smoke. It drifted heavily toward her, but she was not disturbed, because a prairie fire could scarcely make headway on land as denuded as theirs. As far as she could see in every direction, Circle B longhorns were trotting eastward like a vast army in full retreat.

Off to the east she discerned her brother Augie slicing toward her in his wagon through phalanxes of eastbound steers.

"A prairie fire!" he bellowed as he braked. "We'll need more buckets and burlap sacks and shovels, and all the help we can muster. Load up at the station, and come along!"

"Augie," she exclaimed disdainfully, "I've been aware of it for hours. It's almost stationary, and it's not going to race over naked dirt. I think I should like to paint it. The colors are remarkable."

Her cold calm subdued him. From the moment they had arrived, the brute menace of prairie fires had hung over Flatwillow Station. At the worst, they were galloping infernos that raced ahead of the wind faster than man or beast could flee, towering walls of orange flame and bitter blue smoke that fried and choked everything they overran.

"Quite right, Minnie," Augie confessed sheepishly. "You always get the better of me. Let's rove west a bit and see what's happening. Cattle have been trotting through the station in fear of their lives."

"Capital," she agreed, mildly elated at the adventure. Subduing a prairie fire would make splendid copy for her journal and might even sell to the *Times*. Their hackney horses were skittish when pointed west, but eventually the brother and sister rolled toward the dark sunset. When they reached the downed fence separating Flatwillow range from the Q, they gazed out at a smoldering black carpet that stretched as far as they could see. Musky fumes coiled up from thousands of charred bits of debris. The whole spectacle was much less menacing than Minnie had hoped it would be. She was disappointed.

They wheeled their wagons up to the bench that formed the southern extremity of the creek valley, and there they were treated to a more entertaining vista. Black fingers, mostly along the bottoms of coulees, projected deep into the Flatwillow Station range, and at the head of each finger was a crackling blaze. The fire had died on the denuded prairies, but flourished in every crease of land where sagebrush and chokecherry grew.

In fact, the fire had not expired at the fence line as Quincy Putnam had intended. He had seen what had interested him most — the bunch grass clipped back to the roots. But his keen eye had passed over the brush and debris of the open country, brush that now fed fingers of flame. The sagebrush massed in the bottoms was crackling and spitting like a long fuse leading to a detonation. Quin had burned his fence, but the Flatwillow range was being sliced into paddocks where longhorns gathered, hemmed in by black boulevards.

"It's not doing anything but cleaning up the brush, and that's a blessing," Augie observed. "We'll have more forage in the spring, I'd say."

In their immediate area the various fingers of fire were pursuing the drainage down to the creek and then dying in the wet bottoms.

"We shall have to summon the men and put out all these bottoms, I suppose," Augie grumbled. "I rather think the dangers of prairie fires are exaggerated by the folklore."

Through the marbled twilight they could see several amber blazes dotting the country. No broad lines of fire anywhere. Just glowing dots, like campfires of a militia scattered across the darkening plains. The soft plop of horseshoes on dust drifted up to them, and the faint scratch of distant voices. Far down the creek valley, a murky band of horsemen moved toward them, followed by a wagon. That would be Alex and the crew. In the dusk noise drifted far.

On the northerly slopes, beetles of bronze fire were eating their way down toward the creek, sometimes flaring up when a noble sagebrush burst into flame and shed glowing coals.

"I shall have to paint that!" Minnie exclaimed.

"Let's meet them and report," Augie urged, rattling down the long grade, with Minnie behind. But they were on the wrong side of Flatwillow Creek, which they could not ford because of the cutbanks. They drew up.

"Hoo, Alex. We're here," Augie called.

The Circle B crew halted across the creek in the dark.

Augie shouted to them, "It's just brush in the coulees, that's all. Most of it was on Putnam's range."

"Putnam's range burned?" Alex asked. "Our cattle were on it. The cattle are what worry me."

"Yes, it burned," Augie replied. "As far as one could see. The west wind —"

"The west wind? The west wind!" Alex exclaimed. "And all our cattle are back here. It's not the bloody fire that's the problem; it's the cattle. Pounds, shillings, pence! And not only that; the herd arrived."

"Herd?"

"Whilst you were gone. Two thousand from Texas. A dozen drovers holding them, and not a bloody blade of grass."

"Send them back! Send them back!" Minnie cried.

"How much of Putnam's range burned?"

"As far as we could see."

"I shall have a look," Alex yelled, snapping his reins. He careened westward through the gloom until he reached the charred land, demarcated by Putnam's blackened, smoking fenceposts.

He stalked out on the burn, black in the black night. Heat licked his boots, and sulfurous fumes seared his throat. But sooner or later, he guessed, he'd emerge onto rank, silvery pasture. West wind!' Putnam had waited for the west wind! Alex thundered over the charred earth for so long that he began to doubt, but at last, ahead of him, pale in the moonlight, was a carpet of high, rustling grass. He stepped over a plowed furrow onto it, exulting savagely. Deliberate, then! He stormed north along the furrow as it curved around the head of a coulee and circled a copse of cedar. Putnam had taken no chances with a shift of breeze, he realized, with grudging admiration. But Putnam'd pay. Oh, how he'd pay!

Nowhere on all that moonlit grass was the bulk of a longhorn visible. The Q Ranch crew had driven them all east of the fire before lighting it. His mind raced. There'd be no driving his longhorns over this stinking wasteland for weeks. Putnam had built a fence without wire! But surely there were other ways . . . Through the nesters north of Putnam? Risky. They were voters; the Birkenheads were aliens. Through the Little Snowies? He'd never been up there. But his men had talked of dense forest, fallen logs, thickets . . . Surely there was a way through all of that. Up a creek. Over a game trail. Down a canyon. Twenty or thirty head at a time, guided by watchful drovers.

Alex calculated quickly: the burned strip was a quarter of a mile — no, maybe half a mile — wide.

Four or five square miles of excellent feed, gone. Enough for his whole bloody herd, probably, until it rained. An outrage, burning public grass like that! Putnam must pay! Let him keep his few acres; Q Ranch was doomed.

He stalked east again, kicking aside live embers.

How fortunate that the fire had burned some of the Birkenheads' range, Alex thought. That put him on high ground. There'd always be some salty stockmen who would forgive Putnam for burning his own range — but never for burning someone else's. Not in a drought like this! Alex took savage pleasure in the brief he would lay before the district cattlemen soon.

He found Natividad Rourke beside the creek, holding the crew at Putnam's fence line. Natividad, the darkly handsome son of a Mexican mother and an Irish father, had trailed north with the first herd the Birkenheads imported from Texas, and Alex had hired him as his foreman. He knew longhorns and spoke Spanish and Texican, a variant of English that none of the Birkenheads could comprehend, although Minerva was slowly learning to translate it. Rourke had been a wise choice. Christmas, as they delighted in calling him, could cajole, vet, and bully longhorns expertly, out of years of intimate association. His ready smile, and ready fists, had transformed him into a respected segundo at the station.

"A blaze half a mile wide. But there's still good bunch grass on the other side. It was deliberate," Alex informed him quietly. "We've got to cross it somehow. I've ruled out the nesters, at least for the time being.

That leaves the south flank of the Q, over the Little Snowies. Can you do it?"

Christmas smiled.

"There ees nowhere the longhorn will not go," he said, with just a trace of his beautiful mother's accent.

"Good! I knew it! We'll move the new herd first, and then the rest. Tomorrow, find a passage." Alex peered across the creek into the night gloom.

"They drove back to the station, sir," Natividad explained. "Miss Minnie was very tired."

"Very good, Christmas. You go on back with the men. Tomorrow we must move the new herd. I'll leave the details to you. Find a passage, a game trail or whatever. Don't fail!"

"We'll be off at first light — on the Q by dusk." The foreman grinned as he wheeled away with his men.

Nip and tuck, Alex thought. But he'd pull it off. He turned his hackney toward the station. Odd, how they always called it the station, rather than home. By rights, after four years, it was home; it had come to seem like one. And all three had actually enjoyed the place, and the rude life, far more than they had anticipated. The American prairies grew on one.

The master of Flatwillow Station rattled on through the night, his shrewd mind coldly calculating every angle.

It was war. He'd be ruthless, of course, but less so than Minnie. She was a terror. He had a fair claim to grass over on the Q, same as anyone else. A man had to protect his property; he had to get his longhorns onto

84

that public grass. Next year they'd fetch sixty thousand quid, even if prices stayed low. Enough to go home . . .

He'd try the southern flank over the mountains first. If that failed, he'd tackle the northern flank, through the nester cropland. He hated to do that — oh, he hated the very idea. The nesters were a feisty lot, and there'd be political trouble because the Birkenheads were aliens. But he'd do it, by God, if he had to! He'd do it even though there was scarcely a gun-smart man on his immigrant crew. He'd do it at night, probably. Several thousand beeves across nester cropland and through the north fence.

And after that he'd see to it that Putnam was nailed to the blacklist. That'd kick the last props from under the chap. And, of course, he'd file a complaint with Sheriff Earley over in White Sulphur Springs. That'd be just the thing! Get Putnam to cooling his heels in the pokey for a couple of months — until it rained. That would be the short-range solution. Tie him up for a while. The blacklist would be the long-range one; it would ruin Putnam and secure the Q range for Circle B. Every herd-building buckaroo in the county would be lassoing Putnam's shorthorns, saying they had strayed, and Putnam would be helpless to stop it. By autumn Putnam would be off and gone, folded up like a Parker House roll.

But all this would be done through the stockmen's association, of course. That's where Alex differed with Minnie. The Birkenheads would stay in the background, stay invisible, pull strings, let those rough frontiersmen do the dirty work. Oho, Putnam! A couple of months in the hoosegow for you and grass galore for the longhorns!

Alex sighed contentedly. If all else were to fail, he held yet another card, the ace of all spades: Texas fever. Those longhorn herds trailing north were full of it, and most were resistant to it. But if he were to drive the sick ones into Putnam's shorthorns, the contagion would scythe them down, and by midsummer Putnam would scarcely have a live animal.

CHAPTER
EIGHT

The young trail boss, Abel Hitchcock, eyed Alex quizzically. Nineteen hundred cattle and no feed. The starving beasts were bawling their complaint to all within earshot while they scrounged browse and bark and cactus down along the bottoms.

The crew had tallied over nineteen hundred in the new herd that morning. Twenty-one hundred was what the Texans had started with, but the grass had petered out north of Cheyenne. One by one the weak critters had capsized, Hitchcock explained. The laggards were left behind, alive, and some of them would survive and be gathered by other roundup districts. Some would eventually be credited to the Birkenhead accounts at the Chicago stockyards.

"I should like to employ you and your colleagues for a fortnight," Alex proposed. "There's good grass off to the west."

Hitchcock ruminated a moment. "You might nab a few, but ah doubt it. They're free agents; ah have no more authority over them after this mawning. And they're all steaming to jog to Miles City."

"What's so urgent at Miles?" Alex asked genially.

"Why, I s'pose they all want to git to church, suh."

"I see. And how about yourself and the cook?"

"We're employed permanent by Goodell and Knight, and we'll be sailing downwind with the chuck as soon as possible — at least, after a little visit to Miles."

"I suppose you're eager to get to church also, eh?"

"Yes, indeed, suh. We were a right religious outfit, ah'd say. Sort of a floatin' All Saints parish, suh."

"Well, Hitchcock, I need some drovers urgently."

"You might engage three or four," the trail boss ventured. "Older men. Some of those old fellows up above thirty, they ain't got religion anymore."

"I see. What if I pay a bonus?"

"Mistuh Birkenhead, they're all itching to squander money, not earn it. Never saw such a tithing outfit. They've been on the trail since last March, suh."

"What shall I propose to them? I'm quite prepared —"

"Double."

"How much is that?"

"Double their trail wage of fifty and found. Some might last you out a few days afore they get religion."

"A hundred dollars for a fortnight?"

"If you can hold 'em for a fortnight."

Alex bagged four. One was gimpy. Another lacked an eye and crabbed about everything. Another had the most preposterous lantern jaw, at least as far as Alex's tastes were concerned. And the last was a gaunt scarecrow loaded with boils. These Texicans were the oddest-looking lot Alex had ever seen, save perhaps some of the Welsh.

The rest bolted down Flatwillow Creek, boiling up dust and whooping like wild Indians. Four days of grueling riding would land them in the queen of the cow towns, the mecca of every trail-beat cowpoke on the northern plains. The ones who remembered to ante up their fare first would catch the Northern Pacific and ship back to Texas; the others would jostle down with Hitchcock and the cavvy wagon. And when they quit Miles, they wouldn't have a dollar's change among the whole lot.

Ten of his own men. And maybe four Texans who might linger a fortnight. Alex weighed the odds coolly. With these he had to funnel the new herd over the Little Snowies and then gather his home herd and push it over the mountains, too. So few men and so little time! He would take every necessary risk.

"Christmas, I intend to ride along."

"It's not wagon country, sir."

"Then I'll ride the chuck wagon."

"There'll be no chuck up above; only below, sir."

"Then I'll pull along as far as I can, and you may send a man back periodically to report. I wish to make the decisions."

"I think we'd better scout a passage first," the foreman demurred. "We'll be moving a large herd through several miles of dense forest and thickets along the crest, sir."

"No time. No time for that! We'll take our chances. Surely there'll be trails — deer, elk —"

"These are longhorns, sir."

"I see. Well, let's be off by dawn at the latest, eh? These hungry beasts —"

"Sir, I'd suggest we send a man ahead to ride along the burned strip. He might find a break in it where we can push through. Or even a narrow spot where we can stampede the herd across."

"Very good, Christmas. Start him off at once."

They rolled at dawn, while the air was cool and sweet, and the quiet was pierced only by the bawling of cantankerous bovines. The Texans took over: the Circle B men were rank greenhorns when it came to trailing large herds. They drove the panting beeves southwest through the day, pounding up so much dust that it coppered the sky.

The advance rider reported there was no passage through the burn: the Q Ranch had artfully fired clear to a steep cliff that angled off to the southeast. So it would have to be the hard way, around the eastern shoulder of the mountains and then up the long slopes, probably in the Jones Creek drainage, until they hit big timber. After that, it was anyone's guess.

They ranged ever farther from water, while the animals' tongues slobbered out and dust caked them all in the searing heat. Alex rode point in his wagon, while close behind lumbered a giant roan steer with a span of hooked horns over seven feet across. The doughty animal had led the herd over seventeen hundred miles and was still game. At the rear, men suffered cruelly in yellow dust so thick that the bandannas over their noses were useless and their eyes watered shut. Unruly bunch-quitters darted out, intent on a retreat to the

90

creek, and some were lost in the haze. Only the long conditioning of those thirst-crazed beeves on the northbound trail kept them together.

They rounded the eastern flanks of the Snowies through the afternoon, climbing all the while along dry shoulders, barren of brush and timber and mowed to the bone by sheep. High above, the cool pines met the prairie, first in outlying sentinels, then in copses of juniper and ponderosa, and then in park-like slopes where the yellow pines were carelessly scattered.

While the sun boiled the blue out of the heavens, the herd pushed southeast of the Little Snowies, closing in on the Jones Creek Valley. Dusk found the flagging cowboys steering the silent cattle into a broad coulee where the creek should have run — but didn't. At least there was brush in the bottoms, and the long militia staggered down into it, savaging twigs and leaves and stems. There was an eerie silence upon the herd.

Alex Birkenhead had never spent such an unholy day or night. The ground was a frying pan, and all of his two hundred eighty pounds of beef ached and steamed. He sucked at his canteen greedily, while sweat furrowed the yellow gumbo that caked him. But he, riding point, wasn't half so miserable as the yellow scarecrows who had tailed or flanked the herd, eating grit until their throats clogged and their lungs hurt.

"We'll need to lullaby these dry cattle all night," Natividad said as he hunkered down beside Alex. "They're primed to bolt back to the Flatwillow. Wouldn't take much. The Texas lads will take the first shift. That's because ours have never done it and should see how it goes, yes?"

"Of course. As you wish," Alex said shortly.

"And tomorrow we'll scout for a passage, maybe along the creek, before we move beeves, yes?"

"No time, no time!" Alex wheezed. "Take a bunch with you, for heaven's sake, man. Take fifty whilst we hold the rest."

"That would bind us up, sir. You can't just highball two thousand longhorns through timber."

"The woods don't look so thick, Christmas. Those pines up there are rods apart. Surely there's a way."

"The next mile, yes. But on top —"

"Well, try it my way. Those poor devils are dreadfully dry. We've got to cut corners, Christmas. Courage, man!"

The foreman retreated morosely.

They were all sullen and growly as the dawn broke. After a gritty breakfast, Natividad gathered six men, cut out forty irate beeves, and started up the creek bed in the long slant of the coppery sun. They had no trouble for a couple of miles, until they approached a basin where the headwaters of Jones Creek gathered in wetter times. The ponderosa grew thicker there, and juniper thickets formed impenetrable barricades. At the bottom of the basin they boogered the lumbering animals up a steep, rocky slope and into a timber-choked vale, rank with lodgepole, pine, fir, and spruce. On the shaded forest floor, there grew a little grass, green, moist, tender, wherever it could commandeer some sun, and the cattle snatched at it greedily in passing.

The cattle funneled into a saddle at the crest of the slope, hemmed by vaulting massifs on either side. Deftly they whipped their giant horns through the narrowing passages among the rank pine, leaping over fallen logs and struggling under scratching limbs in the process. Then the critters began to scatter. There was no way man or beast could follow a straight trajectory in the deeps of the forest. The drovers were slowed by murderous limbs and flailing needles, dense thickets and waist-high barricades of log. They twisted and turned through the maze, hoping to regroup ahead in some alpine park or sunny glade. The clatter of horn banging wood astounded them; the whole area was alive with a rattling staccato mayhem.

It was then that Natividad Rourke knew he was in trouble. He had lost track of most of the others; the cattle had splintered off every which way, vanishing from sight in a place where one could see only a few dozen yards. And the enraged bawling of the beasts told him they were wedged in tighter than an ax handle. He drew his six-gun and fired three times. There was an answering shot above and left; others rang out from various corners of the big timber. He fired three again, and men began to materialize, picking their way on foot and leading their mounts.

Natividad steered his way toward the loudest bawling and found a bull wedged into an arc, horns trapped so that his big head aimed east and the rest of him, pinned by four trees, aimed north and south. If they were all like this, Nativided thought, he had real trouble. He spotted Arne, the giant Swede, and sent him back to the cavvy wagon for an ax. And then he put his scratched and bleeding little crew to work.

Lem Eakins stripped the saddle from his sweat-stained cayuse and led it to the trough. Oh, he had a story to tell! He wanted Quin and Bull Durham and all the fellers he could rustle up to get an earful.

"I was riding high in the mountains, looking for sheep on our range, like Bull said to do," he began after he had cornered an audience. "And I shore did see some sights. I got to hearing an all-fired powerful racket off there to the southeast, down in the corner of our range. Couldn't rightly make out the why of it, but it was coming to me, soft on the breeze like that. One moment I'd hear something; next it was quiet as a church. Then I heard some shots, seems like, and something odd — a rattle, sort of — so I thought maybe those boys at Fort Maginnis were practicing with this new Gatling gun, or maybe even there was a war over yonder. But 'twasn't that a-tall. No, sir, not a-tall.

"I was kind of leery, not knowing what in tarnation was stewing over yonder. I saw them crows overhead, all upset and fussing, and I heard more of that rattledy-rattledy sound. All of it coming from over the summit, down the other side, looking over the Musselshell Valley, you see."

Quin smiled patiently. He knew what was coming. Lem was having a leg-pull, and soon he'd go heehawing off, after flummoxing the whole ranch. This was probably going to be another one of the abominable snowman tales that the drovers yarned each other with all winter around the potbelly. So Quin listened quietly, enjoying the music in a cowboy's yarning.

"I tied my bronc back a piece. Woods were coming at me too thick to ride in that country anyway, and I'd have likely brained myself on a limb. And I set off on my dogs, climbing out along a big old promontory that shoots off thataway, to the south, where I could get me an eyeful.

"I got out to the end there," Lem went on, "and had me a swig on the canteen, because it was almighty hot even up there. And cross my heart, down below, all little dots, is a bunch of cattle. Miles down the hill, I reckon. I could hardly make out what I seen, and the men down there was all little dots, too.

"Except there's one little dot twice't as big as the others, and he's sitting in a wagon, and I says, Lemuel, any little dot setting a wagon like that has got to be a Birkenhead, none other. And I scratch my haid a little, because if'n it's him over in that sheep country and he's there with a mess of beeves, all restless and giving him what for 'cause there's no water in that frog pond, and the beeves are chewin' brush and otherwise misbehaving so's I can pity them clean up on my peak, well, he's up to something, you bet.

"So there I am, wondering about all that and listening to all the racket up close on top, off to the east a piece. Just the most awfullest noise a man ever did hear — a rattle such as I can't tell. It's making me antsy, and I check the loads in my iron just to make sure, and start hiking that direction. Wish't I had my horse; I hate walkin'. But I get over there to where are the noises, and there is lodgepole pine country down below me. And men yellin' and steers grumping, and once't or twice't a shot or two, and something that sounds sort of like cussin' — beggin' your pardon, Missy — only I can't make out the words.

"Well, anyhow, after you sit awhile you get so you can kinder peer down into the woods a little, and I slowly get to see what all the ruckus is about. I'm maybe fifty yards away, up on a cliff, studying down in.

"Sure enough, there's a few Birkenhead men in there, all collected around a big old cow, watching her. And she's in a fix. She's got her horns stuck between four lodgepole. How she got that way I cain't imagine. There's two trees behind her horns, and two more ahead, so she cain't go backward and she cain't go forward neither. And they ain't got a saw to cut her horns.

"Everyone knows how them beasts can flick their heads so one horn flies up and the other down, and they'll drive right through some hole about as wide as their shoulders. Well, she's done that all right, but then she got almighty stuck. So I peer around some, down into those trees, and I see she's not the only one. They got others stuck like that all over the parcel from here to Kentucky.

"Well, Christmas Rourke is there — I recognized him — and he's directing the men what to do. Only there ain't nothing works. That cow is all-fired mad, boxed in like that. She gets a notion to pull back out and she slams backward like one of them Missouri riverboat paddle-wheelers with all them paddles churning backside ahead. And then she gets the notion to go forward and lowers her big old skull and slams in, Keerack! She hits her horns against those lodgepole up front, and she's got one sore haid, sort of dizzy-like, let me tell you.

"Then all them cowboys get aholt of her horns. They're going to twist her loose so them horns are up and down instead of crosswise. Three fellers, they lift up on one side, and two other fellers, they push down on the other side, twisting that cow's neck until she's getting a little bit irate and will have none of it, and she flips them off like pesky flies, and those fellers, they go rolling around and slamming into trees and whatnot, like nothing I've ever seen.

"Now I thought I heard it all. There warn't no words I never heerd before. But one of them strangers — a Texican, I figure — he eddycated me like I never knew the half of what he was yellin' at that cow, he was so het up. And that cow, she just done what I'd do if I couldn't go neither forward nor back. She lifted her tail — oh, sorry, Missy.

"Them fellers, they move on to the next stuck beeve. It's the same story all over again. Them critters are jailed in there for life, seems like. And I watch all this fussing for nigh onto an hour, and it's a sight, just a sight.

"Then that big Swede, he shows up from below with an ax, and they all go back to the cow to free her out. The trouble is, there's noplace to take a swing except up and down, so that's what he does, whacking down into that old tree until he's all out of steam and there's only a little white dent in the tree. A couple of others take a crack at it, but it's no use, so they all stand around jawing. And then Rourke, he pulls out his iron and puts down that cow. Then they all go off every which way and put the critters out of their misery. Then they all go collect their broncs down below where I can't see, and I hear them heading down the slope, mad as hops.

"So I skeedaddle over to the lookout place again, and pretty soon the bunch of 'em show up below, clattering on down. The trouble is, the Swede's got a thirsty bronc under him, and the bronc snorts and goes to bucking and fishtailing some. Well, sir, quick as a flash the whole herd is up and gone, off for the Flatwillow, I reckon. Every last bumpy-rumped one, with the crew trying to head 'em off and not even catching up with those hell-for-leather steers, and then they head 'round the bend out of sight, and there's no one there but that one big dot on the wagon, Mr Birkenhead, one or the other. So I come along home."

They all laughed, but Quin was saddened, too. He grieved over the loss of any stock, even those destined for his range. He turned contemplatively toward the house.

They would do better on the next attempt, he thought. There were trails enough, even for a longhorn. Elk trails, creek beds, high meadows. It would simply take them a few days to scout them out, and then they could move the herd over, single file, onto his high grass. So . . . the burned line hadn't really stopped the invasion, only delayed it a few days.

Quin boiled. His wintergrass would be decimated once Alexander the Great flanked his charcoal fence. And no hay. No way to feed those shorthorns next winter. He could either sell his entire herd at ruinous prices or see it starve to death. Either way, Q Ranch would collapse — unless it rained, rained for six solid weeks, which he couldn't count on.

He had to find some way to drive those longhorns off his land and keep them off. Rebuilding the fence would be futile. Law? Too late, too expensive. He already owed Miss Nicole over a thousand. War? The association would gang up and make quick work of him, and put him on the blacklist besides. And he was going to have to let his crew go, anyway. Shoot the trespassing stock? That'd only bring the blacklist, and the sheriff. The blacklist would finish him faster than all the bad weather in the world.

Things had never been so dark.

CHAPTER
NINE

"Fencing the open range is a crime against nature. We shouldn't permit it, and we should pull down wire as fast as it's strung up!"

The orator was Amos Clapp, a florid, meaty man with powerful arms and thighs and stubby hands. He ran longhorns along with Hereford bulls along the north fork of the McDonald, near Grassrange.

"They learned the long and short of it down on the southern ranges last winter," he continued. "When those blizzards hit down there, the stock couldn't drift with the wind the way it usually does. They can stand 'most any sort of a blow, as long as they can get their tails into the wind and keep moving. But when they hit those fences down there, they piled up and died. Now that's the unvarnished truth."

Clapp was addressing fourteen of the twenty-three stockmen who formed the Maginnis grazing district, including Alex and Augie Birkenhead. They had gathered at the rambling log home of Silas Stone, up on Ford's Creek, nestled into the paws of the Judith Mountains.

"When the range is open, the way it was in buffalo days, the stock grazes a little here, a little there, at random, and the grass is never damaged by anything. That's nature's own way, I say. A little here, a little there. That tough grama leaps back almost as fast as the herd passes over. And some areas don't get grazed for three or four years running. That's how it should be."

"Wait a minute, Captain," demurred Orville Pickett. "That was before we overloaded the range with all them cattle. There ain't hardly a spear of grass doesn't get et three, four times a season now."

They addressed Clapp as "captain" only as a courtesy. He held no such military rank. In fact, back in Ohio he had been the proprietor of a military academy that had failed. And now, three years later, he still affected military ways. He wore a gray tunic with brass buttons and used a McClellan cavalry saddle. Behind his back his neighbors joked that he made his steers line up for roll call and dress parade every morning.

"This range isn't overloaded!" Clapp glared. "The plain fact is, a man could ride all day and never see a steer. It's underused. We could double our range animals without any trouble at all. This little dry spell has persuaded some of us to retreat at the very gates of prosperity."

"Well," Pickett pressed, "them steers look almighty thin to me, and I'll be danged if I can find a blade of grass."

"It's the fences," Clapp boomed. "Our trouble in this district started exactly when Putnam began fencing public range. Exactly. It's a plain fact. Over sixty square miles of it fenced off. If he hadn't done that, the whole district would have been grazed evenly. And that's a plain fact."

"Could be, but sixty square miles are a drop in the bucket," Pickett persisted.

"Then why did our grief start when that fence went up?" Clapp demanded. It was a telling point: the overgrazing did in fact coincide with the fencing, and the stockmen connected the two in their minds.

"I think," objected their host, Silas Stone, "that the two aren't connected. Quin Putnam simply saw what was coming and acted to protect his range."

"What was coming! What do you mean, what was coming?"

"What was coming was obvious to any man with eyes," Stone rejoined. "Grass has been short for two years now, and was getting short long before this dry spell hit us."

"What's obvious to me," Clapp retorted, "is fence on our range. Those nesters north of Putnam, too. Putnam's the worst offender, but those farmers have fixed it so we can't water stock in the south fork of the McDonald, so that area isn't even grazed anymore. Why, if our stock could water down there, there's whole townships of grass they'd start chomping. It's the water, Silas. The minute the creeks are sealed off, the whole range shrinks down."

That was another sore point with the stockmen. There was a lot of country the range cattle scarcely grazed because it was too far from water. Clapp's logic was hitting home.

"The nesters are squatting, same as everyone else on the western lands," Stone replied. "Surely you don't begrudge them the bit of land they've farmed in that narrow valley."

"Of course I begrudge them!" Clapp thundered. "Every inch of public land under fence I begrudge because it reduces my living. We should tear down those fences for good."

"That would put range cattle into their cropland."

"Well, that's not our problem. They've preempted public land; let them pay for their mistake."

"It sounds like you're hoping to fatten your stock on another man's barley or oats under color of some principle or other," Stone needled. Several of the stockmen laughed. "But I guess Congress will give squatters much of the land they've preempted, eventually. Now let me ask you something, Captain. Are all your buildings on patented land?"

It was a telling thrust. Clapp's headquarters, too, were on public land. Only Silas Stone, among all of them, had filed claims.

"Well, that's different. Temporary structures until Congress gives us some law to live with. Holding the fort, you know."

There was laughter, but Clapp broke into it: "Every square foot illegally under wire hurts us. Don't you ever forget it."

"A moment ago," Stone rejoined, "you were telling us the range is understocked and we could double the load. How, then, can you say the opposite — that the fencing is hurting us?"

"Fencing stops the random grazing," Clapp replied triumphantly. "The whole range has got to be grazed hit or miss, like in buffalo days."

Silas Stone sighed unhappily. Before the meeting he had spent an hour in his rocker, trying to sort things through. The young man liked Putnam. They both had settled here in 1880 and had prospered. But he didn't like Quin's fence, either: it cramped the open range by as much as was enclosed. But he concluded that if a man was going to grow blooded stock like those Durhams, and winterfeed them, it had to be done Putnam's way.

"Captain," piped a new voice — that of Oliver Henry, who ranched north of Stone. "What do you propose to do about it?"

"Tear it all down. Every strand. Rip out the posts. All the nester wire, too."

"What about hay meadows?" Stone asked laconically. They all knew he had a thousand acres of it under fence, stretching clear to Fort Maginnis. And not a foot of it patented.

"Hay meadows is different. I'm talking about fencing open range," Clapp explained.

"Your principles are a bit selective, Mr Clapp," Stone retorted. "You're going to tear down open-range fencing because it's on public land, but not hay-meadow fence, even if it's also on public land. Mr Putnam's fence doesn't even enclose his range, but my hay-meadow fence does. I have an illegal enclosure, and so do you, and others among us. It just seems to me your feet are standing on both sides of one of those fences you want to tear down."

Clapp smiled and bit off the end of a cigar.

"And that's not the end of it, either," Stone continued. "You're squatting, Mr Clapp. 'Most every man here is squatting. We can't even lasso a surveyor! My point is, the one man who isn't squatting is Quin Putnam. I think he's over five square miles of patent land now, and the tally goes up each year. And as for the nesters, they've got homestead claims on file, and some Desert Land Act claims, too."

Clapp knew he had already carried the day. "Well, Silas, let me put it to you as a plain fact," he drawled. "It's us or them, and the niceties don't matter much. I'll tear down illegal fence when I'm ready."

Silas Stone knew how the affray would end. The sledgehammer force of Clapp's argument would gain more credence among those desperate men whose backs were to the wall than any ethical point ever made. Quin Putnam was in for some hell.

He stood, a lithe and slender man, and looked around at his guests. "Georgeanna's baked some rhubarb pies," he announced.

That was all they needed to break for the ranch kitchen, where hot pies, still bubbling from the wood-range oven, and thick hot coffee in blue and white speckled pots burdened the table. They all lined up for a feed, and a good eyeful of Georgeanna, too. They could never state their curiosity about the buxom, wide, dimpled, flaxen-haired girl who was Stone's mail-order bride. She was Armenian, and she had

105

married Stone soon after debarking at Ellis Island in 1880. Stone had sluiced a good poke of placer gold at Virginia City and Confederate Gulch, and then decided to ranch. About the time he settled at Ford's Creek, after systematically examining much of Montana Territory on horseback, he had sent for a mail-order bride through a New York broker for twenty-five dollars. He sent her money for rail passage to Bismarck, North Dakota, the Northern Pacific railhead then. He met her there, and they couldn't speak a word to each other. She liked him, though: she read people through their eyes, and his hazel ones were frank, honest, tender, and courageous. They were married on the spot by a Methodist circuit rider, and then drove a buckboard over several hundred miles of Indian country to the new ranch on Ford's Creek. They were lovers before they were friends, and she bore him a son before they could say much to each other. And now they were both lovers and friends. In fact, she adored him. She beamed as the stockmen dug into her juicy pies and her thick, aromatic coffee.

The stockmen settled down in the shady sitting room while hot August breezes eddied through open windows and flies tormented them. They expected Birkenhead to unloose a real stem-winder about Putnam's grass fire. But Alex understood taciturn frontiersmen and was wily enough to recite the bare facts in less than a minute. Putnam had burned a strip at least a quarter-mile wide on his land. The blaze had sliced deep into Circle B range to the east. There was ample evidence that it was deliberate: a plowed firebreak that wound artfully around thickets and coulees for anyone to see. The fire had driven Circle B cattle off range sequestered by Putnam, and had demolished two or three square miles of excellent grass.

Silas Stone stood up. "Tell me, Alex, how Mr Putnam's land got to be such excellent feed."

"That's an idiotic question."

"The grass behind that fence," Stone persisted, "stood nigh to three feet high in places, cured on the stalk. And even the new grass got up a foot this year before it burned off. I saw it myself. It looked as good as it did in the buffalo days."

"Oh, I know what you're driving at, Silas," said Alex impatiently. "Putnam practiced a sort of husbandry, eh? And now we all want to take advantage of his prudence, eh?"

"Oh, something like that."

"Well," Alex retorted. "I agree with Mr Clapp. The husbandry was at our expense. By the amount he set aside, he shrank public range."

"Three square miles of feed lost to a criminal," Clapp boomed from his corner. "The feed on Q range could keep us all going until it rains. That fellow should be blacklisted."

"Which is what you'll end up doing," Silas added drily. "And then you'll run your stock on the blacklisted man's tall grass with no thanks to him for setting it aside. Who else among us set aside feed against a drought?"

"Criminal, I say. We've a right —"

"And," Stone added mordantly, "you'll auction Mr Putnam's strays to compensate for all the grief he caused by saving out his grass for us to appropriate in hard times."

Augie smiled beatifically. The Birkenheads both loved a well-aimed jab.

"I move," Amos Clapp interjected suddenly, before the debate turned to Stone's ground, "that the district association blacklist Putnam."

There was no need for a vote. They had gathered for a lynching of sorts, and mere argument wouldn't waylay them. Putnam was to be blacklisted; his name would go down among the names of thieves and running-iron artists and odious men of all sorts. They agreed to sign a complaint, all save Stone, that would lead to the arrest and probable conviction of Putnam for maliciously setting range fires. Silas Stone, as secretary, was requested to deliver it to the authorities. They agreed, off the record, to pull down Quin's north fence and all the nester wire along the south fork of the McDonald, but not until after the fall roundup. After the beeves were shipped, the remaining stock would be driven onto the Q Ranch grass, which would provide excellent winter pasture for them all. Putnam's strays would be gathered at the roundup, auctioned, and the proceeds applied to funds to support range detectives. Clapp was delegated to ride to Helena to lay the case before the territorial legislators and officers, as well as the Montana Stockmen's Association, just in case Putnam or the nesters raised hob about fences and crops.

They rode off, then, in the August heat, while Silas Stone, his arm around Georgeanna's ample waist, silently watched them clatter away. He was melancholy, almost bitter. The association he had built for the mutual protection of open-range cattlemen had flooded its banks like a rampaging creek in spring.

He squeezed Georgeanna affectionately and then stalked out to his barn, where a man could think in the cool. Silas was a man of stern and uncompromising rectitude, and this manifested itself in a passionately held sense of justice. That justice was double-edged: it cut against horse thieves and rustlers, now it worked on behalf of Quin Putnam. It was Silas Stone's onerous duty to deliver the complaint to the law, but maybe he could soften matters a little by informing Quin first. The trip down to Q Ranch was a tedious detour, but he wanted to check on Quin's frame of mind and maybe avert further trouble.

"Georgeanna," he announced, back at the house, "I'll be away on association business for a few days."

"I listened from the kitchen," she said. "You stop first at Quincy Putnam and tell him. You take a good pie for him. He tired maybe grows of Chinese food, and Armenian vittles maybe enjoys." She smiled and patted her man on the cheek.

The two had become one. She knew better than he did what he would do and why. She would have his saddlebags packed for him at dawn, and he would find some little treat in them, as he always did when he traveled. That was her delight. That, and the two boys romping around the barnyard. Her heart overflowed, here in the New World, and she scarcely knew how to spend all the love inside her.

Silas's route took him due south, across the north fork of the McDonald, then through Coffecan Pentecost's mule factory — for that was what the farm amounted to — on to the south fork, and over a low divide to the Flatwillow. He rode before dawn, hoping to get as much land behind him as he could before the blistering heat, and halted at a hitch rail beneath Coffeecan's noble cottonwoods just after noon.

Then began a ritual that took place each time they met.

"Coffeecan, those are the awfullest-looking mules I've ever seen," Silas yelled at his deaf host.

"Every cotton-pickin' one of 'em's better than that sway-back sickle-hocked plug yer riding, Stone," the ancient Missourian bawled back.

"Coffeecan, I wouldn't give you a wooden nickel for the best of your pea-brained blue mules. They're nothing but juicy meat for the Apaches," Silas hooted.

"Well, I wouldn't sell ye one for yer hull spread. Light and set; it's nooning time."

Silas offered the old muleteer some pie, which Coffeecan wolfed down.

"I'm heading down to Putnam's," Silas yelled. "There's trouble. The association is going to tear down fence, and I can't head 'em off. And they're all jumping on Putnam because he's ranching his own way."

"Anyone pulls down my fence, or Putnam's, he'll be pulling bird shot out of his bustle for a week," Coffeecan snarled.

110

"Just thought I'd warn you. Maybe you'd better fence in your corn patch," Silas roared hoarsely.

"I got double-barreled fence inside the door," the man snorted. "Say, wanta buy a mule? I got the prettiest little jenny you ever did see, with the longest eyelashes ever did grow on a four-footed beast. Her name's Miss Beverly Smartass, after my late wife."

"Coffeecan, I'm struck dumb," Silas yelled, retreating south.

"I've spoiled her rotten," the man yelled as Silas boarded his cayuse.

He pulled up at the Q Ranch late in the afternoon, looking forward to Quin's bountiful hospitality and Dingdong's sumptuous feasts. He admired Quin's place.

Quin welcomed him with a strong grip and delight in his eye. The bond between the older settler and the younger one renewed itself through dinner. Silas waited until Dingdong had cleared the dishes away to recount the events of the previous day. He had intended to confer privately, but Quin resisted: "Let's palaver right here, Silas. I want Missy to hear. She's old enough now to share my problems."

Missy smiled, feeling the burden of adulthood upon her.

"It's worse than I thought," Quin responded after Silas had laconically described the meeting. "I didn't figure the others were coveting my grass, too. The Birkenheads, of course. But the others . . ." He shook his head. "Now don't you feel so bad about taking that complaint to the sheriff. It's your duty."

Silas studied his host pensively, reading the face.

"The law's going to have a time of it catching up to me," snapped Quin. "I'm off to Billings tomorrow with over a thousand beeves. Most of my herd. I'm keeping about eight hundred; all brood stock. Silas, these shorthorns . . . I'm in bad shape. Worse than the rest. I didn't get a hay crop this year, and I have to winter-feed those shorthorns."

Silas sighed unhappily. "You'll pretty near have to start over."

"If it winters bad, there won't be anything left to start over with. I'll be finished. I'm letting my crew go, most of 'em. They know the score. I haven't told 'em yet, but they know . . .

"The Birkenheads, they've got their stock back on, and a Texas herd, full of fever, too. The grass fire didn't stop them as long as I hoped."

Silas nodded; he didn't need to be told what the news meant.

"We're trailing to Billings at dawn," Quincy continued. "It'll walk off a hundred pounds an animal in this heat. No water now except the Musselshell and hardly a blade of grass the whole drive. If we don't get our Durhams off before the fever hits them, we'll likely lose the whole herd. So we'll sell them for peanuts before they die of contagion. Those are my options."

Silas was silent, staring into his cup.

"I've got a fifteen thousand annual payment due on my stock loan November fifteenth. Normally I can ship about seven hundred of these heavy Durhams and meet it, with enough left over for the next year's working

112

funds. This year, Silas, with prices the way they are, I have to ship a thousand just to meet the loan, and that won't leave me payroll.

"What's worse, I'll be selling brood cows and yearlings to do it. That's like selling the seed corn. And with no hay and Birkenhead stock eating my grass, if it winters up badly and the Texas fever cuts down my remaining brood stock, I likely won't have a beeve to ship next fall, and another payment's due then. Texas fever, Silas! Everything we've built here is being blown to smithereens by fever and a cut fence."

He slammed a fist into the table.

"Silas, that blacklist, that's like a noose tightening around my neck. It's hard enough fighting drought and Birkenheads and low prices. Now I've got the list, too. Why, I couldn't even ship beeves on the Northern Pacific! And you know it's a license to steal my calves. My stock'll disappear . . . *Strayed*, they'll say. Well, I'm mighty glad I've got this drive going to the rails before the thing gets published. Silas, it's war! There's ten, twelve of 'em going to close down the Q. This place . . . why, if I don't get off that list, in a year the wind'll be whistling through these windows, and the pack rats'll take over."

Quin grimaced. "Well, I'll tell you something plain, and you can tell it to the association. I won't bend. What I have'll be Missy's someday, and let me tell you, I'll fight like a cornered catamount. I'll — I'll shoot every beef they shove on my grass. That's just for starters. That blacklist — Have they ever heard of libel? I'll attach every dime they have. I'll —"

Quin sagged slowly into his chair and suddenly smiled. "Silas, it's neighborly of you to give me a little warning. That list, that's worse than all the bad weather put together. If they ever publish that list with me in it . . ."

The younger man nodded gravely. When quiet, educated men like Putnam get cornered, he thought, they start holocausts. Always the unexpected. Like that fire. Like a libel action.

CHAPTER
TEN

Quin's crew stood expectantly in the amber dawn light, knowing in advance what he had to say and how tough it was for the boss to say it. Most of them were sumptuously adorned in their going-to-town outfits. Some had stuffed everything they possessed into duffels that were tied down behind their cantles. Two had their own pack mules, fully loaded.

A thousand fat cattle sprawled contentedly up in Horsethief Canyon, high in the little Snowies on the south fork of the Flatwillow. There, at one of Quin's line camps, the crew had cut out the best brood stock from among the beeves they had driven down from the high country. Everything else was going on down the trail. It had been unusual work for August, but it was cool up there, so the men had enjoyed it.

Quin and Missy arrived while the crew was breakfasting, and Quin walked silently through his herd, pleased with its condition. But mostly he walked to collect himself for the bad moment to come. When he could tarry no longer, he did what he had to do. At least, he thought, none of them would be surprised. That would make it a bit easier.

"The parting of friends is always one of the saddest moments in a man's life," he began quietly. The morning sun had not yet pierced the gloom of the deep chasm, but the first glint of it burned from a lip of rock high above.

"You're all friends. I've come to know and enjoy each of you in the course of our labors and trials together. I expect some of you I'll never see again, and over the years ahead I'll wonder where you are and what life has dealt to you. It's a long trail into a broad world."

He absently rubbed a hand over his scalp and went on.

"I don't need to tell you — this shipment says it all — that the Q Ranch has its back to the wall. We've cut out what I believe is good brood stock to rebuild with. But what's going down the trail, here, all these calves and young stuff, is what I'd normally sell over the next three years, along with the aged cows and bulls and steers we'd be selling anyway in two months.

"It's the drought mostly. No hay at all. Somehow, I've got to winter-feed the eight hundred we're keeping, and I hope it's an open winter because that's the only way we can. Not enough rain since spring to settle the dust. That can really hurt an outfit, I'll tell you . . . And the bottom out of the market . . . and we're facing other difficulties," he added stiffly.

They would know, he thought, and there was no sense sending them off with a bitter accusation ringing in their ears. He paused unhappily. The worst moment was upon him. He glanced over at Missy, astride

116

Snowflake, darkly sharing his tension and torment. He knew she felt his every ache.

"I'm unable to maintain my present crew," he said abruptly. "I've tried every way I know to hang on. Now, I want you to listen closely and think about what I'm saying when you're on the trail. No one has to be in a rush.

"The only fair way to handle this — this situation — is by seniority. There are four who've been with me from the start and have built Q Ranch from the ground up, right beside me: John Durham, Lem Eakins, Bunions, and Billy Jones. Those are the four I'll keep if they'll stick with me."

That was no surprise to anyone, either. Quin espied a few grins and a wink or two among these knights of the saddle, and something inside him released. A little wrinkle of good humor built up in the webbed flesh around his eyes.

"I want you back. Every one. You've been hard workers, except" — he grinned — "for the Texans we had to send down the trail because they couldn't bestir themselves to make hay."

There was a ripple of knowing laughter.

"In Billings, John will pay you a full August wage, so you'll have a three-week bonus. Then I hope you'll come back. I can offer you the bunkhouse and chow for the winter. You can hunt or fish, write long letters to your dear old mothers, or just snore in bed. And maybe we'll see better times in the spring. Think about it. Chew it over. You're welcome here.

"Now I've been racking my brains for ways to keep you on. I've a notion that may appeal to some, if you want to stay in this country."

Some did want to stay, and they listened intently.

"I need wood. I need firewood, I need fence posts, and I need sawn wood planking to build irrigation flumes next year. We've got timber here on the slopes, and I've got the pony sawmill, the axes and saws and sledges, and all you need. I can't pay you cash money because I haven't any. In fact, I'm heavily in debt and owing my Boston bank. But I'll work out some arrangement to pay you in beef if you're interested. Put in a winter, and next year you'll have your own brand on some of our steers. That's the best I can offer — beef for your labor. But it's a way for you to stay hitched here, if you have the notion.

"Of course" — he grinned — "lumberjacks don't cut such a fine figure with the ladies of Lewistown. And I'm sure there are some of you who'd rather climb into a tin bathtub than cut wood. But my offer's made, and you can think about it. If you've ever dreamed of starting your own spread and building up your own herd, maybe here's your chance."

Quin's hands fumbled about, looking for something to grip.

"Watch over my herd, now. Walk them slow in this heat. You'll have two dry camps, and only the Musselshell for water. And a tough day now threading them over the mountains.

"I hope to see you again, but if not . . . Godspeed."

"You're not coming?" Lem Eakins asked.

118

"I had planned to, but I changed my mind. John Durham's in command, as always."

That was it, then. Silently Quin gripped the rough hand of each drover. Then he turned his face away into the deepest shadow he could find, and stood apart, needing to be alone.

The drovers hoo-hawed the grumbling cattle to their feet and then hazed them into a moving mass of beef and headed them up the creek. There was no cavvy because there was no wagon trail over the mountains. But they had pack mules to heft the gear and chow, and two water barrels.

Quin found Missy's hand and squeezed it while they watched most of his worldly wealth amble around a bend and vanish. A jay chattered, and then a kildeer screamed its lonely cry. The morning sun marched down the shadowed slopes.

"Why aren't you going?" she asked at last.

"I changed my mind in the night."

"Because of Silas?"

"Mr Stone, Missy! When you're a little older you may call him Silas. Yes. Our talk last night was illuminating. Of course, I know how much the Birkenheads want our grass, but what I didn't understand, until Silas rehashed the meeting for us, was that every other cattleman in the district wants it, too. All that knee-high bunch grass behind Quin Putnam's illegal fence! Their mouths are watering. My grass is going to be their salvation if it doesn't rain. They think I've been hoarding it. Hoarding!" Quin laughed.

119

"Papa, we haven't hoarded grass from them! We've just taken care of it. It wouldn't even be there if —"

"Of course, Missy. But those niceties get lost in desperate times. All they see now is square miles of tall, succulent bunch grass, cured on the stem, that will fatten their starving cattle this fall. It's not hard to foresee what's coming. They'll round up and ship as usual this fall — or maybe ship out more than usual — and then, sometime in October, they'll drive a mixed herd, thousands of cattle, onto the Q Ranch grass. And tear down our north fence — and the farmers' enclosures, too — in the process."

"Oh, it makes me so mad!"

"It's not pleasant to think about, is it, Missy? We won't even have feed enough for our eight hundred bulls, young cows, and heifers, not even if it stays open this winter. All we'll have is what's in our hay meadows."

"They'll steal that, too," she said darkly.

"Yes, that would be stealing. But the public range . . . I guess you'd call it appropriating." He gazed expectantly at the girl. "What do you think I should do? What would you do in my shoes?"

"Shoot all the stock on our land!"

He laughed, savoring her youthful indignation. "What else?"

"Sue them! Oh, I don't know. They've all ganged up on you. They've got you treed."

"No, not yet," he replied softly. "Right now, I'm riding up to the east slope of Big Snowy Mountain. There's an alpine meadow there, maybe twenty acres, surrounded by such heavy forest that the sheepmen don't get to it and may not even know about it. I've been there once. Waist-high grass, maybe thirty or forty tons of it, if it were cut. Mostly timothy, not bunch grass, and so thick it's a jungle. It's full of elk, too. They roll in it, play in it, nest in it, and eat a bit of it. I'm going up there to look for a way to get our hay wagons in there and cut it. That's one thing.

"I'm also going to try mowing our winter pasture before it gets chewed down. It's year-old grass and won't make very good hay because it's just stalks. But it seems to me we could make some sort of feed out of it if we get cracking. Just harvest it right off the range and haul it close to the house where we can keep an eye on it.

"Another thing: I'm going to swing by the nesters north of us and see if I can board a few beeves. They always have a little spare hay. Coffeecan and Lars, in particular, ought to be able to winter fifty or sixty for me. So, honey, we're not licked yet."

"Well, if they wreck our range, you should wreck something of theirs," she said.

He sighed. "I'm not in the vengeance business, Missy. I'd like to avoid trouble. Have you ever seen a man with a bullet in him, or a ranch house burn? I'm sticking to other tactics. But if they corner me, if they start a war, I'll finish it for them. Those fellows on the trail, they'd come back and fight if I asked."

He stared into the hanging dust where the herd had been. "All the same, I'm glad they're gone," he muttered.

She studied him contemplatively, gauging her chances. "May I go?" she asked. Her eyes fixed him so eagerly that he laughed.

"I don't see why not."

"I have to go get ready!"

"I was planning to start from here; that's why the mule's loaded. Tell you what: you lope Snowflake back and tell Billy Jones and Dingdong — tell them both, now — that we'll be gone for a few days. Then pack your duds. Warm things, mostly, because it gets cold up there in August. And some things for Lewistown, too, because we'll be stopping there to see Miss Nicole. And bring an empty tick, and I'll show you how a girl can sleep on the ground and think she's at the Ritz. And bring back the walking mare; we've got to make tracks."

She bolted for home, and he eased down beside the creek to enjoy the solitude. It would take her awhile, but what of it? he thought, watching the ripply current. He relished the jaunt, and her company would make it all the more delightful. The daily inferno was grinding him down, along with all the rest, and he yearned for cool pines and time and space to mull things over . . .

Was there any way to defend his grass without triggering a tragedy? Men got killed in this country for less than what was at stake now . . .

Quin's humor veered in odd directions now and then, and the more he puzzled about the sullen malice aimed at him, the more amused he was. What a conniving creature a human being could be! Captain Amos Bidwell Clapp, late of the ABC Cadet College, Canton, Ohio, coveted his grass. The man was indignant that there was so much as one blade sequestered from his stock. What was that joke about him? Oh, yes, that he had made his bulls noncommissioned officers because they commanded —

Missy materialized then, winsome on her cocky mare, eloquently pleased by the adventure. An insight swept Quin: his whole life — failures and all — was worthwhile because of her.

They rode swiftly up-canyon and then branched off on a trail winding west. Quin knew long before they reached the high park that they'd never drive hay wagons up there. Chasms assaulted the way. Rocky slopes blocked passage. And finally, there was the dense forest they were penetrating along an elk trail.

They ascended steadily through shadowed woods and then burst out onto a sunny meadow. The rippling grass lay thick and indolent in the sun, and the transparent air was pungent with the incense the sun cooked out of the pitch pine.

A dozen elk stared at the intruders invading their secluded sanctuary. A bull elk snorted as Quin and Missy rode into the thickest grass Missy had ever seen, so rank that the horses had to press through as it caressed their bellies. She jumped down into a field waist-high, a carpet unlike any bunch grass she'd known. She could scarcely push through it.

"It's what I remembered!" Quin exclaimed.

The whole pasture was naturally irrigated by a creek, which broke into a dozen sparkling rivulets that crisscrossed the plateau and then collected into one stream again as it danced down the grade.

"Wild timothy mostly," said Quin, studying it from his mount. "As soon as we get back to the Q, we'll drive a hundred up here for the autumn."

"A hundred!" Missy exclaimed. "In here?"

"Yes, and they won't clean the platter before snow flies. We can feed that many from now into December if it stays open. And I think it will. A hot summer means a warm, open winter if I understand cycles correctly. Of course, it's a gamble. They could be trapped up here if there's an early blizzard. But everything we do now's a risk. It might be a worse one to stow them below where there's no feed at all."

Missy ran a hand through the awesome grass, but doubts nagged her. "I think we should bring them down sooner," she said.

"Perhaps we should. It's likely that some cold and light snows will drive them down without our help, and we can collect them down below when the time comes. If not, we'll ride up here before Christmas and fetch them back to the Q."

"What about wolves?"

"You're right, Missy. Using your head. You'll be running our spread someday! We'd better run a few tough old longhorn cows in with the shorthorns. A wolf thinks twice before tangling with those horns."

They camped on a rocky bench above the park in an amphitheater where the night breezes would be few. Quin stripped the gear and the packsaddle from the mule, and then Missy led the three beasts down to the meadow.

124

"Let them eat just a little," Quin warned, "or else we'll be fighting colic in the morning."

The pitch-pine smoke of the cook fire lingered fragrant in their nostrils. As fast as the sun slid below the mountain, a sharp cold descended, and Missy shivered. It wasn't so frightening as long as Quin was here. She threw more dead-wood on the fire until it crackled up and the amber light flickered on the cliff above them. Maybe there were Indians lurking just above, ready to spring . . . "I'm glad you're here. Otherwise I'd be afraid."

"There's very little to be afraid of these days," he said. He reached over to squeeze her hand, watching her fear in the wavering light. "Suppose something did happen to me, Missy. Do you think you could handle it alone?"

"I — I don't know. Do we have to talk about it?"

"You're fourteen, now, girl. Of course you could handle it! You could ride back to the ranch, or get Miss Nicole in Lewistown without any trouble. You can saddle up, ride, cook, hunt, shoot, light fires, read, sew, deal with strangers, fish, gut and clean game, defend yourself with weapons. Why, you're almost grown up!" He paused. "It's a lot different from when you were nine."

She bridled.

"Don't you see, honey? When you were just a mite of a girl, camping out like this on the prairies with your folk, you still needed their help. But you don't need help anymore. You're almost grown up."

125

She shrank down inside herself for a while, and then beamed suddenly at him.

"A few weeks ago," she said solemnly, "you told me that we have to let go of the past to grasp a better future. Well, I'll let go of being nine now. It's scary to camp, but I'll remember I'm grown up."

Quin smiled. He found a bowie knife in his kit and disappeared upslope into some cured grass. In a minute he dropped a huge armload of it at her feet and motioned toward her empty tick.

"May as well sleep in style," he said, going for another load. Then, while she stuffed, he smoothed the earth of their bed-grounds, carefully plucking away pebbles. When she climbed into her bedroll, it was into a velvety softness and coziness that transformed the mountain camp into her private nest.

"The sky certainly is busy tonight," he said, staring upward. "You can't really pick 'em, though it looks like you could . . ."

She didn't reply; she was asleep. He watched a few sparks eddy upward in the night breeze, wishing he could spend a week here. But he'd gotten a whiff of autumn in the high air, and it jabbed him like star-roweled Mexican spurs in his flanks.

In the morning they packed reluctantly and jolted down through the forest until they emerged onto ponderosa-dotted parkland, huge ribs of the somnolent mountain sweeping down toward the Judith Basin, simmering below.

A while later they descended into a regiment of dun sheep undulating along the slopes. They were instantly circled by three sheepdogs, growling and springing around, just out of kick range. Quin tugged back on his snaffle bit and quieted the sidestepping gelding.

A sharp whistle echoed up from behind the bend below, and the dogs whipped away as fast as they had come. Then a sheepherder appeared, limping upslope on a game leg, using his staff as a crutch. He inventoried Quin and Missy with liquid brown eyes set deep in a face weathered to chestnut and stubbled with gray.

"A Q on the right shoulder," he said resonantly. "You are Quincy Putnam."

"Correct."

"A hard man but a polite one. We encounter your hands from time to time, and all they say is, You're on Q Ranch range. Nothing more . . . unlike the other beef outfits."

"That's what they're instructed to do."

"Then you're a gentleman . . . It's a hard year. This band's doing well, but I've had to push them into brushy bottoms and holes where we've never gone before. Look at those coats, will you? I've never seen wool so thick this time of year. Have you?"

"I can't say," Quin replied. "I'm not familiar —"

"It's the odd weather. I'll show you."

He hooked a lamb with his staff and lifted it tenderly into his arms. "See that coat, sir? I've never seen the likes of it in August," he said, parting the wool with his hands.

"Yes, it does look rather heavy —"

"It's going to be a bad winter, sir. They're getting ready for it now. My band's fat, but the others . . . I'm with the Montana Sheep Company, yonder toward the Musselshell, your neighbor to the south. They're talking of shipping all of us and our bands to the Idaho country, or Nevada. And with cattle on our range —"

"Cattle?"

"Yes, sir. Other side of the Little Snowies. We can't keep them off in a year like this. The Birkenhead brothers, sir. I wandered into them nigh onto a fortnight ago. A huge herd, right up from Abilene. The foreman, a very civil gentleman, Natividad Rourke, visited with me a bit. Three thousand, he said. All poorly. They were quarantined for a month near Cheyenne because of a Texas fever outbreak, and they were fighting blackleg and splenetic fever, too, and some other ailments they hadn't a name for, along with plain starvation and a few cases of jimson-weed poisoning and the like. They were taking the herd up over the Little Snowies and onto your range, Mr Rourke said."

Quin closed his eyes for a moment.

"The second herd," he muttered. He rubbed his blistered scalp absently.

"I understand, sir," the sheep man said kindly. "The pressure is severe just now, sir. Well, I, for one, have always appreciated your husbandry. We must all do as you do, or perish. If it's any consolation, sir, you have friends where you'd least expect them — among the herders. But I'm sorry to bring you such hard news."

128

Quin reached down over the gelding's withers and proffered his hand, and the herder gripped it in his own hard, scaly one.

"You'll pull your band through, I'm sure," Quin said. "There's grass up above the timber, on the peaks. You might try it."

They jolted on down the slope in grim silence.

"I want a lamb," Missy said.

"Blackleg, too," Quin muttered. "I'm glad we shipped when we did. Won't be any left by spring."

"I want a lamb," Missy repeated, but he didn't hear her.

CHAPTER
ELEVEN

For once, Nicole dreaded to see Quin. She had rehearsed the little speech all summer, but now she was petrified. She owed him that: she had to tell him face-to-face, and not just write cold letter.

Her decision to escape to Saint Louis had solidified all through the heat of July and August, and along with it, sheer anguish. Quin and Missy were the only two people she had on earth. She couldn't just leave them — and yet, she had to. The summer had torn her to ribbons as she had been flung from one horn of her dilemma to the other. Sometimes, when the crabbed closeness of Lewistown cramped her meanly, Saint Louis glistened lucently in her dreams. That's where she was born. That's where she had prospered sixteen years. She pined for cobbled streets, gaslights, and velvety green parks overarched with elms. St. Louis! Trolley cars and wharves and silks and steamboats and parasols, theaters and libraries, town houses and paving stones!

Bit by bit through the summer, the heat and her wrenching dilemma sapped her vitality. She remarked the decay of her constitution daily in the looking glass. Sleep eluded her, and food had become sawdust. She gulped down nourishment standing over the drainboard and didn't bother with proper meals. She dozed sometimes the whole night in her parlor chair, dreading to go to bed and cope with restless dreams. She grew wan and gray and taut and tense, and blackness smudged the flesh below her burning eyes.

But now Quin and Missy were seated before her, and she was concentrating her rattled mind on a certain camouflaging crispness.

"If Sheriff Earley rides over here and nabs you, and if there's some legal shenanigans that delay your trial and tie you up in White Sulphur . . ." She shrugged.

"I'll be stuck there while Birkenhead beef eats up the Q," Quin concluded.

"Sheriff Earley will come," she said. "He's got to do something. It's a stockmen's association complaint — the most powerful group in the county."

"A hundred-mile ride to serve a misdemeanor warrant?"

"No. A hundred-mile ride to serve his political masters."

"He'll have a time of it finding me," Quin snapped.

"And you'll have a time of it keeping Birkenhead beef off your ranch while you're on the lam," she retorted. "Either way, you lose."

"Earley's had plenty of time. Why hasn't he come?"

"I don't know," she said.

"Silas," he muttered. "Silas must have said something. Am I on the blacklist? Is it published?"

"No," she said.

"I treasure my good name. I have never before felt a shadow on my reputation. It hurts. That means more to me than the loss of my stock, or the Q Ranch. I don't belong on that list!"

"Tell me what's happening," she said tautly.

"It's simple. I've got grass, and the other outfits want it."

She waited him out, easing back stiffly in her vast chair.

"Sixty square miles of it, Clapp contends, but that's the usual claptrap. I've got twenty of winter range, a few in hay meadow, and the rest in timber and high summer pasture."

"Whatever you have, it's all they've got. Quin — have you considered that they might resort to violence to get it?"

"Now, Miss Nicole, every one of them's a sensible, salty man. There's not a harebrained one —"

"Of course, Quin! In normal times! But don't you understand the madness that grips desperate people? I've seen it over and over in the casebooks. They'll hate you for doing the right thing, saving grass!"

"Well, that's enough melodrama," Quin snorted. "Let's get at my remedies in law. What about the blacklist, first? That list is big trouble, the worst thing I'm facing. Have I got a libel case? Even though I set that prairie fire?"

"Yes, you certainly do, if they publish a list with your name on it. The fire's nothing — a misdemeanor that you haven't even been convicted of. You're innocent until proven guilty. That list makes no distinctions. Your name will be thrown in with the names of rustlers, horse thieves, murderers, and bad men of all sorts. What's more, that list is intended to damage you, make you an outcast, so you can ask for maximum damages, even though the list isn't circulated widely."

"Well, then," Quin snapped, "do it. Prepare a suit against them all. Leave Silas Stone out, but all the rest. And sue the association itself. And sue them for as much as you dare. And have those papers ready to slap on them the day they publish that list."

Nicole stared at Quin. She was seeing a man she had never seen before. "I would suggest," she said quietly, "that I write each association member warning him that such actions will be brought if you are blacklisted. A little prevention is a lot cheaper than prosecuting a score of libel actions."

"Yes, of course," he snapped. "I'm in hock to you enough as it is. But I'll go into debt to my eyeballs before I'll let them strangle the Q."

She continued to stare at him for a moment and then wrote a note to herself.

"Have we covered everything?" she asked, peering at him over her spectacles.

"No," Quin said. "Are you well? You look awful, Miss Nicole. As sure as I'm sitting here, you're in some kind of trouble or some sort of grief."

Nicole was nonplussed. "It's just the heat," she countered. "I'm worn to a frazzle."

"Why don't you come out from behind the barricade and talk with Missy and me a bit? When you're behind that desk, you're all lawyer, and when you sit here, you're all friend. The rest of this meeting will be among friends."

She gazed oddly at him and then wordlessly circuited the barrier and joined them.

"That's better," Quin beamed. "I think you should come out to the ranch for some country air. It's cooling down a bit now. Come stay awhile. You can close down this practice for a holiday, certainly."

"Quin — I can't." She gestured helplessly. "I can't." He waited for more.

"Don't you see? I can't leave here to visit —"

"A single man? Why, Nicole, I'm old enough to be your father. Of course you can."

"No, that's not it. Quin — I haven't told anyone. I'm thinking about — leaving. I've decided to. I'm going to wind up this practice November first and go to Saint Louis. I'll leave about December first after I ship my household goods and sell this place. I'll take the stage to Billings and then the NP . . . Quin, I can't stand it here any longer, don't you see? It's like a prison to me." She fumbled helplessly. "You're the first to know."

Quin absorbed the startling news desolately.

"I think you'd better come out to the ranch for a good visit," he persisted.

"No, you don't see. Not at all," she said. She eased back, wondering how to explain so many of her most private thoughts, wondering whether to bother, staring into her lap. Then she crossed some divide in her mind and began to speak in a throaty monotone, the words forming a river of despair and need. "I'm a freak here, a complete oddity. I haven't a single friend, male or female."

She caught a glint in Quin's eye.

"I mean — you're here infrequently, but in town there's no one. I live utterly alone. The women avoid me. The men all seem to be — afraid. I've gone to ice cream socials and dances, and they stare. I guess I really don't have much to say to a cowboy, but at least it would be nice to dance, or just joke a little or — They stare at me on the street until I hate to leave this house. I — It's very strange. I'm a prisoner here in Lewistown, and I've got to escape to a city where I can be anonymous. There's no compelling reason for me to be here now, with my father dead."

"At the Q Ranch," Quin interrupted, "you'll waltz with Lem Eakins, Billy Jones, and me, while John Durham fiddles."

She smiled fondly. "It's too late for all that, Quin. I'm going. Don't worry. I'll sell my practice to a good man. With the new county seat here, it'll be lucrative for someone with ability, and I'll make sure, for your sake, that my replacement — Oh, Quin, there's so much you don't understand. Barriers, subtle walls. When my father was alive, but failing, everyone knew I was doing his work, and doing it very well, too. As long as I could prop him up at his desk and get him to sign things, everyone was satisfied. What a smart girl, they said, and things like that. I guess they thought I was cute. They knew I was practicing law for him, Quin!

"But now I do the same thing — exactly the same — and it's different. Oh, no one's rude. Just uneasy. The women avoid me because they can't think of a thing to say. Land sakes, how are you, they say, and then back off. It's my fault, really. I'm just not thrilled about the latest recipes — and things. The men trouble me even more. Oh, so polite. But always watching. You'd think I was either a saint or a bawd, I don't know which. And the worst of it is, I don't really have anything to say to them. What do you think of Molière's plays, Mr Westring? Do you enjoy the Brandenburg Concertos Mr Clark? So you see" — she hunched her shoulders in a petite Gallic shrug — "I must go."

She paused, collecting more thoughts in her orderly mind, her violet eyes glowing luminously. "I don't wish to be a what's-her-name — Susan B. Anthony. I like our civilization the way it is, mostly, and I abhor firebrands and reformers. I just want to practice law. I'm a good lawyer, and I just want to be — to be accepted as one in the middle of this — this tradition or whatever it is that defines what men and women may do. I don't — want to turn the world upside down. I just want a little niche for me, and there's none here, don't you see? Law is all I know, Quincy. Everything. I grew up in Papa's office. I — I'm just different. No one taught me to cook and sew or run a house or have — I didn't — Those things aren't the ends of my life! I can't stand it here anymore!"

She sat tautly in her chair, her face etched with desperation, staring sightlessly at Quin. "I've said more than I ever intended. Please forgive my breach of decorum."

136

She stared at him bleakly, awaiting whatever rebuke would come. But it was Missy who responded. The girl simply beelined into Nicole's arms and hugged her. Nicole was utterly unprepared. She had scarcely known what it was to be hugged; yet here was Missy's warm cheek against her own, and the girl's arms squeezing out a message of caring.

"Oh, Missy dear," Nicole gasped, tears welling up at last from eyes that never wept.

Quin fidgeted and cleared his throat. "You pack up," he said at last. "Write notes to your clients and maybe put an ad in the weekly saying you're on a holiday, and I'll go over to the livery and rent a buggy —"

"Quin!" she gasped. "I can't go out there! I've got a deposition, and — I haven't said I'd go."

"Maybe let the people next door know, too, so they can keep an eye on the place. Or tell the marshal —"

"Quin, I didn't say —"

"If you stay in this heat, you'll come down with Texas fever, or mange, or blackleg, or maybe splenetic fever, or pleuropneumonia, or maybe all of 'em at once."

She laughed suddenly, and Missy did too.

The next morning there were plenty of eyes watching Quin hoist a trunk into a buggy and then give Miss Nicole a hand into the seat beside him. Word had spread fast when Nicole talked to the Weedens next door, put a small boxed vacation notice in the *Argus-Miner,* and posted a dozen or so letters to local clients. When Quin trotted his blood bay out on Main Street, with Missy towing the mule alongside, those censorious eyes were watching, watching.

Nicole knew they were all there, peeping, and suddenly she didn't care. She'd soon be gone, anyway. So let them! She smoothed down the cream linen of her long tailored skirt and sat bolt upright until they were out of town.

"I don't know a blessed thing about Molière, either," Quin said slyly, and chortled. She slipped an arm through his, then withdrew it clumsily. Quin chortled again.

"We'll be stopping to see my neighbors on the way," Quin explained. "I want to see them about boarding some stock this winter."

They rambled up and out of the Judith Basin, into high, rumpled plateau country where the Big Sky engulfed them. Only then did some inner tautness in Nicole begin to yield a little.

"You know, Quin," she said throatily. "I never said yes. But I'm going to love this. It won't change anything. My only hope is a large city where there aren't so many walls."

"We'll see about that!" Quin snorted. "Meanwhile, we have to cure you of foot-and-mouth disease, ticks, and scours."

"Quincy Putnam!"

"We've got some bag balm and pinkeye medicine out there —"

"Quincy Putnam!"

"We could dehorn you, too, but then you wouldn't have any protection against wolves . . ."

There was a warning glint in her eyes.

"We'll be stopping at Coffeecan Pentecost's in a bit. Just remember to stay upwind of him."

The mellow shade of Coffeecan's giant cottonwoods was delicious after the ferocity of the cloudless day. Quin leaped down and stroked the pump handle until he got a good flow of cool water for Missy and Nicole to splash in.

"Them's the worst-looking rat-tailed thorrybreds I ever laid eyes to," Coffeecan yelled as he erupted from his garden.

"Not half so ugly as those hammerheaded blue mules you raise," Quin bawled back.

"Is that thing there supposed to be a mule, Putnam? Looks more like a poodle dog to me. Say, wanta buy a jenny —"

"Coffeecan, I wouldn't sell my mule for the entire lot of your knock-kneed lummoxes," Quin roared into his host's better ear. "Meet Miss Aumont from Lewistown."

"You that lawyer lady?"

"Yes."

"Don't know what the world's coming to. No good, I'd say."

Within an hour, Quin had negotiated for the boarding of twenty heifers through the winter. The price was dear, but the animals would be safe, come what may. And as part of the bargain he was forced to buy a jenny mule he didn't want, for thirty-seven fifty.

"Why the odd price, Coffeecan?" Quin yelled.

"Thirty-five for the jenny and ten bits for her copyrighted, patent pending, trademarked name, Putnam."

They rode on down the intimate valley of the McDonald south fork, where Quin was greeted warmly at every stop. Little Lars Hilleboe agreed to board ten bulls in exchange for stud service. The shorthorns were good milkers, and he was building a dairy herd. By the time they reached the road from Grassrange down to the Q Ranch, Quin had found havens for seventy of his brood stock. Not as many as he had hoped, but a little more safety. They rolled over the low divide in the bronze dusk — it had been a long day for Nicole — and then up the Flatwillow to the Q and some comfortable beds.

It was too dark for Nicole to see much, but she knew that the next day all the legal descriptions, surveyors' charts, plat maps, contracts, business letters, vouchers, and lawsuits that had been the Q Ranch to her would spring miraculously alive. She could barely wait to see in the concrete what she knew so intimately in the abstract.

They pulled up before a spacious white frame house, with a welcoming porch awaiting friends and family, and tugged her inside. Missy led her into the stilled home while Quin put the buggy and animals away. By the light of a kerosene lamp, Nicole glimpsed a handsome parlor — elegant with period furniture and an Aubusson rug, she thought.

"Do you like it?" Missy asked, and Nicole sensed that her answer would mean a great deal to the girl.

"It's striking, Missy. It's just the house I've always imagined Quin would have."

The girl beamed in the warm light.

Quin was a meticulous man, and he took his time rubbing down the weary horses and the mule, watering them, and forking them a good bait of hay, along with a can of oats.

Missy led Nicole to the guest bedroom that would be her cloister for a while. It was an austerely male room, Nicole thought as she gazed at the golden oak double bed, dresser, chair, and washstand. A white vitreous china pitcher and basin rested on the stand. Plainly, Quin had expected male visitors. But she was used to all that: not until after Jean Aumont died did she live in a feminine room.

Quin hefted the black leather trunk up the stairs with a great clatter and deposited it in a corner of Nicole's room.

"Welcome to the Q, Nicole," he said rather shyly, something bright in his face. "Welcome home."

He clicked shut the door, and she marveled at how young he looked in the lamplight, all bronze and male.

She awoke to the chime of a clock somewhere downstairs, and sunlight catching motes of dust in the air above her bed. She counted to eight, and knew there had been more chimes before she started. She was shocked, but she felt rested, and she stretched happily under the blanket before she threw it off.

A place was set for her in the dining room, and Missy bounded from the kitchen with a bowl of steaming oatmeal, examining the guest curiously.

"Quin says you'll be on your own for a few days," she announced. "He has to get all sorts of things done as soon as possible. Move a lot of cattle up to a meadow,

141

and see about haying some of the winter range. He says he'll be back about dusk, so we'll have a late dinner. And" — she giggled — "he said go do something silly."

Nicole liked being on her own at the Q, the luxury of freedom, and not having to say all the right, polite things to her hosts — not that she needed to here. This was a new universe to explore, one she understood in a curious way through her law, but didn't really know at all. Missy had vanished, too, busy, no doubt, with her chores. So Nicole was alone once again, but it was a different sort of aloneness, for here there were people about, and no invisible walls to seal her off from anyone.

She grew aware that Quin's character permeated the whole ranch, from its grand design to its most minute detail. And that fascinated her more than the ranch life itself. The gorgeous views from the windows, framed by ponderosa in the yard, bore the stamp of Quin's taste and sensitivity. The study fairly shouted of him, with its burnished rolltop desk, great Morris chair, and vaulting walls of books. She could envision him there, penning the dozens of heavy-stroked letters that she had received from him over the years. She poked through his library and discovered virtually every branch of learning exquisitely represented, including some old, familiar legal tomes. She enjoyed books, really; it was only when she was trapped with them in her Lewistown prison that reading became unbearable.

She peeked into his bedroom and found it as austere as her own guest room: a plain cane chair beside a sturdy black walnut bed. On a small table sat a kerosene lamp and a much-thumbed Bible, beside the *Book of Common Prayer*. Yes, she remembered, he was an Episcopalian, and the religion seemed to flourish in him. There was some spiritual quality evident here in this chamber that was as austere as a monk's cell compared with the handsome parlor below. Quin was a man who could enjoy life's bounty and beauty, yet withdraw into a spiritual life where he needed no more than a bit of bread and a window to the sky. It fit him: the quarters were imbued with the very man she had known in law, a man who had sometimes frustrated her with a carelessness about things or with a conscience that blocked all reasonable solutions.

How unlike her father Quin was! Her father had had ravishing lovers, one after another, who slipped into their Saint Louis brick home again and again. Sometimes she heard them or saw them when she was little, but she always knew when they were there, murmuring, usually in the night, but sometimes in the afternoons when her father gave her a quarter to go to the soda parlor or the park.

She always wondered about her own mother — whether she had slipped in and out of her father's house like the other women. Nicole hoped she was legitimate. When she was old enough, she had checked. Her baptismal certificate indicated that she was. It listed her mother as Annemarie Campaigne Aumont, but her father had never spoken of Campaigne relatives. After he died, she had combed his correspondence looking for clues about her mother. But there had been none. She would never know how

143

long her parents had been married, who cared for her when she was an infant, or how she came to be in her father's care.

Now she would return to her childhood home and begin anew. Jean Aumont had fled to the Montana frontier to escape a scandal, she knew. She had found tantalizing bits and pieces of that story in her father's correspondence. There had been a doe-eyed blonde Hungarian woman, with two lovers — one of them Nicole's father — and a murderous betrayed husband, a furrier who catered to the carriage trade. Her father had fled up the Missouri River in fear of his life after an eleventh-hour warning from his lover. But now . . . Jean Aumont was dead, and the affair long buried. There was nothing to keep her from reclaiming her ancestral home.

Nicole wandered from the springhouse to the barn and the outbuildings, then down to the pole corrals to watch the brood mares for a while. It was inexpressibly quiet there, rather like the gardens of a convent, she supposed. And everywhere she looked, from the orchard to the shining mountains far across the wide, wide valley, she saw the faith and works of Quincy Putnam.

CHAPTER
TWELVE

"How do ye want t' have it — the happy news first, or the bad, or all in order, as it happened?" John Durham asked, settling into the chair in Quin's study.

The foreman had returned from Billings, seen the lamplight still yellowing the windows of the house, and slipped in to report before going to bed. That was Durham's way: almost any other man, after a hot three-day ride, would have reported in the morning.

Quin sighed restlessly. "Let's hear the worst."

Durham's eyes widened ingenuously. "The terrible truth is, I squandered a hundred and twenty-nine dollars without ye authorizing a penny of it," the wiry foreman announced.

Quin eased. That was calamity he could live with.

"I got t' thinking on the ride doon, the way I often do when languishing in the saddle, about the donkey engine and sawmill ye palavered about before we left. Cutting the timber, ye know.

"And I got t' supposing that maybe that boiler could drive a pump, the way they do on a fire wagon in the cities, and maybe we could employ it, if we got t' moving our butts a bit, t' pump some water upon the parched-up hay meadows."

A drowsy Quin awakened with a start.

"I was meditating," the Scot continued, "it's terribly late in the year t' be watering grass, but still it's mid-August, and a good soak might put a wee bit of growth on it before the frost. So after the other duties were done — I'll get to that — why, I began t' hunt around Billings, and I found a pump that will spin off the belt, same as the saw blade, and three lengths of canvas fire hose. 'Twas all I could find, but coupled together they'll allow us to drench about a hundred yards of meadow, either side of the creek, for all the miles of it."

"John, you're a genius!" Quin exclaimed.

"Well, I've spent a little ye didn't intend, and I'll ask ye to slice it from my wage . . . and of course I'll pack my kit the day the accounts are settled, if ye do. At any rate, it'll work. We can bolt on the pump in the morning, and in an hour we'll be laying water on the meadows. I'll put one mon — Bunions, I suppose — on it steady, tending the firebox and moving hose and tugging the rig along behind the Percheron."

"If that's the worst news, what's the good?" asked Quin.

"We trailed the herd t' the shipping pens with no loss, in spite of the heat and dry. It's a fine thing they were fat and strong. I was about to let the laddies go when I ran into that livestock broker, Horatio Bowler, and he was telling he had a buyer out in Oregon country for shorthorn bull and heifer calves. Building a herd there, it seems. And the mon would split the freight instead of our paying it all, which means a three-dollar bonus per beast for us.

"So I read the laddies their death sentence: they'd have t' suffer a wee bit more before rampaging on doon t' Montana Street, and you never did see such universal disgust disfiguring all those innocent countenances. But we cut out four hundred and twenty-one calves for the mon. And I says to Bowler, I says, get me cash dollars, because the buyer is unknown, and by the by, it arrived on Western Union, and I have a voucher for ye here. So ye got an extra twelve hundred for the young stuff, minus a broker fee of four bits per.

"The laddies, ye never saw such contumacy in so many froward divas, but I held the cudgel, namely the payroll, which assured me their undying fealty, at least for an hour or two, all maledictions aside, and so we got it all done, all loaded properly. So I cut the gentlemen loose, and they forayed off like a cavalry charge for all the glittering and heinous palaces of Montana Street, where no Presbyterian like me has ever set foot, at least not recently.

"I haven't seen a laddie since, not even a one sprawled down in the gutter, and canna tell ye whether they'll drift back up here like ye wanted, or not. I had a tedious trip back with Bunions and Lem, the pair being swollen-headed and antisocial after their joust with the devil, and being a bit weary myself with the arthritis that's been clabbering me these days."

The voucher looked like manna to Quin. It and the Chicago proceeds would defray a winter's expenses and perhaps be a corner on a fresh herd in the spring.

147

"What an unfeeling despot you are, John," Quin yawned. "Exasperating the boys like that. And now you're going to pain the rest by making them tend the steam engine!"

"Aye, mark my words, mon. The day's coming when a cowboy will spend more time mothering machinery than mothering cattle!"

"That it will, John. Well, now . . . there'll be a bonus for you at the end of the month for a job well done. Tomorrow I'll tell you about some notions I have. We'll try to cut some hay, after all, right off the prairie. But not tonight. I'm glad you're back safe . . ."

He tiptoed tenderly past Nicole's door, noting that no lamplight glowed from under it. She had been sleeping late and was looking more rested each day. And obviously relishing her stay, too, asking myriad questions and gamely experimenting with everything from milking a cow to riding a horse.

Quin smiled, disinterring the memory of her first ride the day before, with Billy Jones fussing around the barn, manfully trying to avoid hee-hawing all over the place, and Dingdong's beady slant eyes lurking behind the kitchen window.

Missy had saddled a gentle mare, and Quin had lifted the compact young woman aboard. But the mare, so docile under other riders, assessed Nicole her own canny way, and wouldn't budge. Neither her polite tapping on the mare's ribs nor her polite giddyaps yielded any motion. Nicole took to tugging at the reins and tapping at the same time, and that produced movement, but a backward one, so that the little mare eventually backed around a full circle. Billy obviously couldn't suffer it any longer: he retreated into the barn, and from that sanctuary there emanated great hawking and spitting noises. Nicole haughtily proclaimed her preference for walking, anyway, and braved her way back to her room where she disported herself for some time.

By the time Quin sat down to poached eggs and a slice of beef the next morning, the steam engine was chuffing in the nearest hay meadow and a great charge of life-giving water was fanning out on the parched earth. The sight of it lifted Quin with a moment of heady joy. From his window he watched the boys stuffing firewood into the firebox, and he decided to send Lem down to Roundup for a load of coal, and to have a dozen more loads freighted up. That would save the firewood for the house stoves.

Quin itched to start cutting the prairie-grass hay. He loped out to the bottoms east of his hay meadows, where the bunch grass lay thickest and tallest, and waited there for Durham and the boys to show up with the mower and dump rake.

He was fascinated by grass. There wasn't much of a literature about it, especially the western bunch grass varieties the cattlemen lumped together as grama grass. What he knew was largely the result of his own close observation. He had a reverence for it, an awe of it, and he saw those swords of green as the very wealth of nations and the vaults of all prosperity.

He knelt down in the midst of it, seeing what he had. It wouldn't make very good hay, he realized. It might not make hay at all if it was so brittle that it disintegrated when cut: Standing the way it did, cured on the stalk, it was a marvelous feed for cattle on the hoof. The clump under his gaze was silvery dry. The stalks of the old growth stood upright, hip-high, and could easily be mowed and raked. But there wasn't much nurture in them; it was straw, really.

The old sere brown leaves still stood, brittle in the heat. And down around the base was this year's growth, bleached white now but still tinged with green. Most of the new grass would be lost, he knew. It was too short for the dump rake to pick up and would fall between the tines. Much of the brittle old grass would disintegrate, too, and escape the rake. Yet he had to try.

"Set the mower as low as it'll go, John, and watch out for that patch of cheat grass," he directed.

The foreman hawed the paired Belgians into action and began an experimental swatch through the tawny bunch grass, with the mower teeth clacking beside him. The spears of tall grass tumbled behind like fallen soldiers, and then Billy followed with the dump rake, leaving dun heaps every few yards.

"Now let's see what we have here," an eager Quin cried, scooping up a fistful.

"It's mostly straw, mon. But 'twill keep the beasts alive," concluded the Scot.

"We lost the new grass," Quin sighed, rubbing his scalp. "At least we don't have to cure it. We can rake and stack immediately."

It was the best he could hope for.

150

"I tell you what, John. Experiment with this today. Then tomorrow, when Lem gets back with the coal, we'll pitch in. Maybe there's a hundred tons — at least that, I hope — we can get out of this. I can even put the girls, or Missy anyway, to driving the hay wagons, and Dingdong to forking hay back at the barn. But we've got to clean this off before outside cattle get in here. They're mostly around Durfee Creek now, but that won't last. We'll cut the closest meadows first and then work down the Flatwillow."

They were desperately shorthanded for such a vast venture. They needed a dozen men and had only four, with Lem operating the pump. The most brutal part, in that August sun, was forking the hay onto the wagons and then pitching it up on the haystacks. Every forkload rained a cloud of disintegrating grass on them, which itched and bit. They rotated the tasks, with Quin toiling alongside his sweating crew. They ate before dawn and began cutting at first light to take advantage of the cool. At the nooning they broke for three hours, and then strained and sweated again into the dusk.

Nicole at last mastered a buckboard and began to bring them cool spring water and bountiful sandwiches, watching thoughtfully as the gargantuan labor of ranch life revealed itself to her. She wished she could do more. Yet succoring thirsty, weary men was important, too. They gulped down her refreshments while rivulets of sweat drenched their shirts, which they wore against the merciless sun. Time and time again her eyes strayed to Quin, older than all save John, but working rhythmically on the hardest tasks, perduring against time and calamity.

When each wagonload was topped, a bonneted Missy drove it back to the haystacks, and Dingdong, dragooned from his pots and kettles, helped her fork the harvest to its final destination. At first it was easy when the stack was low and the pitching was downhill, but it became a staggering job for a girl when each forkload had to be pitched high above her head. She worked ferociously at it, heart hammering, and then collapsed for ten minutes before she was able to drive her wagon back to the fields. But little by little the stacks began to grow — a ton, then two, then ten.

"I'm sorry," Quin apologized to Nicole over dinner. "I didn't mean to make a galley slave of you. I can't afford your fancy fees unless I make hay." He grinned at her like a pixie from under his sun-blistered scalp.

"Nothing is free," was her enigmatic reply.

Two days later the rubicund carcass of Pinky materialized, with a still-besotted ghost of his former self in residence, and beside him the cadaverous hulk of Sleet, a refugee from voluptuary excess. The pair had envisioned a lengthy bunkhouse siesta, followed, perhaps, by a little woodcutting through the golden days of the equinox. But Quin hectored them both into immediate gainful employment on a weekly basis, and after several groaning days, during which they fermented the last of the juices of Billings out of their fevered flesh, they became a great help. Ton by ton, the prickly stacks near Quin's ranch yard grew.

152

By the end of August Quin supposed he had fifty tons of the bunch grass put up. A pitiful amount to spread among eight hundred beeves through a Montana winter. But at least something. It was a wasteful harvest: in an open winter the cattle could have eaten it all. At times the steamy toil was so brutal that Quin wondered if it made any sense. He could sell his entire herd and start over. But when the Circle B longhorns began drifting in and crowding the haying crew, they goaded Quin into a fury of renewed labor. He would cut all he could while he could.

Wherever the hay meadows had received the benediction of Durham's pump, they greened ebulliently, the mixed bluestem and fescue and native rye rejoicing to be alive. But the growth, what little there was of it, disappointed Quin. It was the season when grass is virtually dormant, and now it vegetated comfortably in the summer breezes, fattening up on the moist clay but growing very little. The quest for tall grass put him in mind of his alpine meadow, and he decided the time had come to move cattle there for a harvest feast. On the final day of August he pulled his crew off the haying and set out for the high country, first to gather any hundred shorthorns they could discover, and then to drive them to the mountain pasture. It took four days.

Nicole fretted restlessly as she waited for him to return. It was time for her leave-taking, time to fold up her Lewistown practice and begin a new life. Her stay at Quin's ranch had been restful, but it had also

153

multiplied her pain. The man she loved was no closer to her than before. Saint Louis, she knew, would be no remedy for her anguish. She doubted that she'd be admitted to the Missouri bar. Urbane lawyers would suavely deflect her petitions in that civilized arena until she yielded and settled into a diminished life as a legal secretary or, at best, a law clerk buried in some firm's rearmost cubbyhole. So, at most, she could look forward to some ladylike labor, providing she mastered dictation and one of those typewriting machines.

She had no connections in Saint Louis, either, apart from a few distant Aumonts. She would be alone, as solitary a woman in Saint Louis as she was in Lewistown. But at least, she thought, Saint Louis tendered the freedom of anonymity. She could come and go as a private person, and that was something to treasure. And there would be opera, theater, libraries, parks, and excursions to occupy her. She could be free and busy, and those activities would make her lonely life bearable.

Still, the decision left her deeply melancholy. When she thought of the impending journey, she immediately thought of Quin, so that she maintained a sort of balance on the fulcrum of her will. She was torn between buoyant hope and a ripening sense of futility . . . He hadn't the slightest romantic attachment to her, she supposed. She was unsuitable: she was a bluestocking, and worse, she earned a living in a mannish profession, and that was obviously too much for him. And besides, she was too young . . . She ached for him to see her as . . . a woman.

154

How she cherished Quin's gentle intelligence, his learning, and all his little humorous sallies. And even his stubbornness! His very character had cushioned her Lewistown practice, and she had often pined for him to ride in from his ranch. She had needed someone like him, someone who endured, who weathered well. That was his forte, that weathering. There were other types of men — more reckless, dashing, cavalier, bold, brawling — but Quin was merchant and priest in whatever odd conjunction the two traits fit together. But it was his way of transcending suffering, his spiritual depths, that had; in the end, blessed and inspired her own life.

"Quincy, it's time for me to return to Lewistown," she announced after he had returned from the uplands. "I must find a replacement and close my practice."

"You're going, then," he said, daunted. "I wish I could persuade you —"

"Yes. I simply must. I'll miss you both . . ."

"I'd hoped the ranch, the freedom you needed —"

"It did help. It really did. And I'm so grateful."

"I've been thinking. How about bringing in a partner? Aumont and Smith or Jones. It might make things easier for you in town."

"It'd be worse! They'd only gossip about Miss Aumont and Mr Jones. No, Quin . . ."

"Well, you could marry young Mr Jones. That'd settle their hash." He chuckled at the thought.

The grief that swept her then was nothing he could see. "Never, Quin. Never," she whispered. "I can't marry — a Mr Jones. There's no man would have me, a pariah, a woman full of torts and habeas corpuses, and . . . Oh, Quin, oh Quin . . ."

"A dazzling damsel like you? Miss Nicole, don't be so pessimistic! Find a man, love him, and let him love you, and all the rest will work out!"

She felt the sting of sorrow cut through her.

"Well," he sighed, finally, "I'll miss you terribly. I had such hopes . . . You're just getting doors open here, and roots down in the Big Sky country, with a county seat for a practice. You'd trade the Snowies for the gaslights, would you?"

It was all too much for Missy.

"Miss Nicole, don't go. Please, Miss Nicole . . ."

A desolation deeper than anything she had ever known seeped through Nicole. Through all the weeks at the Q Ranch, Missy had been glued to her side, showing her Snowflake, and where the hens laid brown eggs, and — don't tell Quin! — the tobacco-plated inside of the bunkhouse, and the fragrant hayloft, and trout in the creek, observed by stealthily peering through chokecherry brush. Missy had led her into the cool springhouse where the food was kept and into the gardens to dig potatoes and pluck raspberries. And they had talked — no, chattered — all the while, sometimes about things Missy had been too reserved to ask Quin about.

"Please, Nicole —" Sudden wet glistened on her cheeks.

"I'll come back," Nicole responded miserably.

"No, not ever" was Missy's dark premonitory response. She bolted up to her room, and the door clattered shut behind her. Nicole winced. She felt so needed, just when she was determined to put Montana forever behind her. She found Quin observing her, apparently waiting for something.

"Quin, I — What shall I say?"

"That you'll send us a postcard," was his wry response.

"I'd like Missy to come to town with me for a while. We'll manage very well, although I'll be busy and she'll be on her own at times. It'll be good for her."

Quin leaned back in his chair, avoiding Nicole's eyes. "I'm afraid I need her here, Nicole. She's almost another man for me, just when I need help so much. I don't know how I can let her go until after we've made hay and driven down the stock. Mid-October, maybe, when we're done . . ."

"I understand. That's when I'll be packing, but we'll find time."

He smiled uneasily. "I'll be asking John Durham to drive you back. Same reasons. I wish I could spare the time, but everything's urgent."

"I'm upsetting things! Would it help if I waited —"

"No. We're picking up some stock salt in town anyway," he said, feeling the gulf widen each moment.

"These have been precious days, Quin. Every one. I'm glad you asked me. Do you understand why —"

"I imagine," was his laconic response.

An awkward silence enmeshed them, and they could no longer reach across it. Nicole bumbled away and fled to her room.

The leave-taking on a colorless autumn dawn was much harsher on her than she had any inkling it would be. Missy descended into a severe silence. Nicole couldn't think of anything to say that made any sense. She felt she ought to be saying grand, momentous things, mountains and streams and big skies full of words. She couldn't imagine what was upsetting her so much unless it was Quin's own melancholy silence. His eyes raked her as she sat in the buggy, lingering on her face, the cameo at her throat, her creamy linen suit. He gazed so intently, his face a mask, that she couldn't bear it. She was too contained, all bottled, corked, sealed, tied, and roped.

Then they were off, she and old John Durham, rattling up the grade. She turned to see Missy staring mutely while Quin slumped over a hitching post, looking terribly old.

I tried so hard, she thought, hiding her tears from John Durham. I tried so hard to stay.

"I think, lass," he said gently, staring straight ahead, "ye'll be coming back someday."

CHAPTER
THIRTEEN

Quin waited until the eve of his departure before telling anyone where he was going. He knew what Missy's reaction would be, and he was right.

"No, Quin! Don't go there," she begged.

"I'm going there to do business. That's all there is to it," he soothed. "I have an offer I'm going to lay before them."

"But they've blacklisted you. It's like being an outlaw."

He touched her gently on the cheek. "Maybe they'll wipe my name off the list as fast as they slapped it on, after they hear me out."

The district's fall roundup was under way. As always, it began on Silas Stone's S-over-S spread and then transcribed a huge circle, moving clockwise at about twenty-mile intervals. All the ranches in the district and some outlying ones, too, had their representatives, or reps, on hand for the tallying, and many of the cattlemen themselves were present.

Quin threw his rimfire saddle over the bay one heady September morning, just when the sun was deviling the cold, and lashed his saddlebags over the cantle. Missy held the reins silently, her eyes riveted to the old pearly handled Peacemaker in Quin's black holster.

"What do you think, that I'm riding off to a massacre?" he joked. "You mind the store, now. John's going to cut more hay from the bottoms, what little there is left of it, and I'll see you in a day or two."

The gelding danced along, enjoying the fresh breezes as much as Quin did. The roundup would be at its second camp now, he knew, up north of Fort Maginnis a piece, hard upon the Judith Mountains. If Silas's ranch was at ten o'clock in the clockwise progression, they'd be at eleven now.

He wished he could do it another way. What he really wanted was to visit each cattleman at his home, individually, and talk things over man to man, over a little sippin' whiskey. People were at their best that way, with all their hospitality and reasonableness governing them. But that was scarcely possible. It would mean several hundred miles of grueling riding and two weeks of travel. Two weeks he could be haying or completing his own gather of the beeves up in the high country. So he was constrained to do this the other way, visiting the roundup itself, where he could catch ten or twelve of them at once.

That didn't bode well. Men who were reasonable alone formed a solid phalanx in a group like that. It took only one old bull, like Clapp, to keep them all in line, leery of busting the ranks even when something inside them was bawling to cut loose. Even worse, he'd have to catch them in the evening, around chowtime, when they were exhausted after a rough day of gathering, tallying, branding, and castrating. They'd be owly and short-fused and not inclined to give him even the ten minutes he needed. But Silas would be there, and Quin was counting on the young man to bring them together. All he wanted was to be heard out.

Well, he mused, circumstances were never ideal for any project, but it was sometimes best to proceed as if they were, even when nothing good was on the horizon. That was the real test of a man's mettle, that ability to carry the day when things were stacked against him. He remembered how he had vegetated in the Union army under General McClellan, the Hamlet temporizing on the Potomac, awaiting a textbook perfection in his ranks and a plague upon the enemy.

Well, this wasn't war; it was business. And he was on a mission of conciliation, not a showdown. He was riding there to offer them something of value, not to threaten them with disaster. They had more grief than they could use; what they lacked was hope. He intended to offer them hope, and on terms that wouldn't embarrass them. Whether he succeeded would depend on how high a wall Clapp and the rest had built — Clapp, the soldier manqúe, whose life was a march and a strut and whose mode of enterprise was a clash for the spoils of war.

Clapp was no merchant, Quin knew, and scarcely comprehended the peace that often results when merchants and entrepreneurs trade for their mutual benefit. The webs of trade, Quin held, spin networks of benefit to nearly all — until they are slashed by politicians, soldiers, and fanatics who want the world to

161

whirl their own way. Well, this was a business foray and nothing more . . . unless succoring desperate men was a religious act, which Quin thought it might well be. He'd fail, probably. But his offer, of fine-spun gold, would echo after him, embedded in the annals of a man's life.

He angled north across Silas's barren hills, past the distant fort, and up along the flanks of the Judith Mountains, scaring up antelope herds. The orb dipped behind the western peaks, and immediately a chill lowered from the slopes, reminding him that it was mid-September and frost was lurking near.

He jolted down the long grade to Little Box Elder Creek, where the gathered cattle formed a lowing black mass in the brushy wastes. The amber glow of cook fires was a night beacon in the early gloaming. Something in him was taut, and he wished he could recover the ease he'd need to address these men genially, as old friends.

They greeted him somberly. The wrangler led his bay to the remuda. The drovers nodded, awaiting a cue from above. They were all loyal to their brands, and that fealty transcended old and mellow friendships with Quincy Putnam. The crew, fifty strong at this point of the gathering, had devoured its sowbelly and beans, and now men were hunkering down against their saddles, enjoying a cheroot or a chaw. Quin spotted Oliver Henry and old Clapp and some of the others around the cavvy wagon. But it was Silas he wanted first, and he found the young stockman in the spreading Sibley tent he had purchased in 1884 for these bivouacs. The fall roundups were plagued with nasty weather in their latter weeks, and for all the cowboys' braggadocio about slumbering under the stars, they were often sick and miserable in the icy rains. Silas had been the first to remedy their distress with a Sibley, a round tent that accommodated a sheet-metal stove at the center. The drovers slept around it like wheel spokes, feet to the fire, and stayed healthy and rested through the entire ordeal. And Silas was convinced they worked better, besides.

Quin found Silas wolfing up bread and beans from a tin plate. The young man gripped Quin's proffered hand silently, a question on his face.

"I'd like to powwow with the association men for a few minutes," announced the visitor as a plate of chow was thrust into his hands by a cowpoke. "Can you arrange it?"

"I imagine. But they'll be wanting to bed down after a day like this one. Have you something in mind?"

"Peace talk," muttered Quin. "Or just a plain business offer, I suppose. And I came a few leagues to say it."

"Well, you came to the right place," Silas agreed, finding mettle in Quin's visit. "I'll see who I can rustle up." He vanished into the twilight while Quin rehearsed. There would be only a moment to sway them before their portcullis clattered down. Every word, every second, was going to count.

One by one the association members straggled in, irked by the intrusion, expecting war, recrimination, or threats, and chary of all of it. Clapp darkened the flap door, itching for a brawl, radiating belligerence. They nodded curtly, and settled themselves in an arc around the tent wall, feet to the radiant stove. Fifteen in all. More than Quin had expected. There were no Birkenheads, but their rep, Natividad Rourke, had invited himself in.

Quin pressed his eyes shut a second, girding for a fateful encounter. Then he began, falteringly: "I'm here simply to make a business proposal," he began hoarsely. "You're all in desperate shape, same as I am. I've got something you need — tall grass — and I'm here to offer it. To share it."

He cleared his throat. The tension in it twisted his voice up into him so that he could scarcely speak clearly. It wasn't the easy calm he had wished for himself.

"I'm not here to talk about public range or private range, or the right or wrong of anything —"

"Well, you'd better talk about public range and the wrong of it," snarled Clapp, "or I'll be walking out of here in thirty seconds."

"I'm here to talk about capital. Our capital. My capital investments," Quin scraped on.

The novelty of that quieted Clapp for a moment. Silas studied Quin intently, a faint amusement playing around his mouth.

"Our capital is grass," Quin continued. "Some of you have exhausted your seed capital fast to make a profit fast. I haven't earned much of a profit over the years, because I've tried to keep my capital intact for the future, for times of trouble as well as for the good

164

times. But grass is our real capital, not livestock. I could have earned as much as some of you have just by using up the capital on my range as fast —"

"Oh, get on with it, Putnam! I want to go to bed," Pickett snapped.

"All right, then. The grass capital is my investment. Every blade of it I've saved out for future use is dollars and cents to me. I own that grass because I fenced it off, no matter who owns what's underneath."

He hurried along, not wanting interruptions now.

"I have the grass you need to survive this winter. And I'll share it, but at a modest price, a return on my investment. I'll — now listen well — I'll winter five thousand head on the Q Ranch for a dollar a head . . ."

He let the impact of the offer settle home. "That's dirt cheap. I'm virtually giving my grass away. If I were in your boots, I'd welcome the offer and the price. A dollar a head is a price you can live with. That five thousand dollars is a lot less than I'd get if I used my capital myself, feeding my own stock on it. Five thousand is a lot more stock than the Q can properly winter, actually. There's less than twenty sections of it —"

"Sixty!" a voice boomed.

"Twenty of ungrazed winter range, the rest forest and high country, heavily grazed this summer by sheep men."

"None of it patent!" that orotund voice proclaimed.

"At any rate, it's an offer. Fair to you, fair to me, and a resource in a troubled time. You can prorate your herds until you come up with the five thousand total.

But you'll have to move Birkenhead cattle off; there's that many Circle B's on the Q right now."

"We can't deal with you. You're on the blacklist," Clapp retorted.

"Well, take me off. There's a quorum of you right here to do it." Quin's response was acerbic.

"When you're on, you stay on."

Quin addressed them intensely: "How does a man get off? Are you a judge and jury? I'm here with a fair offer, straight business. I'm not complaining or fighting or arguing."

He let the matter languish there for a moment. They all knew he had a point; the grass was his capital, and he had conserved it with care.

Silas Stone stood up, bumping his head on the low canvas. "Let's think about this," he said genially.

"Let's not. I'm going to bed. I don't see why we should pay cash dollars for what's ours to take anyway," Pickett grumbled.

The words thickened the decision in them until it hardened into concrete, and Quin saw his chances ebb away.

"Now you beat it, Putnam. We don't trust blacklist men in camp. And don't try sneaking off with that cow," Clapp grinned malevolently.

"What cow?"

"The shorthorn stray of yours we collected," Clapp purred.

There was a season, Quin knew, after all conciliation had failed, when a man had to stand his ground. This wasn't a good place to do it, surrounded by antagonistic men. And a thirty-dollar Q Ranch cow wasn't much of an occasion for it, either. But it had to be done. It had to happen because it was fitting; because, after making a generous offer, he couldn't leave this place like a whipped dog who would be kicked again and again in years to come. There was no relish in him for the task, as there would have been in warrior men whose joy rose with the scent of battle.

"If there's a cow of mine here, it's not a stray. I'm here to collect it," said Quin tautly.

"She belongs to the association now." Clapp sprung to his feet, relishing a confrontation. The rest sat be mused.

"Let's get something straight," Quin snapped. "That cow's my property. You're a private association of private men — not the law — and you have no more rights than I have. If you confiscate that cow, I'll call it theft."

"Criminals don't have rights, Putnam." Clapp took a step toward him, all brawn and meat and peacock tail.

Quin started to shout something, then stopped abruptly. Trading epithets here would get him nowhere.

"I'm going to pay the two-fifty the association charges to return strays, and then I'll take her with me," he proclaimed. He pulled two greenbacks and four bits from his jeans and handed the money to Silas.

"I'll record that payment," Silas said.

"I'll be leaving now," said Quin in a deadly, dulcet tone. "With my cow. Anyone who tries to stop me will have to resort to violence."

There was a long, taut silence.

"I'll help you find her, Quin." Silas's genial voice snapped the tension. The young man threw an arm around the older one and eased outside into the biting black air. No one followed.

"That was a generous offer, but you were wrong on one particular, Quin," Silas remarked as they strode out to the herd. "It wasn't fair to yourself."

Quin laughed shortly.

"I'm not going to be a part of the rape of the Q," Silas continued. "Matter of fact, we're pushing half our beeves up above the Missouri, on reservation land, for the winter. There's grass up there, a little bit anyway, with the buffalo gone and only a few scrub Indian cattle."

"Think you can swim them across the Missouri?"

"Sure, if we're careful. The water's low and slow now. It's a question of getting them to swim straight across at the ford and not paddle downstream where the bluffs could trap them."

"You'll manage it with that savvy crew of yours."

"We've got the strays penned yonder. There's only a few," Silas explained. The thick bulk of the Durham cow was plain, even in the gloom. "I guess she didn't need too much finding," he said with a wink.

Quin dropped a lariat over her head and tugged her to the remuda, where his gelding was waiting, courtesy of the wrangler. Quin mounted and reached down to grip Silas's big hand.

"Well, I failed."

"No, you didn't, Quin. Not at all. There's things a man does just for the record."

168

"Well, they didn't teach me any of it in those business courses I took," Quin joked. "Thanks for siding me, Silas."

Quin trotted off into the night, his fast horse braked by the lumbering cow. It was a long way home, twenty-five miles south over high plains. He could cover a lot of ground with a horse that walked at five miles an hour or better, but the lamenting cow — she must have had a calf pulled off of her by a slick, herd-building cowpoke, he thought — would have none of it. He was tired, anyway. The meeting, scarcely ten minutes long, had drained him of his vitality, and the gelding could use a rest, too, after hauling him all day. He'd hole up at Fort Maginnis, an hour ahead, if it wasn't too late.

The fort had been erected in 1880 on Ford's Creek, not far below Silas Stone's ranch headquarters, to keep the Indians on their reservation north of the Missouri and to suppress rustling. It had never achieved either mission, largely because it was staffed with two companies of the Third Infantry, foot soldiers rather than cavalry. Mounted Indians — Blackfeet, Crow, Nez Percé, Flathead, Pend d'Oreille, Bannocks, and Sioux — wandered through the Judith Basin and the adjacent plains almost at will, eluding the plodding columns with ease. Outlaws and rustlers had no more difficulty than the Indians. A bad lot of wolfers, ex-buffalo hunters, breeds, and former woodhawks populated the Missouri breaks, appropriating old wood yards on the river that once supplied firewood for the streamers before the NP Railway brought river traffic to a halt in 1883. Quin, along with other selected men, had

169

followed Silas into the breaks in 1884 and performed a little rough justice, largely because the hapless soldiers at the fort had failed to do it.

In fact, the cattlemen joked, the day the soldiers caught anyone for doing anything, they'd eat their red long johns.

The fort loomed up ahead of him, a quadrangle of log buildings without a stockade, and Quin presented himself to the sentry. He was escorted to the corrals, where he left his horse and dolorous cow, and then to the bunkroom reserved for civilians.

"Guard," a salty voice rasped outside, "I hear a cow. Tell me why I hear a cow!"

A moment later there was a rapping on Quin's door.

"Well, Putnam! So it's you and a cow full of lamentations. Welcome to quarters," Captain Wiley McDaniel muttered from behind his red Vandyke. "All quiet down on the Flatwillow?"

"Quieter than here at the moment," Quin responded. "She's a stray shorthorn I picked up at the district roundup. Lost her calf, I'd guess."

"Must have been an only child. How mothers do dote on an only child. That's what I am — an only child. So she's fresh, eh?" The captain paused thoughtfully. "Some of our boys have been asking for milk and butter. Shorthorns are good milkers, aren't they?"

"Pretty good."

"We've got a contract with Pickett for beef, but that wouldn't cover a milch cow. She for sale? I'll give twenty-five if she's really fresh."

170

"Captain, after dragging this dowager at the end of my rope for seven miles, I'm ready to donate her to charity. Sure, I'll peddle her for that."

"I'll have the voucher ready right after roll call. Say, Putnam, do you have an enclosure down there? Interior Department wants us to report —"

"Far from it. At the moment, one line under wire. I had two, but the east line got torn out."

"Trouble?" McDaniel inquired solicitously, his store open for business.

"Nothing I can't handle."

"You're sure? I've been hearing things —"

"I'm sure."

"Well, fetch us if you need us. We got word from Fort Keogh that you've had trouble."

"Keogh?" Quin was astonished.

"Sure. You discharged most of your crew recently, didn't you? Well, they had a little celebration in Billings and then bummed an NP boxcar to Miles City to continue the soiree, and now three are in the congenial custody of the sheriff there, and one devil is in Keogh's calaboose. Ever been in there? Putnam, that's one awful calaboose. At any rate, they were all jabbering about the Q and the fence cutting. So the intelligence came my way. My district, you know."

Quin rollicked. "Well, send my boys a valentine on your telegraph," he chortled.

The captain retreated, and Quin lowered the wick until the lamp blued out.

He was one of those men who summed up his day after climbing into bed. The practice had begun as an exercise in self-improvement but had deteriorated into flagellation because of Quin's youthful intolerance of his own weaknesses. But now he was gentler with age and wisdom, and the review had become a kind of prayer and a moment of gratitude for a day lived as well as he could, among the many days.

Nothing much was accomplished by all that hard riding and hard talking, he thought. But it wasn't so bad. He had only practiced the golden rule, offering desperate men his tall grass at a giveaway price that, more than anything, salved their pride. And in doing it the record was written, though Quin had no notion who kept records, or why, or who cared anyway, except maybe God.

So, he thought, he'd just go back to the Q and plug along, day by day, doing all he could to keep things together. And it'd come out all right if he persevered. He'd transcended hate today: Clapp had hazed and riled him, but he'd come out on top, standing on his rights. Well, thank God for that, and for Missy, and for Nicole . . .

CHAPTER
FOURTEEN

Nicole took one look at the ashen-faced, travel-weary man and the stricken girl and led them into her office. There were times, she thought, when the practice of law wasn't law at all, but succor for desperate people, times when she felt she really was a nurse or a priest. Those were moments when she felt the burden of her practice most heavily on her small shoulders, because more often than not, there was nothing she could really do. People suffered, and the law was of little avail.

Quin handed her a letter, and it took only a glance at the name of Henry L. Dearborn engraved in an upper corner, and the Chicago postmark, to tell her much of what she needed to know. She began to read:

Dear Sir,

I am writing to inquire about a young woman in your custody whom I have reason to believe is my granddaughter.

Mr Andrew Bird, a private detective in my employ in respect of a stockholder suit, laid before me some material he had been carefully gathering for years, no doubt in the hope of winning a consideration from me.

The girl in question is named Antonia Novak and would be fourteen or fifteen. In 1871 my daughter Ruth eloped with one Anton Novak, causing my family great suffering. The man was a recent immigrant, of low birth, suited only for menial work, and filled with the strange notions and superstitions that, I understand, prevail in Eastern Europe.

Such was our distress at Ruth's willful rejection of us, and the privileges we accorded her, along with the highest ideals of character and comportment, that I felt constrained to forbid her further presence in our house, to forbid my family from further contact with her, and of course to strike away her inheritance.

Mr Bird's information about the expiration of my daugher and her husband at the hand of savages seems solid enough, as does his account of your rescue of the girl.

I have given considerable attention as to my responsibilities in this case. Clearly, if the child is a granddaughter, I have some obligation and duty, especially as a man of means, able to care for her and relieve you of your burden.

I don't wish to inflict the girl upon Mrs Dearborn or anyone else. But I have made inquiries, and have located an excellent home for young women, a place that has had particular success with intractable and difficult cases, modeled after the various cadet academies for young men. Not only does the home instill virtue and industry, but it takes pains to disabuse its wards of any superstitions or nonsense such as the girl may have inherited from her father, that would impede her full Americanization.

I plan to place her there until the age of eighteen and then find a suitable employment for her. Given her limited background, I presume she could be a ticket-taker in my company or perhaps a telephone operator.

In any case, I feel a strong sense of duty toward her — we Dearborns are a responsible clan — and will see to it that she receives an adequate training suited to her limited abilities.

I propose to journey west to relieve you of the burden of bringing her east. And of course I shall compensate you, at the rate of $200 per annum, for her care these five years.

Sincerely,
Henry L. Dearborn

"He seems to have a narrow view of what constitutes a good American," said Nicole drily. "I don't suppose I'd meet his lofty qualifications, either."

They sat across from her, eyes riveted on her, waiting. They wanted hope from her, she realized. Well, she could give them that. But first she would clear away the underbrush so that she could see where they stood.

"Missy, what do you think of all this?" Nicole asked gently.

The girl remained silent.

"Missy?"

"I want to stay here with Quin. I don't want to be taken away and put in some home."

"I showed her the letter when it came," Quin interjected. "Or rather, she saw me — and picked it up and read it."

"Quin, what do you want?" Nicole asked.

"I love Missy as my own daughter."

"Well, then, we'll make her your daughter" was Miss Nicole's crisp response. "I've already completed the adoption papers, but there's a snag."

"A snag?"

"Missy's parents aren't legally dead. No one saw them die. They've been missing for five years, but it takes seven before the courts can declare them dead. Of course, proof of death isn't entirely necessary in adoption proceedings, but it helps. You see, Mr Putnam, the courts don't wish to make a terrible mistake."

She saw something sagging in Quin.

"I've written the commanding officer at Fort Keogh, and also the Indian agent at Pine Ridge. Something may turn up in the patrol reports for that period, or the agent might get an affidavit from one of the Sioux in the hunting party. But it's going to take time, and we'll have to stall Mr Dearborn.

"I've looked into legal guardianship — making Missy your ward — and I've found that that would leave you vulnerable. If Henry Dearborn were of a mind to, he could go to court, terminate your guardianship, and take Missy."

"He's not going to take her! He'll put her in some home over my dead body!" Quin exploded. "We'll disappear. I'll sell the Q, and we'll go somewhere. It's a big world. We'll go somewhere that'll take another two years to find. I'll move. I'll keep her free until she's of age, I'll —"

"Quin, you're talking wild."

Quin subsided slowly. Nicole had never seen him so distraught, so impassioned. The intensity of his passion, radiating from him, awed her. And somehow it pleased her, touching something feminine inside her.

"Quin, Quin." She shook her head gently. Then she lifted the little spectacles to her nose and read the letter again.

"Quin, did you notice anything strange about this?"

He shook his head wearily.

"Well, it's a strange letter for a man professing to do good and offering to perform a duty. It's cold, ice cold. There's a lack of concern about Missy's happiness . . . as if she weren't a person. What would you do, Quin, in such a situation? You'd wonder if your granddaughter is happy where she is, and whether she's well cared for. In short, you'd make inquiries first, before tearing her life apart. You'd intervene only if you knew she was miserable . . . Don't you see?"

He nodded.

"And that's not all. He's jumped to a lot of odd conclusions, too — presumptions that spring from his own narrow views. He thinks Missy lacks intelligence and is fit only for a life of menial labor. Imagine that! The nerve of him!"

Missy bristled. "My father could dance circles around Mr Dearborn. And play the violin, too. And hug me with great big hugs. And laugh, too. He always made my mother laugh until she gave him a big kiss!"

Nicole and Quin both laughed.

"There's another thing about this letter," observed Nicole. "This lack of affection, this coldness. I don't think he's mean; the dear man's too full of his own rectitude to be mean. But he's cold and hostile . . . That's a female opinion, not a legal one."

"I think he means well."

"Yes, according to his lights! But this talk of a home for difficult cases . . . Doesn't that say something to you?"

"Yes, it does, Miss Nicole. It says I'll defend Missy at gunpoint if he comes after her!"

"Oh, Quin." She was annoyed.

"I'm almost fourteen now," Missy said. "If he takes me away, I'll come back when I'm eighteen and of age."

"I'm afraid," Nicole rejoined, "that he can govern you to the age of twenty-one. That's true in most states."

Missy blinked solemnly. "I'm old enough to take care of myself, Quin. Don't be afraid for me. He can't hurt me very much, because you've taught me to take care of myself."

"Missy!" Quin exclaimed.

"I just want you to know I'm not nine anymore."

He patted her hand.

"As for the adoption," Nicole said, "I think we should plan the proceedings for early December, as soon as the new Fergus County Court opens here. If there's information to be gotten from Fort Keogh or from the Indian agent, we'll have it by then. Landrum Lipsett is running for the judgeship unopposed, and he knows Missy's story perfectly well, like everyone in Lewistown. If we don't have proof of death by then, we'll just have to take our chances with Lipsett. I think those chances are good, but of course I can't guarantee it."

"We'll risk it," growled Quin.

"Fine. I'll try to make it number one on the docket — the first business of the new Fergus County Court, December first."

"You were planning to leave before then."

"I'll delay my departure for a few days. It makes no difference, really."

"What if he refuses?"

"Landrum? That's rather unlikely. But if for any reason the court resists, we'll have to stall Mr Dearborn, that's all, and try to find out about Missy's —"

"Stall for two more years."

"There are other procedures — circular advertising, for instance. Quin, leave it to me. Right now, all we have to do is stall him until we go to court in December. I'm going to draft a letter for you to copy and sign. I'll need an hour; it's dinnertime, anyway. Perhaps you could dine at the Traveler's Rest . . . ."

Quin rose wearily. He and Missy had ridden hard all day on a worrisome mission. Nicole saw a terrible melancholy in his face, and she fretted about him.

"Quincy!" she chided. "And Missy. This can all be worked out with an excellent chance of success. You don't understand how strong your case is, even if he could prove that Missy is his granddaughter. You've been her parent for five years; a court is not likely to change that."

A kind of thanksgiving spread across Quin's features.

"Now go have a relaxed meal, you two!"

It's the burden he's carrying just now, she thought as they left. Almost despair in him, but not that deep. Those fierce moments! He'd surrender all he has, and is, to help Missy! And how she's blossomed this year . . .

She settled down to her work. It was late and gloomy, so she lit the lamp and drew it close to her foolscap. This letter would be a stall; the next, if there had to be one, would be a warning, a shot across his bow. And of course this letter would direct his attention to Missy's welfare and happiness, in case those elementary considerations had escaped him. But long before the situation got very far, Missy would become Antonia Putnam. She picked up her pen:

Dear Mr Dearborn,

I was astonished by your letter and curious as to why, at this late date, you have assumed such interest in a child whose origins remain obscure.

My daughter, for such she has become to me in these five years since I recovered her, has had a sunny and comfortable upbringing here. I have the means to support her easily and with every advantage, and my Harvard education ensures her schooling. I have shown her your letter, and she is strongly opposed to any change in her life, such as you propose, and assures me of her happiness with me. Surely, if you value her tranquillity and comfort, you will not attempt to pluck the girl from an eager parent and shut her in an institution of any sort.

There is grave doubt that the girl is any relation to you at all, or the child of your estranged daughter. The recollection of a frightened nine-year-old as to who her parents were would never satisfy a court. There is no linkage of dates, places, or names that I can see, that would establish you as a blood relative of hers.

I think it would be wise for you to drop the matter entirely. Your concern for her is certainly benevolent and upright, but any further action would lead only to heartache for you. Let the girl, whoever she is, reach her maturity in a home where she is loved and enjoyed.

Yours sincerely,

"I'm tired, and it's not as concise as I would wish," she apologized in her throaty voice after Quin had perused it. "But it'll do."

"It doesn't sound like me," he grumbled.

"If it did, I wouldn't be earning my lavish fee as your lawyer," she snapped. "You'd give the game away, trying to placate your unreasonable conscience. There's a limit to self-abnegation, and I'm drawing that line for you. Now don't be a mule."

"It's misleading. I don't have any doubt that Missy's his granddaughter," Quin balked.

"The courts would. There's really not a shred of solid evidence. Airtight legal evidence. Something like Missy's baptismal certificate stuffed in her blouse, when you got her from Little Calf."

Quin sighed uneasily. "Very well, then, Nicole. Missy, does this letter suit you?"

"I wish you'd just tell him I don't ever, ever want to go there," she boiled.

"We're stalling now, until the adoption, Missy. We have to keep our kid gloves on until then, dear. But if the time comes to say it, we'll say it just as you've said it."

After Quin had transcribed it in his own heavy, dense hand, Nicole hurried them out the door. She had been tempted for a moment to offer them her guest bedrooms. The two had looked so shaken and drawn. But she had never done that, not for anyone. She no longer cared what the neighbors thought, but inviting them to stay would mean . . . crossing a line. No. Oh, why did Quin need her so much just now? His whole legal business was spinning a web around her, snaring her just when she was breaking free! She couldn't turn them down. Not Quin. Not Missy. Others, yes. Why couldn't things go smoothly when she was about to move?

She snuffed the lamp and slumped back into the big chair in the dark, the chair that wrapped around her petite frame like the love of a father. There was nothing else to hold her, ever.

She had advertised in legal journals for a replacement, touting the advantage of a practice in a new county seat. But it was the same story: they had responded to the blind ad readily enough, but when they discovered her sex . . . She snorted bitterly in the dark. Who would want to assume a woman's law practice? Probably all her clients were lunatics or paupers! So she had found no one. Perhaps she should simply leave: there would be lawyers flocking in to the Fergus County seat soon enough. But who'd help Quin . . . and the others?

Life was such a curse on a misfit! She had been so lonely, sometimes, rattling around in that shadowy house, that she had been tempted to kill herself. But those moments of weakness had been rare and had filled her with self-contempt. In the summers she had found release by hiking along Big Spring Creek and then picnicking beside its rushing waters. But Montana summers were fleeting, and bitter weather could stretch from October into May. She had tried going to mass a few times, but even there she found herself alone, apart. She had no faith anyway. For her father, the church had been a place for baptizing, marrying, and burying; for Nicole it was even less, and her rational, orderly mind questioned the existence of any sort of god, or any authentic inspiration or comfort that she might find in such a harbor as the church.

Why on earth did she let Quin's problems claw at her this way? She always distanced herself from her clients. She had to, if she wished to live a serene life. Once in a long while a client wept in her office, and she couldn't bear it. She fled to her kitchen and noisily brewed tea or fussed with pots until things were calmer. But now she ached with Quin's burdens on her. Worse, her stay at his ranch had only deepened her caring. Like all enterprises, Quin's ranch needed careful nurturing and protecting — and at least as far as the law was involved, she was its shield and defender, its knight in armor. That was a man's role, really. How on earth did the law ever lead her into such byways and alleys? Her every instinct and emotion was female, and the law practice kept dividing her from herself.

She slumped forward over her desk, cradling her head in her arms. There came a wetness to her eyes that she hated; tears were a self-indulgence. But the hot, salty wetness came anyway, rising from springs of unbearable loneliness. What a mess she was making of her face! At least she didn't have to look at herself in that darkness. She was glad Quin couldn't see her this way, couldn't see the woman who had comforted him and Missy, encouraged them, and strengthened them in a time of need. She cradled her head numbly in her nestling arms and let the darkness engulf her for a long time.

There was a knocking at her door. A civil knocking, neither clamorous nor timid, a knock that signaled no emergency but was not to be denied. She rose wearily, rubbing away the stain of tears.

"Quin!" she exclaimed, gazing at the familiar silhouette on the threshold. Instinctively she smoothed her disheveled hair. "Is something wrong? What is it?"

"I was hoping you'd be up. I didn't see any lamplight. I brought you these." He deposited an enormous bouquet in her arms.

"Quin! What are they? I can't see —"

"They're called thank-you flowers. Wild asters, mostly. And wild roses I cut with my jackknife. Still defying the frost, I guess. I was out hiking along the creek — Missy's in bed, but I couldn't sleep — and the three-quarter moon's so white tonight. I picked them for you. Who ever heard of picking flowers at night? I never have. I couldn't even see what color they are, but I got a big bunch —"

"Quincy Putnam, you do the strangest —"

"I got to thinking, no one ever thanks you. Even I forgot to. I was so full of myself when we left that I hardly realized how much you'd calmed us down and pumped us full of hope. And worked out a plan to tackle this Dearborn mess, too. And, you know, it wasn't just law, either. A lot more, Nicole. A lot. So that's my bouquet, but it doesn't really say all it's supposed to . . . Will you invite me in for a minute?"

She led him into the office and lit a lamp. The polished dark woods glinted somberly in the lambent light. She pressed the bouquet into a pitcher, for lack of a convenient vase, and set it on her desk, something wild and prickly resting between them.

"You know," he descanted, as if this whole occasion had arisen so that he might talk to her, "I have some ideas about letting go. We have to keep letting go of things before we can grasp the future. The more we cling to what was, the more we freeze ourselves where we are. Like excess baggage on a long journey. How do we get where we're going, encumbered by it all?

"Well, anyway, did you hear Missy this evening? Saying she was old enough to care for herself now? She's climbed the mountain, Nicole; she's grown, and doesn't need me so much anymore. I suppose I'm leading up to the letting-go part. It's time for me to be letting go of her some, too, for both our sake. It's best to let go voluntarily, but sometimes we get kicked into it. Don't misunderstand, Nicole. I'm not steeling myself to turn her over to Henry Dearborn or anything like that. I love the girl as my own, and we'll be together a long time to come. But you see, a middle-aged man can cling too tight, too, and it's time for papa to stand back and let the fledgling fly, let her go where she wants to go. It's hard, because she's all I have . . .

"But sometimes letting go is — it's like getting kicked by a mule, and then we get all torn up. Now I'm talking about you, not Missy, and how awfully hard it is for me to let go of you, even when I understand why you must go and start out fresh in a happier life. I'd leave, too, if I wore your high-button shoes. But, Nicole — Letting you go, it's worse than a mule kick . . .

"Well, I'll manage. I've managed alone a lot of my life, and I'm used to that. It's pleasant in some ways. I don't always feel so alone, anyway, because I have some sense of a partnership, or friendship, I guess, with God. It keeps me going, that's all. And now time's running

186

out. I've only got a few years left, the doctors told me. Weak heart. I've never told you, but that's why I'm in a rush. I have to finish up for Missy."

Nicole stared.

"Oh, I'm fine. No trouble with it yet, but there will be. Well . . . I came to say thank you, that's all. And to exercise the privilege of a man getting along in years to ramble a bit, never getting things said quite right . . . I'll be going now."

She followed him silently to the door, where he pecked her gently on the cheek, and left. She stood watching him disappear into the dark, feeling filled. She had drained herself helping him, but now she was fuller than before.

CHAPTER
FIFTEEN

When the rains finally fell in October, it was too late.
Frost was already nipping the leaves and whitening the
naked earth. The cold deluge began in midmonth, a
splatter popping into the thick dust, then became a
soaking drizzle, and at last a penetrating downpour
from gloomy autumnal clouds. The parched land drank
it up and then shed the excess in muddy rivulets and
roaring cataracts that sliced new canyons into the
denuded earth.

The deluge caught the communal roundup in its
latter stages, down on the Birkenhead range, and
plunged the fifty cowpokes into a chill misery. They
broke out their slickers, but the water trickled down
their necks in icy dribbles, and puddled coldly on their
saddles. Most of them chose to lope the three miles to
the Flatwillow Station bunkhouse at night, even after
an exhausting day of tallying and riding and branding.
The rest, those who had to attend the gathered herds,
crowded into Silas Stone's Sibley tent, grateful for
shelter and warmth.

The chill torrents caught Quin high in the uplands,
rounding up his shorthorns. He had six men for the
task — his four salaried hands plus Pinky and Sleet on

a weekly wage. The high country was as naked as the plains, even though there had been a few niggling showers up there to entice the grass along. But the sheepmen had fallen back on that grass for their salvation, and it was mowed finer than a squire's lawn. Quin's crew enjoyed the comfort of the line camp Quin had built in the south fork of the Flatwillow, a rude log cabin with a thick sod roof. A crackling blaze in the sheet-metal stove soon steamed the wet chill out of them each dusk.

There were seven hundred-odd cattle to gather and another hundred to be fetched later from up in Quin's alpine park, where they had barely dented the lush grass, even crowded as they were into that small compass.

Quin's Durhams were in reasonably good condition, unlike the longhorns being gathered in the communal roundup down at the Birkenhead range. Both the longhorns below and the shorthorns above were sprouting peculiarly thick, shaggy coats, so thick that they fooled some of the drovers into supposing the stock was fat. Quin studied the drooping hair with malaise: it didn't make sense in a hot year and a warm cycle.

The steady rains sluiced the ash of the burned Q Ranch range deep into the soil and scoured the clay until it was clean umber and sweet-smelling again. After three days of staccato pummeling, the burned-over area resembled the rest of the bare prairie, save for a few charred limbs and stumps and a hint of black around the root hump of the bunch grass.

The burned strip no longer served as a cordon of any sort: the last pungence that might have stayed chary cattle from venturing onto it had vanished. And so the tarrying rains breached the eastern rampart of the Q Ranch range, transforming it into a broad avenue, eleven or twelve miles wide, from the overgrazed open prairie to the tall grass.

As the district roundup ticked around its clockwise orbit, from Stone's ten o'clock to Birkenhead's six o'clock, cattlemen cut out abnormally large numbers of beeves for shipment, and several of these herds had already been driven to the NP rails at Billings. It was a story repeated at every roundup camp in drought-wounded Montana, and its effect was to drop prices to ruinous levels at the Chicago yards as well as at satellite yards in Saint Paul and Omaha.

The remaining cattle, which the stockmen hoped somehow to winter, would have to scrounge a living by munching browse in coulee bottoms and on billy-goat slopes, so short was the grass. A longhorn could prosper on twigs and stems and the husks of weeds if it had to. The green capital of rawboned ranchers, as well as of nations, was devoured for the year. All life is grass, the philosopher once observed, noting the natural system by which the carnivores feast on the herbivores. And it was Alex Birkenhead who added that, in his estimation, the wealthiest nations, by and large, were the ones with the most abundant forage.

Ever since Quin Putnam had withdrawn from the communal roundup, the common task reached its conclusion at Flatwillow Station. In previous years it had ended on the Q range, which stood at seven or eight o'clock on the rotary journey. Quin had erected a stone and mud-mortar line camp on the creek, close to his eastern boundary, for roundup purposes. But that had fallen into disuse after he built his fence.

At the close of the 1886 bivouac, there remained, at last, only the question of what to do with the six thousand starved beeves, of all brands and descriptions, that were to be wintered in that area. And the answer was obvious to them all. For a capstone to the fall's labor, the drovers simply hazed the whole mass of beeves across the rain-scoured prairie to the remaining tall grass on Quin's range; grass that had already been decimated by the Circle B herds. With so many ravenous cattle on it, the grama wouldn't last a month.

And that was how the rape of the Q was accomplished: with a shrug and a few-mile amble, and then a hasty scattering of drovers and reps from a score of ranches, and the ululating departure to Miles City of those who could be spared. All the whispering about a night ride across nester farms, through cut wire on a moonless night, simply vanished, and the simplicity of a short walk up Flatwillow Creek prevailed.

If there was any impact from this, it fell on Quin and his crew as they descended from the upcountry driving their seven hundred shorthorns. They were prepared for the sight of Birkenhead beeves here and there — but scarcely for the vista of thousands of gaunt longhorns across the hills like locusts on a rampage.

"There'll be nothing left!" Quin cried hoarsely, gaping at the regiments and battalions and divisions. It no longer mattered whether there would be an open winter. All he had left was contained in his hay piles, his fenced hay meadows, and the green alpine park miles above. Sixty tons of hay. Scarcely enough for his horse herd, much less his cattle. Pathetic, compared with the fifteen hundred tons he normally cut.

"John," he rasped, "do you remember the name of that breeder out in Oregon who bought our calves?"

"Rathke."

"We've got to wire him. See if he'll take five hundred more, all brood stock. I'll accept terms, if I must —"

"How'll you ship? With the blacklist? The NP won't load a beef, long as your name's on it."

"We'll ship, we'll ship," Quin roared. "We'll ship or I'll sue. I'll —"

"We have to, mon. I'll go talk to the boys."

"Put the shorthorns in one of the greened-up hay meadows, John, please. That'll keep 'em for a week until we have a chance to negotiate, sort things out."

John's sorrel looked poor, Quin thought. All gaunted up. But maybe they all were. No green grass all year. He eased stiffly off his mount and studied his own bay. Like the rest of the stock, it had grown a curiously patchy winter coat in recent weeks, oddly long and bristly. Quin ran a hand along the barrel and discovered lumpy ribs and a shocking cavity behind the rib cage. If his blooded horse was like this, what were the stock horses like?

He strode over to the corrals and studied the milling mounts, utterly dismayed. A man got to working along, day by day, and scarcely noticed change that sneaked up on him. The horses were a sorry lot. Most of them had been penned all summer because there was no pasture for feed. Caved in, ribby, dull-eyed. Was he going blind? Well, most of these would have to go down the trail, too. Not so bad, actually; a chance to unload a few ornery beasts and cull the remuda. The keepers he could put out on good green grass in a hay meadow while he still had some. That was the best tonic he knew of.

He uncinched the saddle stiffly, watching John and the crew snake the long column of shorthorns down toward the easternmost hay meadow. Those jogging cattle, at least, looked fat, fresh from the high country.

It was a foreboding autumn afternoon with a nip in the breeze to confirm his raging instinct to sell off every beeve he couldn't hay-feed, regardless of the price. He could just manage it, ahead of bad weather. He'd load those boxcars at gunpoint, if he had to . . . No, no, no, he sighed. The blacklist was already choking off his operations, strangling the Q. No. He'd go down there and raise hob. They'd ship those steers, or he'd put the fear of God into that division superintendent. They'd load, or the NP would have a few hundred beeves and a lawsuit on its hands, because he was damned if he'd drive them all back to the Q.

A man seemed to end up hostage to the schemes and notions of others, even out here on the frontier, he thought, glaring out across his tawny hills to the dark, alien dots that speckled the range.

The grass would rebound if he could get that fence back up. It easily withstood an isolated sharp grazing

193

such as it was enduring now, even in the growing season. It was unremitting assault and battery that weakened it, especially in the spring and early summer when the grama did its real growing, sometimes an inch a day.

Years before, Quin had decided that the best way to nurture that grass was to keep stock off of it entirely until June. Preferably late June, when the grass had a good seedhead on it. He wanted that seed to start dropping even before the first of his stock touched it. But a goal like that was hard to reach, at least until he could irrigate his meadows and produce a lot more hay.

He had learned to delay feeding out hay until after Christmas or even the first of the year. When the winter stayed open, the stock could prosper on the tall grass in the winter pastures until then, and he could extend his hay-feeding into June. Well, he thought, he'd keep experimenting and striving until he had the ranch he wanted. The key was the grass, not the cattle. If he could control his grass with fencing, he'd prosper, and the ranch would produce year after year, in good times and bad, for Missy after himself.

But so much depended on others, and on the dubious wisdom of Congress. It seemed to him that Congress was moving in exactly the wrong direction. It had outlawed enclosures of public land just when it should have encouraged them under some sort of licensing arrangement. The open-range system had no brakes: nothing but disaster would stop cattlemen from expanding their herds willy-nilly, letting the devil take the hindmost. For years that system had worked, and some had reaped bonanzas from it. But it had worked only because some capacity remained in the vast prairies, and the herds hadn't yet exhausted every corner and cranny of the continetal steppes.

Now the overgrazing was a red flag, in Quin's opinion. There was already trouble, and more was descending. The solution was wire. When a fence circumscribed a range, a stockman was immediately confronted by tangible limits, natural carrying capacities. If he overgrazed his enclosed dominion he paid a terrible and visible price, in both the short and the long term: starved beef, damaged range, sagebrush, cheat grass, weeds, gullies, and gulches. That was the whole case, Quin thought: wire forced responsibility on a man. If the government wanted to keep its range intact, it ought to encourage enclosures.

The rattle of the returning crew broke into Quin's reveries, and he intercepted his men near the barn.

"One more task today, boys, and you can lay off until we drive those beeves to Billings. I'm going to send most of the broncs down the trail, too. The fewer mouths to feed this winter, the better.

"Now I realize," he purred, "that asking drovers which horses should stay and which should go will net me as many opinions as there are men. So I'll ship only those that you all agree should go. When you've decided, you can chowse the departing horses in with the beeves, and we'll put the keepers on hay-meadow grass across the creek."

They rode on down to the corrals and lined up pensively, six black crows sitting on the rail.

"That confounded hammerhead with the roached mane and three black boots is the worst bronc in the outfit," brave Pinky opined.

"Pinky, you don't know sour apples about hosses," Sleet snorted. "That's the best mover I ever done rid. He'll cut me a steer out of a pile of beef faster'n I can cut a girl out of a heap of girlflesh at Caroline's."

"Ain't much of a hoss either way," Billy Jones drawled. "Worse 'un's over in the corner, that humper with the blaze and mooneye. Now that hoss, soon's I'm on, I wanta get off. That's the slowest critter this side of the outhouse."

"Now you whoa up, Billy," Lem demurred, "that's my favorite bronc. I'm always a-saving him till last because he rides easy about the time of day my tailbone is crying uncle. Why, that bronc's so smooth you cain't stick a cigarette paper 'tween me and my hull —"

"Wuthless horse," Bunions interjected. "I side with Billy. Ain't got the speed of a long winter day, and that's the slowest thing I know of."

"Now over there — that cussed strawberry roan with the fatback withers — that thing's a kicker and a biter and a gasser, and he's no good turning, allus wanting to go straightaway, here to there. Most single-minded straight-liner I ever got wind of," Lem complained. "Why, the cayuse, you want him to turn a little bit, you've got to hit him between the ears just to get his attention, else he'll plow straight into a bull or a cow moose or whatever 'tis he's a-going for."

"Lem, you just ain't figgered out how to turn a horse," Pinky snorted. "You got to get aholt of a rein, and if he's a neck-reiner you sort of do the contrary, and if he's a hee-and-hawer, you pull him like this or that."

"Now doggone your pink hide, that's the most insulting line of palaver I ever got to stinking in my ears, worse'n lye soap. Now I ain't gone-ta favor your down-the-trail nags if you backtalk me like that."

"Well, no sense humping your back like you got a cold saddle throwed over you," Bunions soothed. "Let's agree on something. Let's all agree that the blue firecracker with the rat tail here's not even worth giving to the dog-food canner, right?"

"Now you just take 'er easy, Bunions. We ain't considered that nice little blue yet, but —"

Quin jumped off the rail. "Well, boys, we'll keep ten and send the rest down the trail. Ten plus my personal mounts and Missy's Appaloosa. When you get your deciding done, you come up to the house and tell me about it."

Quin spotted a wicked glint in John Durham's eye. "Come on up to the porch, John, and let's chew over this drive to Billings a little," he said wearily, trudging up the grade. "I'll be sending nearly the last of my worldly wealth down there, and I suppose I should give it a decent burial, prices being what they are."

They settled into some generous wicker chairs in the brisk autumn air. It was a place Quin loved, not only for its noble view of the sweeping valley and mountains beyond, but because it overlooked most of his dominions.

"We could ship west, just on speculation, and let a broker or an auction house —"

"I doubt it would help ye," Durham observed. "But ye do have more than just meat to sell with this blooded stock."

They watched a moving dot expand into a large one down the creek road.

"We seem to have company," Quin said.

The dot materialized into two Birkenheads in their chaise. When the brothers traveled together, they took the two-seat chaise, harnessed to an eighteen-hand Percheron. They rode tandem, with Augie usually driving and Alex behind, largely because Alex was the talker and Augie the listener.

"They look like an ale wagon from here," Durham concluded. "It makes ye want a pint."

"I'm not in much of a mood to be a host," said Quin curtly. "I think I'll let you —"

"Ah, stay, mon," Durham objected. "It can't be any worse news they'll bring . . . If I remember history, Alexander the Great offered a generous peace t' all the Persian cities he conquered, t' secure his rear so far from home. That's a thought to make a mon sit and wait, I'll wager."

Quin stayed.

"Well, Putnam, did you contract with God or the devil to send a cloud over your hay meadows? That jolt of green was the most extraordinary sensation when we came upon it," a genial Alex said.

"Neither" was Quin's taut reply. "It was a pump, powered by a donkey engine made in Liverpool."

"Ah! I should have guessed!" Alex eased down into some squealing wicker. "I shall get to the point. In fact, I relish getting to the point. Too often, people doing business don't get to the point at all. I despise small talk, you know. It's the prattle of empty minds, I always say. It's what they do in pubs over a pint of ale all night, eh?"

Quin nodded.

"You're off the blacklist, Putnam. I saw to it myself. A dreadful mistake, you know, and I'm terribly sorry. Midway through the district roundup I went to Silas and proposed that we withdraw the charges. He was more than eager, and so we worked at it together, catching the association men until we had a majority. Working privately, of course, because of the sentiments of Clapp and Pickett. We convened again over on the Pickett range, and I rescinded the charge. We had a majority, so Stone notified the sheriff that we've withdrawn the complaint, and we caught it before it was published. A good bit of work, eh?"

Quin eyed his visitor warily. "Why?" he asked. "Why the sudden benevolence?"

"Why, friendship, old chap. A man likes to get along with his neighbors, eh? Out here a man needs his neighbors in a time of trouble. You're a splendid fellow, Putnam, and it seemed the decent thing to do." Alex leaned forward, fixing his eye intently on his host. "Now that you're off the list and we can do a little neighborly business, I'll inquire about that splendid offer you made in September, a dollar a head for wintering up to five thousand, and all that. We heard about it. Does it still stand?"

"It's a little late for that, isn't it?"

"Yes, indeed, it's late. But if it stands, we'll take it. Augie and Minnie and I will, even if those other chaps don't. Not only take it, Putnam, but pay in advance and rebuild your east fence, all eleven miles of it, eh?"

"But what about all those other beeves? Everywhere I look there's —"

"Oh, we're getting them off, Putnam. We've got half already. Most of them are Clapp's, you know. The man was so obsessed with your range that he ran his beeves down here ahead of the district roundup. I've had my men on your range ever since the roundup disbanded, getting the devils off."

"Getting Clapp's stock off?"

"Yes, and all that other baggage —"

"Off the Q? Off my ranch?"

"Right, old man. Clean off. Every one of those trespassers and interlopers. The whole scurvy lot."

Quin gaped at the two beaming Britons, and then burst out laughing. He couldn't help himself. A convulsion of wild glee simply erupted from him, and then a guffaw and a roar and convulsions that shook him until the tears ran. That caught Durham amidships, and the old Scot started to wheeze like a bellows. Missy stormed out the door, galvanized by the awful clamor, and the contagion caught her until she giggled and chirped, not having the faintest notion of what was so hilarious. Then Alex could no longer contain himself: his vast frontal expanse began to quake. He began to sputter and hiccup, maintaining precious decorum until the bitter end, but his trumpeting delight got the better of him. Then they were all gasping and laughing — Alex's tuba joined by Quin's trombone, Durham's clarinet, and Missy's trilling flute. Finally even sober Augie began his contrapuntal bassoon, a hand decorously over his mouth.

Dingdong skulked in the doorway, shook his pigtail at the sad loss of decorum among these white dragons, and retired to the serenity of his Middle Kingdom.

"I'll accept," wheezed Quin at last. "Five thousand now, and you fix the fence."

"We already have," Alex cackled. "At least, we have the top strand up for ten miles to keep out the heathen."

"Clapp's militia and all the rest," Augie explained.

"We must be off to our front lines," Alex announced. "More barbed wire to string. What a capital invention, a wire full of barbs. Saved by the fellow Glidden, of — What's that odd town, Augie? Oh, yes, De Kalb, Illinois."

Quin escorted the brothers to their chaise and watched them polonaise down the road. Then he collapsed into his wicker and stared at his voucher for five thousand dollars.

Quin shook his head. We'll still have to ship this herd, John. But this'll pay Miss Nicole. I'm seventeen hundred in arrears to her. And maybe provision us this winter."

"What did I tell ye about Alexander the Great?" the Scot purred.

"All they bought was six or seven weeks," mused Quin. "That's all the tall grass that's left. But they got rid of the competition."

"If a longhorn can feed 'till New Year's, it can likely last out an empty belly t'spring if it stays decent. Alex has a chance to pull through at that, and no doubt he's calibrated the pounds and pence of it every which way."

Four bedraggled brawlers emerged from the barn and gimped up to the veranda.

"We cain't rightly figure which broncs to keep," Lem reported dolefully. He had a puffed lip and bloody ear.

Bunions sported a crusty scratch over a cheek and a swollen wrist.

Billy Jones was all in one piece except for a missing incisor and some gore on his lips.

Sleet had a black eye, a bloody nose, one broken gallus, and a ripped collar.

"Where's Pinky?" Quin inquired cautiously.

"He got mad and lit out for Miles City," Lem explained.

Quin sighed. "Well, John, let's you and I pick out the keepers. And remember — *I* run this outfit."

202

CHAPTER
SIXTEEN

A biting north wind sliced into the folds of Alex Birkenhead's greatcoat until he shivered and drew it closer around his massive bulk. The November day really wasn't so bad, except when that bitter wind gusted up and caught him. The low sun still generated a subtle warmth if a man kept his face toward it and turned his backside against the cold, the way the cattle did.

The bottoms had shocked him. All the tall grass had been gnawed down to the nub. Well, he thought, that was perfectly understandable: the stock always cropped down the grasses closest to water. Off to the south, beyond the bench, the grass would be better. None of his cattle were in sight, but that was understandable, too. The October rains had puddled the prairies, and those pools were still open even though the temperatures were plunging into the twenties and teens these brisk nights. And so the longhorns had spread to the far corners, distant from running water.

Alex snapped the reins — his hands were numb, even inside his pigskin gloves — and the gray hackney tugged the wagon south, up to the rugged open range beyond. The grass wasn't much better there, and that shocked him. It was like finding he had only a hundred pounds posted with his bankers when he thought he had a thousand. Even Putnam's grass, it seemed, was finite. There had been so much! Hip-high in the bottoms and knee-high elsewhere! Of course that fox had cut a quantity from the bottoms before anyone had an inkling of it. But even so, that was the tiniest fraction of the whole.

The north wind whistled around his ears, numbing them. He pulled his knitted scarf, the fruit of Minnie's fine hand, up around his neck. These Montana winters! They leaped on a man before he was half ready and hung on beyond all endurance, even into May. He flicked the reins again, and the hackney tugged him even farther south until he approached the long ribs of the Little Snowies. Here were his cattle, chomping without surcease on the dwindling grass.

They looked better; he had to say that much. Many had been here since summer, feasting on Putnam's bank accounts. The man was right: that's what grass was, really, a type of capital. Alex wished he had been present at the roundup camp when Putnam dilated about grass and capital. Christmas Rourke had told him about it, and he'd heard the tale a dozen times since then from grudging stockmen. That Putnam was a thinker!

Still, fattened cattle weren't going to survive a winter without grass, and Putnam's grass was almost gone. Alex grunted up an explosion of hot breath. He was still in deep trouble. He had thought he finally had things under control when he contracted with Putnam for the wintering and drove out the other range cattle. A splendid bargain: for a thousand pounds and some barbed wire he had got Flatwillow Station enough feed for the winter. What a bloody mistake he'd made cutting Putnam's fence in the first place and then stirring up the association against him! He should simply have negotiated with the man.

Well, there was no escaping it. He had cut things too fine, and they would have to ship another herd, even at this late date. Ship at least two thousand to save the remaining three. And fast, before the winter closed in. He perused his hirsute beasts gloomily, then set a brisk trot for the station, arriving there ruddy and breathless from the stinging wind.

"Ha! Augie, I've got some arithmetic for you: when do two thousand and three thousand make zero, and when does five thousand minus two thousand yield five thousand?"

Sober Augie began to churn the conundrum, muttering softly.

"Stop muttering, Augie," Minnie scolded. "It's one of Alex's rotten jokes."

But after ten minutes Augie surrendered.

"When there's little grass!" Alex bellowed, enchanted with his victory. "We've got to ship two thousand so the remaining three thousand on the Q range can survive. We may fetch dreadful prices, but at least we'll have three thousand live cattle to sell, rather than five thousand winter-killed carcasses. The range is stripped. Stripped! We really should sell every beast, but I can't bear it, and it's impossible at this late hour anyway."

Rourke was appalled. "Do you understand, sir, what you're asking the men to do? What it's like to camp outside in weather like this? Ride all day in a freezing rain? Trail a large herd with only half the men we need? Fight off catarrh and the grippe? Camp in puddles and wash in icewater?"

"It's only a hundred miles, Christmas."

"Five days, sir, if all goes well. And a week of gathering the herd together on the Q Ranch."

"There's Putnam's line camp for that. We'll be comfy enough in there. And why sort? We'll just ship the first two thousand —"

Natividad shook his head slowly, patiently. "We'll have to cut out Putnam's shorthorns, in any case. And it doesn't make sense to ship bred cows and heifers only four months from calving."

"Very good, Christmas. You're the expert. We'll sort them out and do it right. Steers, range bulls, open heifers, dry cows . . . very good."

The foreman ran a hand through thick black hair. "I'm not sure the crew will go, sir. They're loyal enough, but they'll be risking too much . . ."

Alex pondered that possibility awhile. "They'd have a holiday in Billings, eh? A little amusement, eh? In fact, we won't need them until well into the new year, Christmas. If the weather holds, it won't be so bad."

"If the weather holds."

"Well, the fact is, we must. We've no choice. Not enough grass, even for a ruddy longhorn. Suppose I went along with our freighting wagon, the one with bows. We'll put the canvas back up and have a cranny to get out of the weather. And I'll load it with emergency gear, blankets, tarpaulins, even some firewood if we get stuck —"

"Eleven men sleeping in one wagon?"

"Well, they'll be rotating, working night duty, won't they?"

The foreman suppressed a rising inner clamor. "I wish we had done this during roundup," he snapped.

It took a week to cobble together a trail herd of two-thousand and fifty-four beeves. Just as Alex had promised, the old line camp was a cozy refuge at night and a good spot to cut out the beeves they wanted. The weather held, climbing to a civil forty degrees by day and slipping only to fifteen or eighteen at the bottom of the long nights.

The drovers broke out their winter gear, especially the woolly chaps that armored their legs against the wind. Some of these were bullhide with the hair still on. Others were sheepskin or angora sewn down to the armoring cowhide. Most were the bat-wing variety, but a few fringed shotgun chaps were being worn as well. A pair of legs stayed reasonably warm, even pinioned in a saddle all day, when encased in woolen long johns, jeans, and those fine chaps. The luckier drovers had Mexican tapaderas on their stirrups, brush-deflecting foot armor that also warmed a man's toes. Good deerhide or elkhide coats, lined with sheepskin, protected their torsos, and the high woolly collars warmed a man's neck and cheeks when turned up. But the wide sombreros of summer had vanished in favor of sealskin caps that pulled down over a man's ears. And a few had fur-lined parkas.

Natividad Rourke noted the steady progress under the lucky sun and decided that his forebodings were merely the stirring of his romantic blood. The fatalistic Mexican side of him whispered that he'd be safe. Life was a shrug of the shoulders. But Alex, ruddy and bustling with good humor, positively relished the whole business.

"They'll weigh out nine hundred pounds average in spite of everything," he exulted. "We should ship late like this every year, after the bloody stampede is over!"

They started down the trail on the bitter morning of the fifteenth, with a north wind building behind them and a low cover of cloud scudding southeast. The cattle were docile and were harried along at an amazing clip by the blast at their tails. As long as a man was moving south, with the wind, the ride was tolerable.

But the temperature dropped all day as arctic air bore down from the northwest, and by dusk it was two below zero on the chuck-wagon thermometer. Rourke halted in the lee of a protective cutbank, where at least the wind was tempered, if not the cold. The hungry beeves hunted down every last twig and bit of straw, and humped against the wind, which gusted over their shaggy coats, rippling their hair.

Alex's men stared at him bitterly, hating the ordeal. They scoured the surrounding hills for deadwood, sometimes hauling a whole log back on the end of a lariat. They huddled over an angry fire, warming one side while the other froze. Natividad built a second blaze close to the cliffside so the bank would reflect heat. And then a third, to form a triangle.

They scalded their tongues on boiling broth that warmed the center while the extremities numbed. Rourke parceled out the spare blankets silently, doubting that dawn would ever come. By common instinct, none claimed the interior of Alex's wagon for a bed, and so it was left to the boss himself. He would need the whole of it anyway.

"You'll each draw two-hour night duty, in pairs," Natividad grated. "Your job will be to feed the fires. Saddle up, but don't circle the cattle unless you have to. I don't think they'll move from shelter, but be ready if they do."

He saw thanksgiving in those haggard faces.

If the cold sinking down from above was brutal, so was the chill rising from the earth. The men hunted brush and straw for a bed, and laid tarpaulins over that, and still the chill pierced through. Men rattled and chattered in their layered clothes, under four blankets and tarps, and barely six feet from fires whose benevolence petered out with every distancing inch. The terrible night air sandpapered their lungs and throats raw. Some gave up sleep altogether and huddled miserably around the fires.

Alex hunched over a mound of blankets and a few pillows he had commandeered at the station, feeling guilty that none of the others shared his roof. In the deepest dark he heard a persistent rattling, a whisper of scattering rice on his canvas, a hundred watch ticks all at once. He lumbered to the flap and peered out on a sullen whiteness: the rattle on his canvas was the daggers and needles of a million whipping flakes. His men, his good crew, were whitened lumps on the whited ground.

Daylight was forever coming, near to eight o'clock in that latitude. But long before then, stiff and sleepless men sucked hot soup and limbered numb muscles in an ominous silence. They saddled their humping, shaking broncs with hands so stiff they couldn't draw up the cinches, and then eased their tailbones down on an ice floe for a seat. Men shook, sneezed, and coughed. But eventually, they hazed the numb herd to its feet and got it creaking south again, while a whiteness veiled the world. Once again the north winds harried the herd into a brisk jogging, but the wind, quartering from the northwest, caused the animals to veer eastward, so that Natividad finally transferred all his men, save one, to the eastern flank to check the drift.

The temperature never rose, and the gray, whirling blizzard never lifted the whole day. Great cakes of snow built up on the cattle's shaggy backs, the innermost flakes melting slightly from body heat until they formed a crystal armor of white that covered each animal like armadillo plates. All the drovers could see was a forest of long horns projecting from a seething white mass. The snow thickened and the horizon shortened until there was no knowing what way was south. The bluffs of the Musselshell were ahead, bluffs that the Indians traditionally used for buffalo drops. They stampeded hundreds of the humped giants off the cliffs and then

210

harvested hides, bone, and hump meat from the few they needed, leaving the remainder for the wolves and mountain lions. Now, in the blinding snow, Natividad worried that his whole herd might trot right off the lip of such a bluff and perish.

And beyond the Musselshell were the western flanks of the Bull Mountains, where the jogging herd could vanish into a forested maze of hills and defy all regrouping by his few men. There was no compass in the cavvy, but the coulees all ran down to the Musselshell, and one of these he employed for his navigation through the storm.

The Musselshell! A thought paralyzed him. In the summer it was an innocuous shallow stream, rarely hock-high, and easily forded. But now, after the rains ... He groaned. If he let that herd swim the Musselshell in zero weather, he would be signing its death warrant. He had to find a shallow ford or turn back into the teeth of that blizzard. A gust of icy air caught him and slapped daggers into his cheek. He had never been so bone-cold, not even in San Angelo, which sometimes got colder than anyone up here ever knew. What mad deity had sent him on this trip? he wondered.

By dusk they were descending an easy grade down to the turbulent river and herding the snow-caked beeves into a sapling-dappled floodplain in the lee of a looming sandstone cliff. It wasn't a bad lash-up, he decided. The critters were already tearing at twigs and bark, and the men could find shelter in the undercut sandstone and fort up a bit. The snow was easing a little, but the six or seven inches that had already fallen could slow the traffic tomorrow.

Natividad eased painfully off of his shaking bronc and collapsed into the snow because his legs refused to function. The others landed in a heap, too, and began thrashing until they could get their pins under them again. Hildebrand, the young Bavarian, hung mutely to his saddle horn, unable to get down. They helped him off and found him raging with fever, shaking with ague, too weak to stand. A dread crept through Natividad: this could be a death march after all.

They carried Hildebrand to Alex's covered wagon and buried him under blankets while the man's teeth clattered. From somewhere inside his coat he pulled an envelope out, pointed to the Munich return address, and wept. Alex accepted it gravely, vowing to do all he could. An hour later Slim Garcia keeled over, just missing the fire, and they found a fever in him as well, and carried him to the wagon.

"There'll be no night duty," Natividad grated. "These beeves won't move from this shelter and feed."

The big Swede, Arne, had weathered the trip best, and took it upon himself to gather wood and build a rude shelter of brush and logs and tarps under the cliff, so the men had three walls and a roof of sorts; a place where a fire could really do some good. Alex was morose. In fact, he was engaged in a wild interior dialogue with his father, scolding Josiah for sending his own flesh and blood into such a wild land. A wheeze rumbled up from Alex's vast interior, and after

212

Natividad had watched one shaking spasm of it, he began to keep a close eye upon his employer.

"A bit of catarrh," Alex rattled. "A little grippe. Never you mind about me; I'm a bullock, a beefeater, and some good scotch in my kit will fix it."

That night was better. The protected men slept a little in the shelter, while the cattle gnawed bark and twigs. But Natividad didn't sleep: he was obsessed with the icy river roiling across the flat and the diminishing crew he had left to move more than two thousand beeves to Billings.

In the gray, clouded first light they rose stiffy to begin the third day. The brutal cold persisted, punishing them to the limit of their strength. Both men in the wagon were alive, but delirious. And Alex looked dreadful, with gray flesh and feverish eyes scowling out at the world. There was a fearsome clatter in his lungs, punctuated by a wheezing cough.

"Let's get on with it," he grated, but Natividad shook his head.

"If they swim, they'll be dead in an hour. We've got to find a shallow ford or turn back, sir."

With a heavy spirit he saddled a blue roan, his fingers so numb he had trouble with the latigo.

"I am sorry," he murmured into the horse's ear. "Perhaps you will have a better life in the next world."

At the fire he yanked off his boots and set dry clothing to warming. Then he mounted stiffly, stuffing stockinged feet into his tapaderas, and rode downstream.

There was nothing for a mile, only the murky green water confined in a narrow, high-banked channel. He turned back to the camp and warmed his feet at the benevolent fire, then started upstream. There was a widening a quarter-mile up, where the river bellied out into rills and rocks parted the water roiling around them. A high bottom — a ford, except for the steep bank on the far side.

He wheeled the roan toward the water. It balked and shivered at the bank, but then splashed in under the foreman's prodding and picked its way gingerly across, the water never up to its hocks.

Natividad had found his ford — if it was wide enough for the two thousand beeves. It would be ticklish, moving all those cattle through the water in zero weather, keeping them on the high bottom because any other passage was certain death. He splashed upstream a few yards and then started his roan across again. The horse was bolder this time, moving confidently until it hit a hole and plunged in up to its withers, while a blast of icy water shocked Natividad's legs and belly. The horse floundered out, and then the numb dead cold outraged rider and beast.

He knew he had only minutes to live unless he reached the fire. He kicked the sopping horse savagely, and they galloped and stumbled back to camp with the brittle air biting at his soaked lower parts. At camp the men sprung into action, pulling the wet duds off the foreman beside a radiant fire and helping him into dry spares.

The horse trembled, then quaked in the cold. The soaked hide turned into a corset of ice over his whole trunk and flanks, sluicing the heat out of him. Tremors traveled through him and his head drooped as the last of his body heat was sucked out of him. He stood stiff-legged, refusing to go down, the pitiful heat of the nearby fire no use at all.

Natividad drew on his boots and buttoned his sheepskin again. He uncinched the soaked saddle, taking it to the fire to steam dry.

"Come on, Chico," he murmured gently, tugging at the spastic animal. "Come along now — *poco, poco.*"

He turned his face away from the men. There were things a man had to conceal, and the grief of this man, who loved horseflesh as he loved all life, was engraved on his features.

"Over here, now," he said to the rasping animal. The bronc's teeth were bared, and his lips distended back into a death grin. "It's over now, Chico."

He shot the bronc.

The crossing went as well as could be expected. The pioneer steers shied at the edge of the water, but the bawling, crowding mass behind them forced them in, and they lurched directly across. The rest followed safely over, except for one idiot bunch that veered sideways into holes and swam to shore dripping wet. They began running and leaping, crazily, madly, at the start of their losing fight against death.

The herd staggered through the snow, numb men and sullen stock, with the Percheron-drawn ambulance at the rear, burdened with heavy cargo. The herd compacted the snow, leaving a dappled, dimpled highway behind for the big dray horse and his wagon, even where the drifting white was mounded two and three feet high to either side.

The relentless north wind hazed the herd south, so that once again they covered ground fast, and the swift movement kept bodies warm and healthy. The diminished crew had little trouble, largely because of the help of the wind, and the men could afford the luxury of slipping one gloved hand at a time inside their sheepskin coats and under their warm armpits.

A line camp on the sprawling 30-Mile Ranch, north of Billings, offered a haven the next night, but they had a tough time rustling firewood on the windswept plains. The cloud cover persisted, and they were grateful because clear days meant snow blindness and aching eyes, and clear nights meant even colder air.

On the fourth day, as early dusk cast a lavender light over the snow, they started the herd down into the Yellowstone Valley, where the thin, desolate rails of the NP glowed silver in the half-light.

"Arne!" Natividad barked. "Go ahead and get a doc. Then get rooms at the NP Hotel and have them warm. Jordan, get this ambulance rolling ahead of the herd, and get those three into bed. And don't spare the horse."

He watched the desperate drover, and the wagon, pull ahead of the herd and race for lamplit Billings. And then he turned the herd toward the pens, pushing the beeves so close together that they lent each other warmth. He bought whatever hay and straw he could find, paying a terrible price. It wasn't enough, so he bought sacks of oats and barley as well, and stayed on

216

in the bitter night until he was sure that every animal was fed and watered.

Then, in a dark so dead that it shriveled him up inside, he staggered over to the hotel. Old Doc Chafee was there, peering out from behind rimless glasses.

"I'm sorry. He's gone. The German fellow, Hildebrand. Too late. Gone before I got here. Not that I could have done much."

Men are predestined, Natividad thought. He had known . . . known up at Flatwillow Station.

"Birkenhead, I don't know. Double pneumonia and a fever of 104, and maybe other things, like bronchitis. He's lapsed into a stupor. Built like an ox, but the chances . . ." He shrugged.

"This other fellow, Garcia. Pneumonia, of course. Catarrh, high fever again. A little better than the others. He might make it; seems tough as nails, young fellow like that."

Natividad stumbled downstairs and then next door into the Big Sky Drovers' and Stockmen's Club, where he demanded a quart of red-eye. He was too numb to sleep. Fourteen beeves frozen to death, and one man . . . so far. And the crew: he knew they were going to quit, just as soon as it was decent to tell him. He couldn't blame them. Too many months at half a wage, twenty and found.

He desperately wanted to quit, too. Right then. He didn't even know what was gluing him to the stool. How could a man be so homesick?

He sucked the red-eye and pined for Texas, and the sun. Then he told himself there was no one left to ride back to the Flatwillow and tell Mr Augustus and Miss Minerva. He worried, and drank, and fretted, and drank, and when they closed down the Big Sky and chased him out, he was cold, cold sober.

CHAPTER
SEVENTEEN

Henry Dearborn tipped the porter handsomely and clattered down from his lacquered parlor car into the snow of Billings. The Northern Pacific Hotel was hard by the rails, so he had only a few bounds in which to tote his fine-grained pigskin valise. He always lugged his bags, disdaining help for anything humbler than a steamer trunk.

It had been a splendid safari from Chicago for the trolley magnate. Once it was discovered that he was a railroad man — at least after a fashion — conductors, brakemen, and even a fireman had paraded into his stateroom for an hour of badinage and camaraderie. He was a bluff and hearty man, and a genial host to all comers. Out in Dakota he had spent an afternoon in the cab of the Baldwin, admiring the stoker and absorbing the bluster of the engineer, who griped about the road's speed limit of twenty miles an hour. And in Montana, his coterie had regaled him with tales of snow so heavy that three coupled engines could barely plow it off the rails.

Dearborn was traveling light because he intended to be home well before Christmas, a season he always reserved for communion with his family. The desk factotum took one look at the fine valise and the craggy six-foot gentleman in the chesterfield coat, and reached for the key to the Territorial Suite, an accommodation of unusual elegance for so rude a frontier town. Dearborn pocketed the key, disdained further assistance, and bounded up to his ornate chamber, which he took as another hallmark of a virtuous life.

In the valise were four items that explained, in part, his mission. One, supplied by Andrew Bird, was a copy of a baptismal certificate for Antonia Novak, obtained from Saint Wenceslaus Parish, in the hinterland of southern Chicago. Another, also supplied by Bird, was a Brady and Wheelock Imperial Packing Plant employment record for one Anton Novak. It listed his address, the name of his wife, Ruth, and most important, the date in 1881 when Novak terminated his employment there — a date, by the best calculations, about six weeks prior to the moment out on the Montana prairie when Mr and Mrs Novak died and their daughter was captured by the Sioux. The two additional items were tintypes Dearborn had pilfered from his wife's escritoire without her knowledge. One — of little value — showed Antonia as an infant in the arms of Ruth Dearborn Novak. The other, which Dearborn considered a great prize, was a likeness of Ruth, Anton, and Antonia, taken when the girl was eight and her features were well defined.

Dearborn also had Putnam's letter, which he pulled from a breast pocket of his pin-striped suit and perused once again after he was settled in his suite. The letter generated a faint irritation in the reader. Plainly,

Putnam intended to keep the girl, so there was going to be an unpleasant clash of wills. Moreover, the letter looked like the handiwork of a lawyer. It was written close to the vest, admitted nothing — not even the girl's name — and discouraged further inquiry.

If Henry Dearborn could have heard Nicole's tart assessment of him and his motives, he would have been incredulous. Nicole was right in one particular: in spite of his bluff heartiness, Dearborn was as cold as an open grave. But she was quite wrong in supposing that there was any malevolence in him toward Missy. Such hostility, even a buried one, was quite beyond Dearborn's character.

In fact the trolley monarch was an idealist, a visionary, and a devoted family man. He idolized Adelaide Dearborn, his wife, of many years, and enshrined her on an altar. He doted on his sons and their families. His ideals were the loftiest and most modern in the history of man. He believed that sterling character lay at the very heart of all happiness and was the true wealth of nations. Right conduct, the strenuous devotion to duty and virtue, ushered a man into an abundant and blessed life.

That was his theology: a man made his own heaven or hell through his own exertions and conduct. He had the free will to become what he chose to be. The biblical heaven and hell, he suspected, were merely the symbols that primitive peoples used to express the same basic idea. The Deity might forgive, but life never did: a man's actions produced inevitable consequences for good or ill that could never be erased or undone. If someone put the proposition to him that scoundrels could have a rollicking good time, his rote response was that the rogues were lying or deluding themselves, or that their riotous good times were at the expense of future happiness, because their world would soon enough tumble around their ears.

Such rectitude and nobility of mind were awful burdens to bear, but worth the price, he believed. And few men there were who could climb such a mountain. He had only to look at himself — the captain of a flourishing enterprise that he had built with hard work, sobriety, and transparent honesty — to demonstrate the iron truth of it all.

It distressed him to think of the flood of immigrants arriving on these shores who hadn't the faintest inkling of the importance of right conduct. They were mostly the dregs of oppressed humanity, victims of church and state, men who never had the opportunity to perfect their own wills and forge their own destinies. If America was to be rescued from that flood, leaders such as Dearborn himself would have to drum the ideal of right conduct into the foreigners. And to do so was the loftiest act, not only of virtue but of patriotism as well, for it would bless the newcomers in their private lives and would benefit the Republic.

This philosophy had impelled Henry Dearborn upon a fifteen-hundred-mile expedition to the frontiers of Montana. He sought to do good; his motives shone kindly out of his very eyes. This was a mission of rescue and responsibility, the assumption on his manly shoulders of one of life's awful burdens. When it came to doing good, Henry Dearborn was not easily put off. It often inflated him with a sort of ecstasy, this knowledge that he was turning the sorry world into a better place. This child of his wayward daughter — how sad that the young sometimes rebelled against the hard-won wisdom of their elders — this child he would gather into the bosom of his protection and then guide her every step — to the extent that she was salvageable after rusticating among Indians and frontiersmen. It would take close and strict supervision to handle the herculean task, but he was prepared for that. Rescuing the girl was his Christmas present to himself and his salute to the Teacher of Right Conduct whose precepts of behavior Dearborn assiduously studied and sometimes rejected.

He had found quite the perfect institution for the girl, a pair of adjoining academies up in Libertyville, one for each sex, run by a manly headmaster, Woodley Thornhill Elliot, whose ideals were inspired by the best modern sources such as Emerson and James. There the girl would be taught right conduct and would emerge so purely American that she could overcome even the stigma of her surname. Dearborn had paid the tuition in advance as a mark of his pleasure. The ecstasy of doing some little thing to bless the world was almost unbearable, and Henry Dearborn thanked Divine Providence for this opportunity to be of service to man and for being led miraculously to an orphan in such urgent need.

All of this, of course, meant extracting the girl from the grasp of this Putnam. Odd that a Harvard man — if such he really was — would hole up in Montana, unless he had a black mark on him, the result of some debacle that had arisen from his weak character. All the more reason to salvage the child, Dearborn thought.

He could scarcely imagine anyone living out here, much less enjoying it. The desolate white prairies had rolled past his window for endless miles, a frozen waste. Well, he'd be away soon enough. He had passage back to Chicago for himself and the child all paid for.

A day later Dearborn boarded a Concord stagecoach that would carry him to Lewistown, a hundred thirty miles distant, by way of Roundup and Grassrange. There was a competing route, through Lavina and Judith Gap, but it had been throttled down for two weeks by drifting snow and cold. The weather was so bitter, in fact, that this coach would be driven by two teamsters in alternating half-hour shifts, so that one would always be warming inside.

Dearborn had a keen eye for all the minutiae of public transportation, and he caught the tensions of the phlegmatic drivers as they loaded in freight.

"It'll be a cold trip for you gents, won't it?" he asked genially.

"Suppose so," the taciturn man responded, and turned away. Conversation with frontiersmen was something new to Dearborn's experience.

After the rebuff he comforted himself with his own shrewd interpretation: the span of horses looked worn, no doubt from dragging the coach through heavy snow in recent weeks. Dearborn was right, but he didn't know the half of it. Snow levels were so high there was no way of knowing where the rutted road went. And drifting sometimes delayed the coach for hours while the drivers, and passengers, shoveled a passage through white dunes.

Just before departure another passenger arrived, that gargantuan fellow he'd spotted in the hotel, who apparently was a Briton. The man looked a little peaked and clambered into the groaning Concord with some difficulty, settling himself across one whole seat, which normally accommodated three. Well, Dearborn thought, it was at least another body to help warm the icy interior. The Briton pulled a heavy buffalo robe over his lap and legs, and belched unhappily.

A classic example, Dearborn presumed, of lapsed character. The man had let his appetites get the better of him. But he was quite mistaken, for Alex Birkenhead carried little fat, and after a month of fever he had lost what little he had. He was simply solid beef in a barrel.

The mustachioed driver swung inside, and then they were off, under a scudding gray overcast and into a rising north wind. The coach lumbered out of the Yellowstone Valley with the listless horses straining into a rising gale that blew the heat out of their bodies. It would be a long, numbing trip, with the coach making barely two miles an hour instead of its usual five. Even within a mile of Billings, Dearborn's feet turned into blocks of ice, and he stamped his kangaroo-leather ankle-top shoes on the floorboards to revive his circulation.

The Briton extracted a bottle of bourbon and a tumbler from his stachel and poured several fingers.

Dearborn blanched: he never touched the demonic stuff that led men to perdition and numbed their senses. In fact, he was an ardent member of an Evanston temperance society that was making noble efforts to close Chicago saloons, especially those that catered to immigrants. But here this Briton was not only indulging but doing so scarcely three feet away! Oh, the waywardness of man, he sorrowed.

Alex burped. "Medicinal. I ruddy well died of pneumonia a month ago. Woke up from a coma, high fever, good as gone, and demanded my scotch. Had to blister their hides before they let me have it. But of course if alcohol is antiseptic externally, then it must be internally, so I started in to sterilize all twenty stone of me. I downed the whole bottle, and started to recover from that moment. Only trouble was, that was the only scotch in all of Billings. Civilization hasn't caught up here, you see. Then they brought me some rotgut called red-eye, and I swilled that until I discovered your good Kentucky bourbon. Tolerably good spirits, I'd say. What a blessing it all is, saving lives and dispensing happiness, eh?"

"I wouldn't know," Dearborn replied primly. "I'm teetotal."

"I see," Alex said, lapsing into unaccustomed silence.

The clouds were again spitting a little fresh snow, which swept across the windows as the coach crunched through the layered litter that had fallen earlier. By the time they reached 30-Mile Station it was close to midnight and the two passengers had whiled away a numbing fifteen hours staring at each other. Three more inches of snow had accumulated.

They warmed at a wood stove while the teamsters hitched another weary span of six Belgians for the long upward haul through the Bull Mountains to Roundup. It was going to be a grueling night, but Dearborn didn't complain. He wished to do the manly thing and endure in silence.

Then they were off again, past the black hulks of pines and into the whistling gray night.

"The winter closed in early," Alex muttered to himself. "We were lucky to get the stock to the rails in time, even if it almost cost me my chips."

"You're a cowboy?" Dearborn asked.

"A cowboy, ha! I'd break the back of a horse. We've Flatwillow Station Ranch, my family. I'll be getting off at the Flatwillow stage stop about a mile from our place."

"I'm going to Lewistown myself. I trust there's a decent hotel there. I'm quite fastidious, you know."

"There's a hotel," Alex responded gamely.

"If you're a rancher you probably know a fellow named Putnam. That's who I'm going to see."

"Putnam? Of course, of course. A friend and a neighbor."

"What's the man like? Rather a scoundrel? What on God's green earth would bring a Harvard man to the frontier, unless some great scandal or terrible failing?"

"That's an interesting question," Alex observed, his interest piqued in the bluff man across from him. "Why do you want to know?"

Dearborn smiled genially. "Oh, just curious is all."

The stage creaked and hissed through the night, halting frequently while the numb drivers exchanged places. When they crept into Roundup at dawn, they found seven inches of fresh powder on the level, piling into drifts under the northern gale. The Belgians slumped in their traces, quaking with exhaustion, while the drivers unhitched them and led them to warmth and succor. They had expended more brute energy in a hundred yards of this sort of travel than they did in a mile of summer hauling.

"We may have to lay over here, gents," said Fawcett, the senior driver. "We're thinking on it. We do have a fresh team here, rested for two weeks, if we push on. We'll have some chow and then see how she looks."

"By all means, press on," Dearborn urged. "I have important business and a deadline back in Chicago." He warmed his hands at the hissing coal stove, sighing happily as its radiant heat chased away his aches.

"Important business, eh?" asked Alex.

"A life is at stake, sir," was Dearborn's dignified response. He didn't much like revealing confidences to the imbibing Briton, but the cold and shared hardship spun him on. "A granddaughter of mine, an orphaned child of foreign extraction on her father's side, deprived of all opportunity to learn proper comportment and true nobility of character here in these wastes. I intend to rescue her before it's too late; make a true American of her."

"Indeed? How extraordinary. And what would a true American be, sir? As a foreigner, I have great curiosity, eh?"

"Character, my good man. Strong character is what divides us from all the Europeans, except, of course, you English-speaking ones. We breed a manliness so magnificent here that it's unexcelled by any modern nation; men who govern themselves, and who accept no lord's collar, and who realize the consequence of their every action, in an unbreakable chain; men who —"

"Dearborn, how can that be, when even the most intelligent of us scarcely understand the impact of what we do?"

"I'm talking about morals and ethics, sir," Deaborn explained patiently. "The results of evildoing are always obvious beforehand."

Alex beamed beatifically. "Ah, I see, I see! I shall continue your case for you, eh? Here in the New World, where they are no longer chained by monarchs and ecclesiastics and hoary tradition, men will fall back on their own character, this rectitude you espouse, or perish, eh? If there's nothing to stop a man from succeeding, then there's nothing to prevent him from failing, eh? Only his manly character."

"I think you're having a little fun with me, Birkenhead. There must always be institutions to help men along and free them from superstitions. I've found just such a one for the girl I'll get from Putnam. There's an academy I've found, where she'll be taught —"

Alex poured a vast jolt of bourbon into his tumbler and swilled it down while Dearborn gaped.

"But what if Antonia — her story is well known here, Dearborn — doesn't wish for all this good to be done to her?"

"Why, she's a minor female and has no say in it," the magnate explained to his obtuse auditor.

Fawcett broke in: "We'll be going ahead, gents. The sky's a little lighter, and we've hitched a fresh span of eight big 'uns, instead of the usual six, to see us through. The temperature's dropping, though. Twenty-three below, it says."

They boarded the creaking Concord once again.

"I'm popping off next stop," Alex said. "Twenty-four miles up, right on the Flatwillow."

They plodded out of Roundup, north on a vast white waste, along what the driver hoped was a road; he didn't really know in a world bereft of all its features. Scarcely an hour later the sky gloomed down again, and the blizzard resumed with such stinging violence that the drivers wrapped their faces and stuffed gloves inside their gauntlets. When that didn't help, they began exchanging places every ten minutes, shivering under buffalo robes.

Alex quaffed a Falstaffian snort and tried again. "What if you're quite wrong? What if some benevolence, some mercy exists in the universe that gives men second or third chances; that props up the weak and renews hope? Or what if some stern force plucks up a virtuous man and shakes him until his teeth rattle, and sends an invading army through his home and his enterprise, or inflicts disease upon him?

Dearborn, what if virtue isn't connected with any reward at all?"

"Well, of course, those are the old notions — magic and superstition entirely. There's nothing but cause and effect. That's what we have to be rid of, these excuses for bad conduct. That's what this child has no doubt inherited, and I'll be driving all that stuff and nonsense out of her, I suppose."

"Ah, but you haven't even met her," Alex demurred. "A delightful, poised young woman, just now blossoming. And intelligent, too. Putnam's not neglected her schooling . . ."

Alex was in mellow good humor in spite of the sullen, numbing cold that invaded the coach like a plague. He dearly loved a scrap, and he was working himself into one like a circling shark.

Dearborn scoffed. "All that's immaterial. Even her apparent happiness is immaterial unless it's based on sound principles. When people are artful at wasting time, they suppose they're happy."

For all his avidness, Dearborn didn't enjoy being grilled about his ideals. Too much was hard to explain to the narrow-minded. But in the end he could turn his own life into an example.

"You know, Birkenhead," he said genially, "I've lived an exemplary and blameless life for the most part, as manly a one as I could, and I've built up a considerable company in the process. I've had one or two reverses, but never a failure. Never a real failure. Not in business or in my private life, either."

"Suppose," Alex persisted, "that someone with just as strong a character as yours suffered all manner of defeats, so that in spite of his strength and optimism and whatever you have, he fell upon hard times and lost his family and health and reputation —"

"I'm not saying it can't happen," Dearborn hedged, "but you'd likely find some weakness under the veneer. The man wouldn't be the true article."

They scarcely noticed that the coach was groaning to a halt. The whole world outside their windows whirled opaquely white. There was a sudden silence, save for a gentle creaking of the coach in the gusting wind. The mustachioed driver clambered out the door and slammed it, leaving a draft of bitter air eddying around the passengers. A few minutes later he dragged the comatose body of Fawcett inside and propped it up.

"Don't know whether he's dead or alive," the fellow muttered, slapping his colleague's face. There was no response. "Don't make much difference now. One horse's dead in the harness, others too weak to drag a mouse, shaking the meat off'n their bones. Maybe one good 'un left in the span. Don't know where we be from the sheep ranch."

Alex suddenly beamed a macabre smile.

"Guess I'll ride the good 'un for help," the driver muttered, yanking his sealskin cap down over his ears.

Alex gulped a massive draft of bourbon and laughed so merrily that Dearborn thought he was sodden with drink.

"Good-bye, then, old chap. Have a short ride," Alex bawled merrily.

232

"It will be. A lot shorter than yours," the teamster muttered. He looked sharply at his two passengers and then bolted out. The coach creaked while harness fell away, and then they saw him outside, clinging to a staggering Percheron as he vanished into a white ground blizzard.

"Well, he'll be back soon with a party," the bluff Dearborn announced. "It's certainly going to be an unpleasant wait."

Alex laughed wickedly. "How does doing all this good to Antonia Novak feel now, Mr Dearborn?" he boomed.

"What do you mean?" Dearborn fidgeted.

"I mean this might be the end of the trolley line. Where's your reward for this bit of good you're doing, eh?"

"Surely, Birkenhead, you're not suggesting —"

"There's a sheep ranch a quarter of a mile from here, if I have my bearings right. But a quarter of a mile in a ground blizzard like this is the same as twenty miles," Alex explained quietly.

"Surely he'll make it. Why, that's only four or five city blocks."

"He might. But then a search party would have to find *us* — a small coach buried in an endless white sea . . . after the wind dies."

The trolley king paled and began shaking in his chesterfield.

"Have a little spirits, Mr Dearborn. Warm up the cockles of your heart, eh?"

"But I never — My heart doesn't need warming, sir."

"Well, if you won't imbibe, at least have a little sense and put that frozen chap's greatcoat over you, and fetch his buffalo robe from the box outside, eh?"

The chattering magnate bundled himself in the dead man's clothing and then pulled a stiff buffalo robe over him, grateful for the warmth that gradually stole through him. Why, he thought, he could endure this for days if he had to, under that heap of wool and fur. He settled into a doleful vigil while Alex hoisted the bottle rhythmically, apparently without a care in the world.

So, Dearborn thought, he was going to pay a price for this good work. This ordeal would make the rescue of his granddaughter all the more noble. Once he got back to Chicago, why, he'd be feted and celebrated . . . It was a thought to keep him going for the next day or two. He'd survive, no matter whether the teamster made it or not. Once the weather cleared off, he'd see the smoke from the ranch house and head for it on makeshift snowshoes. He was agile enough, unlike that drunken Briton dozing across from him. What a story he'd have to tell when he got home, he thought.

CHAPTER
EIGHTEEN

One of the few advantages to growing old, Quin mused, was that it breeds patience. He was surviving the ordeal of being snowbound with some equanimity, unlike poor Missy, who was petulantly storming through the house. Quin had simply holed up in his study, savoring his books, meditating, enjoying the aureole of warmth around the wood stove.

The sullen skies had scarcely stopped unloading their cargo since mid-November, and now the drifts lay heavy across the yard, ribbed and whorled by bitter winds. Lumpy footpaths led from house to barn to bunkhouse, and a triad of avenues ran to the woodpile and coal heap.

A hundred Durhams were trapped high on Big Snowy Mountain, which could just as well have been half a world away, now. Quin and Missy had missed the adoption proceedings on December sixth because of a blizzard. There had been no mail because Grassrange was now a million miles distant. And Quin's cattle, what few he had left, were either making a living on browse and brush or starving to death. Not even the drive to the rails in October had gone the way Quin had hoped: the daunting reality was that there would be no sale to the Oregon Durham breeder, and Chicago prices were lower than ever. The only thing that had gone well was the boarding of seventy head with Coffeecan, Lars, and the others. After the first blizzard the crew had driven the animals over to the McDonald without difficulty.

Quin stretched moodily. "The best-laid schemes of mice and men . . ." he summed up. The recollection of the Robert Burns poem prompted him to pluck an anthology from his shelves, and turn to his favorite, *To a Mouse:*

> *Thou saw the fields laid bare and waste*
> *An' weary winter comin' fast,*
> *An' cozie here beneath the blast,*
> > *Thou thought to dwell,*
> *Till crash! the cruel coulter past*
> *Out thro' thy cell . . .*
>
> *But, mousie, thou art no thy lane*
> *In proving foresight may be vain:*
> *The best-laid schemes o' mice an' men*
> > *Gang aft a-gley,*
> *An' lea'e us nought but grief an' pain,*
> *For promised joy . . .*

He ran a hand idly over his scalp, into the bushy gray hair at the back of his head. His own best-laid plans had fallen around his ears often enough. He thought of his exquisite Abigail, dead of childbed fever in 1863, while he was a lieutenant in Washington. The news had rent him in two.

But an equally terrible disaster befell him after the war. His two infant sons, and a housekeeper, had perished in his blazing home, trapped and roasted there by a mob of bloody-shirt wavers and radical abolitionists. Before the war Quin had made a great success of manufacturing cotton velveteen on a new English loom, and after the ordeal was over he began to manufacture it again, buying southern cotton long before his fellow New Englanders were ready to forget and forgive. He supported the conciliatory policies of Lincoln and Andrew Johnson, even while the hot fires of revenge flared brightest among the bloody, gaping ranks of veterans. Quin had never appeased his local critics or heeded the opinion of the day — until their anger cost him all that was dearest to his heart. After that, years of shadow and drift; railroad right-of-way purchaser, land promotor, small financier wiped out in the Panic of 1873 . . . and finally, a man in the Montana wilderness, racing against his laboring heart.

But Quin no longer reviewed ancient calamities or flogged himself with accusations. He could scarcely imagine a more sterile occupation and wondered how he had spent so many years tormenting himself. The thing now was to pick up the pieces and press on and, if there was a lesson to be parsed, to learn it well. Failure had its uses, but man wasn't put on earth to fail, or to live in frustration or despair.

He loved Nicole. He would ask her to marry him. He'd thrashed around too long, harrying his passion from his mind, fearing that a forty-eight-year-old man with a clouded future had no right to press his suit. But such a marriage was thinkable, and not even unusual, he realized, once he had fretted the question through. Nicole knew the verdict of the doctors; he would not be concealing anything from her.

He could scarcely imagine life with anyone else. Women he might find, but only Nicole could meet him at each frontier of mind and soul and body. Helpmeets, housekeepers, and lovers there might be, but for the communion he had sought, there was only Nicole. Only Nicole for the companion who'd whet his mind while she prospered in his whetting. Only Nicole for whatever time remained.

During the long snow vigil the decision had gelled in him. If a man needed beloved children, like Missy, even more did he cherish a beloved wife to enfold in his arms through the blasts of winter and the high summers of joy. Only Nicole.

Of course there was Saint Louis, and she was adamant. But perhaps she was adamant only because he was reticent. Who responds to an uncertain trumpet? What would stay her departure, if the man who attracted her kept suggesting that she marry another?

There was little doubt in Quin's mind of her love. How women gave themselves away! A flood of gladness at the threshold; a smoothing of the hair; a furtive, fleeting glance into a man's soul! But they had danced their minuet apart, across an empty room — for there were no others — and now the dance was over. And it had been his failing, not hers. He had temporized, wondering what he would find in a practicing female lawyer.

He sighed uneasily. She might laugh at the whole idea. She might already be in Saint Louis, though he doubted it. Stagecoach traffic had probably been suspended for weeks, and wouldn't start up until a chinook arrived. The cold took too much starch out of horse or ox teams.

Lewistown! He had to get there and speak his piece before a chinook, before the warm west winds swept her forever out of this country and his life. He had to go now!

He found Missy huddled beside the kitchen range, mending his stockings, and he beckoned her to his study.

"I'm going to Lewistown in the morning." He took her small hand in his strong one. "For a splendid reason!"

"Now? But —"

"How would you like to have a mother? I'm going to find Nicole before she gets away and ask her to be my bride."

"Oh, Quin!" exclaimed the amazed girl.

"I love her, Missy. I think — if we work it right — she'd be happy to —"

"We're the only family she has! I'd be so happy!"

"You wouldn't feel hurt?"

"Hurt? Why —"

"Never mind. Let's both hope I succeed."

"I want — I'll pray for you."

Quin squeezed her hand. "It'll be a tough trip, but I've handled worse. A man can survive most anything if he's prepared and prudent. I'm sure she's trapped there, just as we are here, waiting for a chinook. It'll take some talking, Missy! That'll be harder than the traveling. How do you tell a woman you love her? That's an eternal question."

"You don't just tell her, Quin. You show her."

In the icy barn the next dawn John Durham was chary: "I don't favor it that ye go alone. A mon should be with another in times like this. I'll send Bunions with ye —"

Quin laughed. "*Amor vincit omnia*," he joked.

"Well, it'll heat ye up, I'll say that much. Be cautious, mon, and hole up along the way. There's places enough if ye go to the McDonald fork."

Quin led the two massive Percherons outside. He would ride one giant, even if its broad girth split him up the middle, and the other would pack his kit, plus a sack of oats that would keep the beasts going in rough weather.

The sunswept whiteness was so blinding that it made his eyes water and forced him to squint painfully.

"I'll get ye something I rigged for the snow blindness," Durham said, trudging to his cabin. He returned with a band of blue flannel with two tiny slits in it that would do a man's squinting for him. Quin slid it over his head and found immediate relief as he peered through the scratchy fabric.

"They'll take me for a train robber," he joked. "Tell Dingdong to keep another place set, just in case. I'll be back when I can . . . Don't count days or fret."

240

"Aye, I won't count or fret, but I'll be praying a wee bit. Ye picked a lunatic time t' go wooing!"

Quin threw his padded bulk clumsily over the eighteen-hand brute and plowed up the hill on a bitter-bright day. The whole country lay featureless and white before his aching eyes: shafts of dazzling sunlight darted in every direction off every crystal of snow. The whole arch of the heavens was a strident, clamorous azure, heavy upon the whited earth. What few trees there were along the coulees formed black periods on the blank page. A fresh north wind gusted up ground blizzards, so that Quin was swallowed into a vortex of white crystals that eddied around him into drifts and pockets as the finger of the wind played its games.

He halted every half-hour to rest the encumbered beasts and to stretch his own numb limbs. An illusion of joy was everywhere in that deadly world. The strident glare was too much even for the Percherons. Their eyes oozed copious tears, which froze on their dappled winter hair, and spasms of pain rippled over their squinting eyes. Quin dug into his kit for some burlap, sliced it in two with his bowie, and wrapped it over the forehead and eyes of each animal, tucking it under the bridle of one and the halter of the other.

The beasts plowed steadily along, crashing and rocking through drifts or mastering them with a series of powerful slow leaps that plunged Quin's stirrups deep into powder and out again. On the road along the fork of the McDonald he hit a broken trail: there had been a little traffic among the nesters. And from Forest Grove, where he nooned with a quiet lumberjack family around the kitchen range, on into Lewistown, traffic had opened a footpath or one-horse trail. Still, he stopped regularly as his inner clocks told him to, husbanding the strength of the plowhorses that could save his life if the weather turned ominous. A lavender dusk caught him descending into the Judith Basin and enchanted him with sea greens and purples and some subtle pinks that were reflected across the virgin snow. He stayed warm, whether because of the nature of his mission or because of his prudence and caution, he didn't know. Love warmed him the whole trip.

Twice in the past he had lost his bearings during a ground blizzard. Rather than a chance on straying, he had simply halted, sometimes for a numb ten or fifteen minutes, until he could gain his bearings again. Once he had dropped the stiff lead rope of the pack horse, his hands too numb to tell him that his grip was gone. But the horse had followed along anyway, his nose in the tail of his colleague before him. At times the north winds were so maddening that a man rode sideways in the saddle and the horses quartered along the path, their heads tucked to the lee side. All of this Quin had experienced in the past, and he endured it stoically.

Lewistown huddled cold in the night when Quin rode in, its amber lanterns defiant against the hulking giant of the north. He rode directly to the livery and ordered a rubdown and double baits of hay and oats. So scarce were both in isolated Lewistown that their prices had tripled, but Quin paid without grumbling. The village had been cut off for virtually a month, and were it not for abundant beef, the town would have been close to famine. Some things, such as coal, weren't available at any price, and the cost of others, such as flour and potatoes, ran five and six times above normal.

Only when he was satisfied that his giant mounts were comfortable in an oversized box stall did he turn at last toward Nicole's home, walking stiffly across the crunching, squealing snow of the streets. The house was dark. He gripped the picket fence, hunting for signs of life, but there were none. No smoke, no light. Only the eerie aura of abandonment. He refused to believe, and stomped to a window, peering in on a dusky barrenness. The room was naked.

He swung wearily to the Traveler's Rest for a bed and a meal and a chance to think things through and inquire. Surely somewhere she had left a message. Surely someone knew. Surely she cared enough about him to let him know . . . Or maybe she didn't. Maybe she had left, long gone on some Concord that had slipped through the web of winter. He didn't despair; long life and an intimate acquaintance with trouble had fortified him for moments such as these. If need be, he supposed, he'd make the arduous journey to Saint Louis to press his suit. Wherever she was on the broad continent, he'd search her out and declare himself, tell her of the choice he'd made, the life he proffered, and the love with which he hoped to envelop her.

She was sitting alone in a corner of the dining room. "Quin! I'm so surprised —"

She rose from her chair, disconcerted, reading the story told by the massive layers of wool and leather encasing him.

"You'll have company for dinner."

"You — got my letter?"

"No."

She looked so tiny and vulnerable there in the yellow light, he thought. She was so special, with a perfection all her own. She had a honed legal mind; yet she was almost a child, an unkissed girl with a catch of fear and joy on her now. Wisdom and innocence, experience and naiveté.

The lamplight caught the flashing violet of her eyes and warmed the olive of her face until it shone golden and creamy, gently framed by lustrous waves of black. She was so small, so petite. He had somehow made her larger in his mind's eye.

"Why are you here? They say the drifts are ten feet high, some of them. There hasn't been a stage — just one, two weeks ago, and they refused to take a woman . . . Why, Quin?"

"Oh, I thought I'd drop in for dinner."

"Quincy Putnam, you're still a mule!"

"Contrary forever."

"That sounds like the family motto, something engraved on your escutcheon. A mule rampant, on a white field."

She laughed, a tentative trill chiming into the brittle night, and he along with her.

"I wrote you that Landrum Lipsett would see you and Missy in chambers anytime; there's no need for formalities. And that I'd sold my house to Seth Westring, and the furniture, too. He resold most of it in Maiden, and has more in his store. And that . . . I

244

wasn't able to — that no one would assume my practice. And that — I'd miss you terribly because — I just would."

"And now you're here, waiting for a chinook."

"Going mad cooped up here. Pacing a tiny room all day, not going out except for meals because they stare so much. Oh, I can hardly wait to get out!"

Something happy shrank in Quin.

"This winter, Quin! It's stopped everything cold! The prices — It's three dollars just for this dinner because everything's so scarce."

"I wish you'd come out to the ranch. We'd have a grand Christmas."

She laughed: "You're still trying, aren't you, Quin?"

"Yes."

"It's too late. Too late. I need what Saint Louis has. I need to be anonymous. Do you know what freedom is? It's being anonymous."

"Give me anonymity or give me death," Quin mocked.

"Yes, Quin!" She spoke urgently. "You're making fun of it, but that's exactly how I feel. Exactly."

Quin paused, catching her urgency. "Will Saint Louis really make you happy?"

"No, not happy. I'll always be too alone. But at peace. And diverted by all the —"

"A man carries his peace with him, don't you think? It's not something he can find here or there or somewhere."

"Quin — no. There's no way I can describe to you the ordeal here. You haven't lived it, so words fail me . . ."

"Nicole, have you ever paused to wonder whether you've exaggerated it all? Taken people's natural curiosity about a unique woman and twisted it into something dark and mean, when really it isn't?"

Nicole exhaled slowly, then shook her head.

Quin pressed on, tenderly. "Mightn't there be a lot of men, and women too, who see you, not as a freak, but as something utterly beyond them, a woman so wise and experienced that they stand in awe of you, afraid to offer their friendship because you remind them of their own limited schooling?"

"Please, Quin, don't —"

"Is the malice really here? Among these people who stormed Helena for you? Or do you feel it because you've isolated yourself so much, ever since you were a bit of a girl? Maybe you've got a bad case of the if-onlys: if only I can get to Saint Louis, it'll be so much better; if only I could be anonymous; if only I could escape; if only people wouldn't stare! Nicole — who's rejecting you? These people or yourself?"

She could think of nothing to say.

Quin smiled, and she saw that light on his countenance once again, that light, whatever it was, that always transfixed her.

"Suppose there's a man who'd consider you the rarest of prizes if he could win your hand —" He stopped lamely. "I didn't put that very well. I'll say . . . there could be someone who loves you exactly as you are, Nicole. Someone who'd be enchanted by a keen mind and ready wisdom in his wife. Someone who wants a lot more from marriage than most men do, because he wants an equal, a companion for his mind, as well as a helpmeet and lover. Someone who'd want to marry you for the very traits that you think men scorn. Do you understand me, Nicole?"

She nodded, wide-eyed, both small hands caressing her coffee cup.

"Suppose there's a man who'd welcome your work and cherish your achievements. A man who'd enjoy seeing you help people out of their difficulties, who'd dote on your ability.

"I think you could even manage it out on a ranch, between raising some fine boys and girls, practicing law for your husband and your neighbors. And maybe for all ranchers, up in Helena — writing the legislature or Congress, or drawing up land and cattle legislation. Fighting the scalawags in office . . . Not subtracting from your womanhood and motherhood, but adding on to it, as freely and flexibly as you wish. Not like those dreadnoughts, trying to convert their private miseries into public policy, but as a woman, a woman who's found her niche, her elbow room, within a loving marriage . . ."

He paused, watching her carefully.

"Oh, Quin." It rose throatily out of her.

"Haven't you ever yearned for children? . . . I know you have. I've watched you with Missy. This man I've described, who loves every bit of you, every whimsy and crotchet, this man lives and breathes for you. He was almost too late. Almost defeated by his age. But he came to his senses, and he's made a long winter's ride to tell you how he feels. He's come here to say I love you, before you go galivanting off to be unhappy somewhere else."

Nicole still didn't trust herself to speak.

He sat easily across from her, with a patience forged out of sorrow.

"I love you, Nicole," he said.

"Quin, Quin . . . may I be alone for a while now?"

He smiled and helped her to her feet.

It was late, and the empty hotel lay chill and desolate, creaking under the arctic wind. He walked silently with her to her door, not asking whether he might. In the dusky hall he kissed her. She stood rigidly while his lips found hers and tasted sweetness. Then he gently gathered her into his strong arms, made a haven for her, pressing her gently, then passionately, until a dam broke and she clung to him fiercely.

"My God, Quin! My God! What am I going to do?" she cried, breaking free a minute later. "I've got to be alone now, please."

Shakily she shut the door, a pleading in her eyes. Quin stood there quietly a moment, listening to the millrace of his pulse, and turned to his own room, full of quiet hope.

CHAPTER
NINETEEN

In a rosy gray twilight a band of fourteen gray wolves circled swiftly down from the Little Snowies and into a long, twisting coulee on Quin's ranch. Beneath the luxuriant fur of each animal was a limber, lithe body weighing one hundred twenty-five to one hundred fifty pounds. Their attention was riveted on a bony old cow that had found herself a little respite from the aching north winds under a cutbank.

The canny cow had stripped away much of the edible brush in the area, gnawing back twigs and bark, and even limbs, pursuing them into the heaped snow. Even so, she was gaunt. Beneath her shaggy coat, with its strange streamers that trailed six or eight inches off her belly, there was no flesh on her ribs, and her heavy pelvic bones almost pierced through the sunken corded muscle of her rump. She had done less well than the steers and dry cows because she was supporting life, a half-grown calf in her womb that would emerge into a cold world in just three months. Her nose was lacerated from nuzzling into the snow, and her legs were covered with frozen blood from wounds opened by razors of ice. In her little refuge, there was no running water to drink, and she was forced to eat snow that had a temperature, on many days and nights, of forty degrees below zero. Her body used so much energy turning that snow into water and raising it to almost a hundred degrees that it had burned up all the fat and much of her red meat to do it. Still, she was surviving somehow, waiting for the chinook that would open more forage for her and allow her to luxuriate a few days in its warmth.

She sensed the wolves before she saw them, and she listlessly swung her giant horns around to face them. In other times she might have been a match. The slashing horns could disembowel a wolf and fling his gnashing carcass far away, and the deadly smack of her cloven hoofs could brain a hulking wolf at her flanks. Such armament discouraged all but the hungriest of wolves, in normal times.

But now she lacked the strength. The wolves weren't particularly hungry: they had never had such easy pickings as this winter had provided. The cow backed into brush so thick against the cutbank that her flanks and rear were well protected, forcing the pack to face her deadly horns. But it was no use. There was no fight left in her. A sleek gray female, with her deadly canines bared, skulked easily under the feeble arc of the long horns and caught the cow at the throat, the massive jaws clamping into the windpipe until the old cow collapsed. Then they all feasted on the hot flesh — leaders first and then the cubs, with the very heat of the cow warming them against the night.

This pack had slaughtered one, sometimes two or three, cattle each day, and so easy were the marks that they sometimes slaughtered for the sheer joy of it, counting coups and howling their derision to the coyotes and the other packs. There were other groups, ranging from ten to thirty, harvesting the cattle on the Q Ranch. They particularly relished the still-chunky shorthorns, which lacked the armor of the tough Texas cattle.

On most nights the eerie howling of the wolves echoed across the naked hills to the morose cowboys in the bunkhouse and to the man and girl in their ranch home, detonating shivers in them all. The imprisoning winter had grown maddening. At first the drovers told and retold yarns, until their inventiveness ran out. Then they wrangled and argued about anything they could think of. And finally, they lapsed into a sullen silence, each just barely able to tolerate the enforced presence of his colleagues. There was little to do but stuff the stove and play casino or poker. Sleet, in fact, was one million four hundred seventy-three thousand dollars to the good, most of it lifted from Billy Jones, who was over a million in debt. In a normal winter they would have ridden the grub line. This was the traditional time of socializing, when a cowpoke could alight in any bunkhouse of any outfit and settle in for a while among new friends. And a time when drovers rode far and wide, all duded up in their fanciest finery, to dances and socials where ladies might be. But such diversions were out of the question now.

Things were scarcely better in the frame house on the slope. It was so chill inside that Quin and Missy and Dingdong huddled close to the crackling stoves, keeping their own dark vigils through the painful ticks of the grandfather clock in the parlor. The thermometer outside Quin's study regularly plunged to minus twenty-five at night, and reached minus ten in the warmer afternoons. So white was the land that there was little to absorb the faint heat of the low sun.

Irritably, Quin watched the hay piles disappear, mostly into the bellies of his horses, whose strength was vital for the men's survival. A few of the shorthorns had drifted in, and these he had penned in one of the hay meadows where they could be fed a maintenance ration. He had intended to pull in the rest before winter, but the shocking November blizzard had caught him, and the thing had become impossible. So wherever they were, out on the blanket of winter, they were devouring their own flesh and little else.

Each day Quin and the crew bundled themselves in layer upon layer of cotton, wool, leather, and fleece to cut holes in the ice of the Flatwillow. The thirty-five-degree water still sliding along under the surface cap was much safer for stock than the colder snow. On some days the difference in temperature between the two was seventy or seventy-five degrees.

Quin moved most of the horses into one of the unused hay meadows. It would be good for the broncs to have some running room. And they were better foragers, in some respects, than the cattle. They had hoofs that were well suited for pawing through snow down to the hay meadow grass, unlike the cattle, whose cloven hoofs were inefficient. The horses could reach higher browse than the cattle, too, even balancing on their rear legs for a morsel if they had to. And they had a hotter metabolism, with a body temperature of about a hundred degrees, to help them fight off the cold. On the worst of nights, when the cold was so relentless and brutal that the beasts quaked and shivered helplessly, the whole horse herd sometimes exploded into a mad gallop that warmed each animal's entire body. The bitter air was hard to breathe and frostbit the tissue of their lungs, but even that was preferable to freezing to death. So the deathly winter quiet of the ranch headquarters was sometimes shattered by a thunderous clatter of hoofs. During the few hours when the sun had any potency, the horses with black or brown or bay coats were more fortunate than their lighter colleagues. From perhaps eleven until three, the dark ones could absorb enough heat from the pale sun to feel almost comfortable beneath their shaggy pelts, and as long as the wind didn't blow, they could stop their quaking.

There were more blizzards between Christmas and New Year's that dampened any Yuletide cheer those isolated people were able to sustain. They all tried, but worry hung heavy on Quin, and he felt deep within himself the suffering of every animal out in that icy inferno. The fires of winter had eaten life itself that year. Each evening the men trudged up from the bunkhouse during the festive season, stomping snow off their boots on the porch and then entering along with an icy blast of air. Quin led them in carols and read the Nativity story one evening, and found some small gift from among his possessions for each.

Quin heaped schoolwork on Missy, rather than have her suffer through the endless days with nothing to do. The brilliant snow-light of day was ideal for tireless reading. He plucked books from his rich hoard, scanned them quickly, and assigned passages for Missy to peruse, always with a deadline, so the weary girl would never escape his pressure. Better to be a martinet through the endless days than to let her sink into melancholia. It was an odd education, but a formidable one, based on Quin's college tests and amplified by other works. In addition to the traditional liberal arts, he introduced her to a variety of disciplines that women rarely learned: accounting, banking, finance, economics, principles of management, astronomy, celestial navigation, surveying, cartography, geology, philosophy, psychology, theology, zoology . . . Each afternoon Quin called her into his study, and they reviewed the day's lessons, she reporting what she had mastered and he adding his observations or questioning her closely. Through it all, a deeper bond was forged between them, so that she could barely wait to enter her classroom and surprise him with her progress.

Then, on January second, chinook winds rose out of the west, bringing exquisite warm air that reached the mid-forties by day, and never dropped to freezing at night. The currents intoxicated whoever breathed them in. Men emerged from the bunkhouse, sniffing the wind, stretching in the freedom of a single flannel shirt. The snow levels shrank under the benign winds until patches of ground showed on the south sides of boulders and trees. Durham detailed men to ride the

254

strong plowhorses out and examine the stock and break trails down to the Flatwillow where holes could be hacked in the ice during the rest of the winter.

On the fourth day of the chinook, Quin stood on his porch soaking up sun but experiencing a peculiar melancholia as he thought about one he loved. The morning after he proposed, Nicole had found him in the dining room. She sat down silently across from him, sipping coffee, fondling the cup in her hands, saying nothing at all while wave after poignant wave of feeling swept over her face. Her eyes simply memorized Quin, recording every hair and wrinkle for some detailed portrait she was painting in the innermost chambers of her mind.

"I need more time, Quin," she said at last. "I need to go to Saint Louis and find out for myself what's true. You said so many things, and some of them shocked me. I remember every word you said, and I'll be able to pull them out and think about them. I need to test everything, Quin. I'm terribly confused about all my connections to others. I don't know; I just don't know . . ."

She had paused, drawing into herself. And then she had pressed her hand down on his.

"I'm so aware of your love, Quin, and so glad for it," she whispered. "Would — would you wait? Would you let me find out for sure?"

"Forever," he said.

That was the last he saw of her, sitting there in the Wedgwood blue suit he loved. He had pressed her hand between both of his and whispered once again, "I'll always love you," and left. He got safely home that night.

Now she'd be leaving. Men and animals would be out these warm days, breaking trails and slicing down drifts. Some coaches would get through, bringing delayed mail and precious supplies — and taking away a vulnerable young woman, on down to Billings and the long, lonely rails of the NP.

He could feel her waning presence as he stood there, feel her rolling farther and farther away, to some unknown address. He sighed, not unhappily, for he had learned to live in hope and patience, but from the loneliness he felt for her. There was only Nicole.

The crew raced to do what it could while the respite lasted. Drovers hunted shorthorns and found a few in the bottoms. They were driven back to the ranch and a good haying. All the surviving cattle were in ominous condition, with frozen ears and tails, cracked and bloodied lips and muzzles, and lacerated legs. Their suffering sickened Quin. While the snow was wet and malleable he had the men build a wind barrier along the north corral fence by rolling snowballs and stacking them up as high as the crew could reach. It was wind that murdered animals, and wind that Quin fought with his snow wall. Only Quin's thoroughbreds, luxuriating in their box stalls, had been spared the wind, although during some of the worst blows Durham had driven as many stock horses as he could into the barn aisle, where their own body heat would warm them. In all of the horse stock, the bones were rising out of the flesh;

256

they were becoming tottering scarecrows. The glorified straw they feasted on wasn't sustaining their weight.

Then, on the ninth, the next blizzard howled in, and on its heels more bitter weather during which the thermometer never rose above minus thirty. Quin had hoped to get more done: there might be a little fodder in aspen branches if a man on a ladder could hack them off for the stock below. But the fresh blizzard put a halt to everything, and men retreated once again to their stoves. The hens froze and died, and Dingdong collected them for stew meat. One of the beeves froze in the hay meadow, and it was too stiff to dress out into usable meat, although they cut off some loin meat with a hacksaw.

Even the spring froze, although Quin had taken the precaution of insulating it in a box of sawn wood, inside the springhouse. So they had to melt snow on the stoves, or trudge down to the ice holes at the creek with a bucket. The bitterness never let up: there wasn't one warm day to ease the torment. The boulevarding north winds slowly savaged all remaining life.

Then, on January twenty-eighth, a blizzard of unprecedented fury broke over Montana. Long afterward, men disputed how long it lasted. Silas Stone swore it raged for ten days, but it probably petered out on February fourth. All who remembered it described it as "the knock-out blow". The polar winds gusted at sixty miles an hour, blowing the last bit of heat out of the miserable stock. Quin's thermometer plunged to minus forty, then minus fifty, but that was as low as it would go; he didn't really know how much colder it got. At Fort Keogh, that day, a minus sixty was recorded. It rarely stopped snowing the whole time, and by the time the storm ebbed away, another foot of icy crystals lay over most of Montana. In early February, Quin's thermometer hung at minus forty-seven or forty-eight, and on one incredible day his barometer reached thirty-point-nine inches; the heaviest air he had ever experienced. Men prepared to die. A winter so terrible brought its intimations of doom. A winter that sucked the heat out of a roaring wood stove so fast that no one could get warm was a winter of the yawning grave, when all life was an inch from disaster.

Desolately, Quin watch it all from his frosted windows. His men shuffled through their minimal tasks and then fled to the corona of their stoves. The snow abated but the cold didn't, and the mocking sun, in its cobalt matrix, spread false cheer through all the glass. On the fifteenth, yet another norther broke over the groaning land, and the red column on Quin's thermometer shrank back into its bulb once again. They lived in mute paralysis: Missy under two comforters much of each day; Quin brooding in his study, his boots hot against the grillwork of the stove. He had never known such helplessness in the teeth of such fury. His puny efforts had come to nothing, and now his cattle were surely dead, and the whole enterprise swung precariously in the north wind. He had struggled and slaved to what end? Persevered to what end? Recognized and defended against the overgrazing of the open range to what end? Risked the enmity of his neighbors to what end? An arctic fist had smashed it all.

He stretched restlessly. He never argued with God nowadays. He never cried, Why have you let this happen to me? The arguing never changed anything. But years before, after he stopped shaking his fist at the heavens, he had found himself changing. And even now he wasn't sure what he was becoming. He knew only that everything which smote him had been put to good use. Everything had worked for the good. An optimism blossomed in him and, along with it, a strange gratitude for all the ordeals he had experienced. He lifted the Book of Common Prayer and turned to the Psalter, where he found the Psalm whose fragments lay tattered in his head:

> Lord, thou has been our refuge from one generation to another.
> Before the mountains were brought forth, or ever the earth and the world were made, thou art God from everlasting, and world without end.
> Thou turnest man to destruction; again thou sayest, come again, ye children of men.
> For a thousand years in thy sight are but as yesterday when it is past, and as a watch in the night.
> As soon as thou scatterest them they are even as a sleep, and fade away suddenly like grass.
> In the morning it is green and groweth up; but in the evening it is cut down, dried up, and withered . . .

Morning grass! His grasses were greener than those of any man he knew. He had Missy, sprouting tall in the sun, waving in the zephyrs; and Nicole, a carpet of the softest and tenderest grass, where a man might rest his head and sleep on the bosom of the warm earth; and all the other doughty grasses where he had grazed and rested, such as the old Scot, and the verdant meadows of Silas and Georgeanna Stone. Green morning grass! He had more than a man could want, stretching out from his windows to the high blue hills beyond. Green pastures: every night before bed he grazed among them, a few verses at a time, nourishing himself with love.

He was bankrupt, he knew. There would scarcely be two hundred head alive in the spring, and only seventy of those, the boarded stock, in decent condition. But he would need seven or eight hundred prime steers by November in order to meet the final payment on his stock loan. It was impossible. And yet ... with irrigation of the hay meadows that covered his patented bottomland . . . he could raise and sell hay. Thousands of tons of hay for all the winter-scorched ranchers in the area — and he could survive. Grass! The blessed grass!

Missy brought him some tea. She had started doing that recently. There was something in her girlhood that was reaching out to comfort a suffering man: a beginning of womanhood growing in her.

"Is the ranch dying?" she asked as she seated herself.
"No, honey, it's barely begun its life."

"But will it be different now?"

"Things never end up the way we intended," he replied. "Things go their own direction, no matter how hard we try. From now on, we're going to raise grass, and not just beef."

"What are you going to do when spring comes?"

"Why, start on an irrigation system for the hay meadows! That was the hard lesson I learned this winter."

"Do you think Nicole will ever come?"

"Yes, I do. I think she loves us both."

"I don't think so. She'll get used to Saint Louis, and she'll like it there in her new position."

"Missy, you're too much of a pessimist. Haven't you ever noticed how beautifully life works out?"

"Like all the stock freezing to death," she retorted morosely.

"Maybe, someday, we'll find a reason even for that, and if we learn it, we'll have another chance."

"I don't think there are reasons for anything. A bad winter just happens. And the cattle freeze and die . . . It just happens, that's all." She shrugged.

Quin laughed.

"Why are you so happy?" she asked crossly. "Because I have such green pastures," he sighed. That struck her as something wildly funny, so she laughed too.

CHAPTER
TWENTY

The waxing sun nibbled black circles in the snow, first around trees and boulders, then around whole buildings and across the southern slopes. Lines of earth peeked through along paths and roads. Heaps of crusted white slid off steaming roofs and collapsed from evergreen boughs. At the Q Ranch the prison walls gradually receded. If the way out was still blocked by sullen ridges, at least the cabin-fevered men could trudge across sloppy fields beyond the creek, or down the road as far as a giant ridge of white that had blown off the northern hills.

Not since before Christmas, when Quin had ridden to Lewistown, had any news reached the snowbound ranch. Quin ached for news. Wars could have been won or lost during his three-month isolation. Friends might have perished in the storms. And how his neighbors and their stock fared through the winter was a question that begged an answer.

He and his crew had endured, day by day, and their enforced proximity to one another had finally ground away each man's rough edges and pressed his crotchets so that there was a March mellowness in them all. The beadle of winter had caned them well.

Crucial supplies were either exhausted or dangerously low. Sugar and coffee were gone, and there was only a little salt and flour. Dingdong had been reduced to providing odd meals, mostly meat and the dregs of the root cellar. Quin fretted about the diet, fearing an outbreak of scurvy or rickets. It was high time to break through and replenish at Grassrange, a dozen miles away. If the stagecoaches and freighters were running again, fresh supplies would be there, along with the ranch mail.

On the last day of March, Quin and his crew, except for old John Durham, set out for Grassrange with a box wagon hitched to four Percherons. Wary of yet another murderous blizzard, they had piled blankets, buffalo robes, and spare gear aboard, along with every shovel on the ranch. Quin drove, while the cowboys rode their own mounts ahead to break a trail.

With that much horsepower and manpower, they made stolid progress through the wet drifts that had heaped along the low divide, topped out on windswept prairie that had blown clean, and then descended through canyons of dripping snow into the crossroads hamlet. Much to Quin's relief, the twelve miles had taken only six hours. They could stock up on provender, feast on the news, such as there might be of it, and reach home soon after dark. They were all rejoicing at the prospect of seeing people and trading blizzard yarns. It had been a winter that would keep the raconteurs among them busy for decades, but a winter that was the nemesis of braggarts and liars, for there was no whopper a man could hump up in his mind that could equal the stark reality, no bagatelle that couldn't be matched by any other veteran of the wars of 1886–87. Billy Jones was the only cowpoke who could think up a whopper worth the telling: he was going to inform everyone within earshot that the winter had been the warmest he'd ever known and that he never did have to don his red long johns. If that didn't get them all to knee-slapping and hoo-hawing, nothing would.

Quin found Nicole's long-delayed letter waiting for him at the mercantile — and another one, postmarked November fifteenth, that suddenly made his blood run cold:

My dear Putnam:
I have irrefutable evidence that the minor female in your custody is my own granddaughter. I plan to travel to Montana Territory shortly to claim her, and restore her to her own family.
I trust you will oblige me in this charitable undertaking, and prepare the child, Antonia Dearborn, for what will transpire.
Should you resist, I would, of course, avail myself of the territorial courts to get custody and obtain damages.
Your obedient servant,
Henry L. Dearborn

He'll be coming soon, Quin thought. He was turned back by the winter, but he'll pounce soon enough, as soon as it's fit to travel. And Nicole gone, too! Well, I'll

264

hide Missy — hide her somewhere good, and pay whatever price I have to pay for doing it. But that man won't get Missy! I'll send him packing! Antonia Dearborn, indeed; she's Antonia Novak, and soon, God willing, she'll be Antonia Putnam!

There were other wagons and teams parked in front of Marshall Mercantile, and one of them Quin recognized.

"Hello, Augie! And Natividad! How've you been?"

Augie and Natividad exchanged a glance.

"You've heard, of course," Augie ventured.

"Heard what? No, we've been trapped since December."

Augie drew himself up and lifted his chin a little.

"Alex died December fourteenth. In a Billings and Carroll Line stage that was caught in that blizzard, scarcely eleven miles from our station, and only half a mile from the Peterson Sheep Company ranch. He and two teamsters and another passenger named Dearborn perished. No one even found them until the January chinook."

The shock of it caught Quin's breath. "Augie! Alex is gone? And Dearborn! Dearborn!"

"Yes, gone . . . Did you know Dearborn?"

"Know him? Why — I suppose I did. After a fashion," Quin stammered. "Missy, Missy, Missy!" he cried.

"Eh, eh?" Augie said. "We sent the deceased back to England in a box, and wrote our family. Father is frightfully upset. Poor Alex! He froze stiff sitting up, and it took a week of thawing before they could lay him flat. Very kindly folk at the parlor, Mathews and Mathews in Billings. They had to build a special box, too, for a man of twenty stone. Alex had only just recovered from pneumonia, you know . . . I shall say something a bit audacious, Quin: Alex was a true Briton, the finest of our island race. A splendid mind. Forever on a great quest for understanding. And a supreme realist, eh?"

Augie halted his eulogy.

"You should be proud of him, Augie. I'm so grieved, so sorry . . ." Quin stumbled. He could never find the words to console anyone very well.

"We're closing up the station whilst we can, in a few weeks, after the cattle have recovered enough strength to ship. We've made a tidy sum at that, in spite of the losses this winter. Going home, Minnie and I. A man gets homesick for his little cottage and the comforts, you know . . . I'd like to see a thatched roof again, and the half-timbered old homes. Strange, eh? Now that the snow's down, we've been out a bit on the range, dodging drifts. The cattle are almost all gone, Quin, and the live ones are dreadful. The sight of them makes a man cry out at nature, red in tooth and claw. Piled up under cutbanks and in coulees like cordwood. Some frozen standing up, with their horns peeking out from a drift. A lot of them ravaged by wolves and coyotes. One poor beast was up in a tree. And the living ones so gaunted and stiff and red-eyed that a man wants to shoot the poor devils. How any of them made it I can't imagine. Makes one a bit awed by the will to live, the tenacity of life, eh?"

Augie stared glumly at the ground. "Quin," he added, "the old way is gone. The open range. You're the man of the future, now. I could never bear to winter another animal without the hay to feed it. Never again!"

"I think most of the stock growers will come to that," replied Quin. "Natividad, what'll you be doing?"

"Closing the station. Then home to San Angelo. I'm as homesick as Mr Birkenhead!"

"Natividad's been our sole help all winter," Augie beamed. "And he'll have his reward for it."

Quin eyed the competent Texan. "If you decide to stay, come talk to me. John Durham's getting crippled up, and he's going to retire soon. So I'll be needing a good segundo."

Rourke smiled. "*Gracias, amigo*, but the warm sun and the warmer senoritas are calling. I'll be five years cooking the cold of Montana out of me."

Quin gripped their hands. "Now don't you leave this country without saying good-bye. I'll want to have a little farewell gathering for you at the Q. And Augie . . . I'm hurting."

The story was there for anyone to listen to around the stove and the cracker barrels in the mercantile, where news was gathered, processed, and exchanged. Quin listened while a clerk filled his wagon and his men hurried around the village on one errand or another, mostly in the saloon. Silas Stone, they told him, had lost seventy percent of his herd, and was so sickened by the carnage that he was giving up open-range ranching . . . The great Niaroba Cattle

Company, off toward the Musselshell, was failing . . . The fresh Texas herds had all perished, but the herds that had wintered once previously did better . . . That English marquis over in Dakota, de Mores, was quitting to go tiger hunting in India, and so was that New York fellow, Roosevelt . . . Stone had seen a white arctic owl last November and figured he was in for it . . . He expected he'd have only nine hundred calves this year, compared with eight thousand last year . . . Fort Benton had thirty-two inches on the level, end of January, and coal couldn't be had at any price there . . . All the blooded stock, the pilgrims and states cattle, had done worst of all on the range . . . Chicago prices were down to three-fifteen a hundred, three cents a pound . . . 'Most every living critter had its ears, tail, nose, feet, and legs frozen up so solid it could still scarcely move . . . Stone's cattle up above the Missouri had died wholesale by falling into the water holes in the river . . . Dry cows and steers had done best . . . Wherever the critters had got out of the wind, they'd done better . . . The spring calves were all runted and sick and twisted up . . . Outfits were folding up down on the Yellowstone . . . From now on, they'd all be making hay and building sheds . . . The Billings and Fort Benton Line had lost a stage over near Ubet in the big blizzard . . .

Quin was so revolted by the whole story that he drove the burdened wagon home in somber silence. None of the crew, who had heard the stories also, felt much like talking either.

In May, the grasses rose lush and sweet, nourished by the waters of winter. They grew into tall plants, thick bunch grass, unmolested by stock because nature had corrected the terrible imbalance in its own way. Quin watched the grass prosper, loving to fondle the moist stalks, rising healthy in the sun. It was his green gold. Apart from a few wretched survivors, there was no stock on the Q to graze it down.

He ordered seed, various varieties to try in his hay meadows once the irrigation system was functioning. He and the crew plowed and dug ditches and built a diversion dam through the lengthening spring days, while the ranch horses fleshed out on the emerald blades that had caught the very power of the sun within them. The handful of gaunted bovine veterans exchanged war stories while chewing their cud on the warm slopes.

Quin tarried until the end of June before cutting his first hay crop. He wanted his grass tall, with good seedheads, to make nourishing hay. If all went well, he would cut about three thousand tons of it before the summer was over. Much of it had already been spoken for by ranchers who vowed they would never again winter stock without reserves of hay. That grass was Quin's salvation: it would see him through until he could rebuild the herd.

Then, on the first day of summer, Bunions brought a letter for Quin from Grassrange. Quin saw the Saint Louis postmark and hastened to his cool, dark study, which was not at all as calm as he supposed it to be.

Dear Quin,

I love you above all else. Am I too late? If you would still have me, I am yours. I will come to you and be your bride.

I have scarcely a domestic instinct in me, and that makes me a poor prospect for you, dear Quin. I want to continue to practice law. I can write a good brief, even if I can't cook a good meal. I dread that I won't meet your expectations.

I think you were right in most respects. The walls in Lewistown were largely ones I built. I found myself building them here, too. Things weren't what I expected in the city. Several firms leaped to make me a partner. I was a curiosity, good for business, and they wanted to exploit that. I had no privacy at all. I didn't want to become a notorious person, Quin. I just wanted to practice law. I resigned a week ago.

I've spent the last week pondering and praying and I believe I know myself better. I want you and law. Would it be unbearable if I were to practice law in Lewistown again, and divide my time between it and you? Would you consider that less than marriage? Would you permit me to pioneer a new kind of wedlock?

> With fear and love,
> Nicole

Quin settled gently into the Morris chair, feeling the steady thump of his heart as he reread the letter. He recalled how it was when he had kissed her at the hotel:

the press of her lips, the fierce tug of her arms, the strange, fond, puzzled look in her eyes when he brought her the bouquet that night, her affronted dignity when the little mare foiled her, her tenderness at the dining table when he had proposed, the cool precision of her opinions, delivered serenely with a faint amusement at the foibles of men, and the suffering he saw when she couldn't cope with a village that was raw and cramped.

He sighed quietly. He would marry her on her terms — indeed, he could not imagine Nicole as anything other than what she was. She would be more than a wife. And what more could a man ask than to love such a woman? He would send Lem and Bunions with a telegram to Grassrange, and instruct them to wait for a reply.

He sat and marveled. Minutes before he had been middle-aged, and now he felt young. He rose to look for Missy and found her in the summer kitchen, scrubbing sheets on a washboard. She glanced up and saw something special in his eyes as he reached down to grab one of her soapy hands. They walked slowly down to the creek.

"She loves us. She's coming," he said, handing her the letter.

Antonia Putnam read it slowly and smiled through her tears.

After a choked moment, he squeezed her hand. "Let's ride into the hills," he whispered. "We'll see how the grass is coming along. It's like love, you know, always springing up fresh, like a gift without end."

ISIS publish a wide range of books in large print, from fiction to biography. Any suggestions for books you would like to see in large print or audio are always welcome. Please send to the Editorial Department at:

ISIS Publishing Limited
7 Centremead
Osney Mead
Oxford OX2 0ES

A full list of titles is available free of charge from:

Ulverscroft Large Print Books Limited

(UK)
The Green
Bradgate Road, Anstey
Leicester LE7 7FU
Tel: (0116) 236 4325

(Australia)
P.O. Box 314
St Leonards
NSW 1590
Tel: (02) 9436 2622

(USA)
P.O. Box 1230
West Seneca
N.Y. 14224-1230
Tel: (716) 674 4270

(Canada)
P.O. Box 80038
Burlington
Ontario L7L 6B1
Tel: (905) 637 8734

(New Zealand)
P.O. Box 456
Feilding
Tel: (06) 323 6828

Details of **ISIS** complete and unabridged audio books are also available from these offices. Alternatively, contact your local library for details of their collection of **ISIS** large print and unabridged audio books.